DATE DUE		

THIS TITLE CANNOT BE
RESERVED, RENEWED OR
TRANSFERRED

OCT -- 1998

Speak No Evil

Speak No Evil

Gary Aldrich
and
Mark Davis

Since 1947
REGNERY
PUBLISHING, INC.
An Eagle Publishing Company • Washington DC

Library of Congress Cataloging-in-Publication Data

Aldrich, Gary.
   Speak no Evil / Gary Aldrich and Mark Davis.
      p.   cm.
   ISBN 0-89526-358-0
   I. Davis, Mark, 1955-   . II. Title.
   PS3551.L3415S64   1998
   813`.54--dc21   98-35210
                                            CIP

Published in the United States by
Regnery Publishing, Inc.
An Eagle Publishing Company
One Massacusetts Avenue, NW
Washington, DC 20001

Distributed to the trade by
National Book Network
4720-A Boston Way
Lanham, MD 20706

Printed on acid-free paper.
Manufactured in the United States of America

10 9 8 7 6 5 4 3 2 1

Books are available in quantity for promotional or premium use. Write to Director of Special Sales, Regnery Publishing, Inc., One Massachusetts Avenue, NW, Washington, DC 20001, for information on discounts and terms or call (202) 216–0600.

To my children, readers all. Everything I ever
learned worth knowing, I read in a book. If your children
read they will turn out just fine—and free!"

Gary Aldrich

For Jada.

Mark Davis

"Call up her father:
Rouse him, make after him, poison his delight,
Proclaim him in the streets, incense her kinsmen,
And though he in a fertile climate dwell,
Plague him with flies..."

Iago's cure, *Othello*

CHAPTER

1

He wouldn't wake up. *Hombre*, the janitor said to himself, you look too nice a man to be drunk in a library.

"*Borracho?*"

The janitor poked the man's arm. No response. He bent over, and could see the profile of the man's face, buried in papers.

His face, though not handsome, was pleasant looking; his nose and long chin came to a point, as if his slender face had been pinched at birth into a half-moon shape.

Was there a reflection in his spectacles? No, it was the whites of his eyes. This guy was out, totally out.

In fact, he could be dead.

The janitor stepped back, almost tripping over the long broomstick he had leaned against the metal filing cabinet. He said a short prayer for the man's ghost and made the sign of the cross to protect himself against malevolent spirits. Then he ran upstairs to find a security guard, someone to call the police to the Nixon Library.

"Five bucks says I can."

"So let me get this one more time. You're gonna line these two shot glasses next to each other, put this hard-boiled egg in one of them, and then move that egg from one glass to the other without using your hands?"

"Let's up it to ten bucks or the next round."

"What about using your feet or elbows?"

"Not even my nose."

"What about using something to push the egg over?"

"I won't push a single solid object with any part of my body."

"You're on." Mike McGuire slapped a sawbuck on the wooden bar. J.D. lined up the shot glasses and the egg in front of him.

They were attracting a lot of attention, but then they always did. McGuire was a six-foot eight black man who wore Tony Lamas with his suit, had an Oklahoma drawl—the legacy of a ranching family that had spent three generations cutting cattle east of Bakersfield—and a Yosemite Sam mustache, which the FBI let him keep on the dubious grounds that it aided him in undercover work.

McGuire's old partner was Joseph P. DeVine, or J.D. to everyone but the Bureau and his mother. He had a mirthful play about his blue eyes, the easy manner of a man who could hold a parole board, or a dissertation committee, or any number of women, spellbound.

J.D. gently set the egg into the first glass, narrow end down. He shut his eyes, face hardening in concentration. He drew in several deep breaths as if preparing to meditate. The bartender whipped a towel over his shoulder, the woman on the next stool gently set down her Manhattan; everyone had to see how he was going to pull this off.

J.D. sucked in a deep breath and held it, his face turning purple-red.

"You gonna do it with psychic power?" the woman asked.

2

J.D. nodded, irritated that his focus had been broken. He took another deep breath and squeezed his eyelids tight.

He leaned forward, his lips almost touching the broad end of the hard-boiled egg. He blew with all his might.

The egg tilted, teetered, then rolled over into the next glass. Cheers erupted up and down the bar.

J.D. snapped up the note.

McGuire ignored him, looking down at something.

J.D. took a minute to catch his wind. "What's the matter? My psychic ability scare you?"

"Beeper just went off," McGuire said. "Message here says they got a chopper waiting for me on the roof back at the federal building."

"A chopper? All gassed up and ready to take you to the Academy Awards?"

"Here's the real punchline: I'm supposed to take you along."

The single engine of the 206B Bell Jetranger cycled into a high whine and the blades whipped into invisibility as the two men settled in the back seats. The pilot pulled off the helipad and into clouds radiant with the copper-penny hue of Los Angeles streetlights. McGuire pulled a phone receiver from a cradle on the interior wall of the craft and spoke for a long time.

J.D. checked the Walther he kept with him always, making sure it was snug in his black ankle holster, the kind with a Velcro flap for quick tear-away action.

He looked outside and could make out the fireplug of the Capitol Records building, saw the giant letters of Hollywood slipping by in the mist to his left.

"We're going to Yorba Linda to look at a stiff they found in the Nixon Library," McGuire shouted over the engine. "The SAC is on this and she wants us there fast. That's all I got."

Years ago, when they had worked together in Washington, McGuire and J.D. had seen plenty of homicides doing the Ten Most Wanted and then the Major Theft Division. But for the past two years, since J.D. had taken early retirement, he'd hung out his shingle as a private investigator in his hometown of Annapolis. The Bureau, overwhelmed by the sheer number of new scandals in Washington, threw white collar crime work his way, making him a special consultant on political crimes.

He was in California chasing leads linking yet another Buddhist temple to illegal campaign contributions to the Democratic Party. Corpses weren't supposed to be a part of his beat anymore.

The pilot cut altitude over Yorba Linda, slowing over wet boulevards lined with the dark shadows of palms, the pavement shiny under streetlamps.

They came to a gentle touchdown in the parking lot of the Richard Nixon Library and Birthplace. A Med Unit sat parked at the entrance, siren off but red lights revolving. There were at least a half-dozen police vehicles and a few unmarked cars.

A police officer led McGuire and J.D. to the library curator, who took them through the Italianate foyer, past darkened exhibits. They exited to a courtyard and trotted down concrete stairs to a hall of offices.

In a room set far to the back, J.D. saw the medics and

the cops standing around, hands on hips. He and McGuire stepped between them. The corpse was bent over a desk. He was a white male, late thirties or early forties, his left-cheek pressed hard against papers on the table, hands dangling at his sides. A spool of microfiche film had unraveled across the floor, curling at the ends like a dying black snake. J.D. stepped closer.

The man's shirt was pure cotton, tailored, with a monogram on the cuffs, TNT. His hair was skillfully layered in a razor cut. His cologne smelled of sweet pine. The first signs of lividity were already apparent in the tips of his fingers, the flesh bruise-blue. The back of his neck was white as bone china. It could be a textbook coronary.

J.D. looked at an ambulance attendant. "Don't you want to get him out of here?"

"Check out the mouth," the medic said. There was something dark there, like a bead of chocolate.

A local detective nodded his permission. "Here, wear these," he said, handing J.D. a pair of rubber gloves. J.D. looked to McGuire, who was officially in charge. "Go ahead," McGuire replied, then leaned over to watch.

J.D. came closer, careful not to step on the microfiche. He slipped on the rubber gloves and touched the clammy white skin of the dead man's forehead. He raised the man's face, gently, from the papers. The man's round, rimless glasses slipped down his nose. J.D. retracted his hand with a start, and the dead man's forehead hit the desk with a hollow-sounding thunk.

"Good move, fed boy." The local detective was amused. "Go ahead and show us how the pros screw up the evidence."

McGuire slammed his boot down and looked as if the Lakers had just blown the NBA Finals with a technical.

But J.D. was too shocked to notice. "I know this guy. He's a source of mine."

Remorse, even revulsion, caused him to close his eyes. It was one thing to look at a stiff that you had never seen before. But someone you had broken bread with, argued with? This was different.

He forced himself to concentrate on just one mantra-thought. It's just another job, just another job. He exhaled and went back to work. Gingerly, he raised the dead man's head again. The eyes were white, rolled up like a broken doll's.

There was something else, something he couldn't quite believe. The dead man's lips were sewn shut.

A thin black thread weaved in asymmetrical zigs and zags, between his upper and lower lips. Tiny black knots protruded from the corners of his mouth, tilting the lips upward into a grotesque smile.

On the table where the dead man's face had been, was a message written in a clean, squarish script on a yellow tablet with a blue felt-tip pen:

SPEAK NO EVIL

J.D. gently returned the man's head to its resting place. He turned to McGuire, the cops, the medics, the curator. "All right," he said, taking charge. "Nobody saw this. This evidence is classified information. Nobody talks to the press."

Everyone nodded. The medics wouldn't tell anyone,

just their wives and their drinking buddies tonight, and next-door neighbors tomorrow. He had no realistic hope that this could be kept secret for more than a day. At least he could buy time for the Bureau before the news cycle hit with hurricane force.

I know you. The monogram on your cuffs stands for Todd Nathan Thornburgh. You had many admirers and more detractors, but everyone called you Doctor Dirt.

CHAPTER
2

Anne Carlson plunked her stockinged feet on her small desk. The other desk belonged to Jack Brauer, her deputy bureau chief, who had sensibly left for the evening. Only Anne would dream of coming back to this florescent-lit, plywood box in a Pasadena strip mall, where her only company were two word processors, a photocopying machine, and an industrial-sized coffee machine that gurgled for fifteen minutes before spewing a brew as black and resinous as crude oil.

She told herself she had to return to keep tabs on a story, although she just as easily could have done that from home. The fact was she couldn't stand to be alone and not working, to know that the Metro-East bureau of the *Los Angeles Times* could do without her being continually at the office.

That morning she had filed a story on an insider deal between a city councilman and a developer. But, in truth, it wasn't yet a story. It was a stream of electrons, arranged in a precise order—her order—that she had sent to the newsroom some thirty miles away. Those electron-words, reviewed and approved by copy editors, would have to make it past Herb Smith, the national affairs editor and chief of all domestic bureaus.

Anne needed to be right here, in her office, where she could monitor the office e-mail network and complain if too much violence was done to her work.

The good news was that her piece had already made it to the rim, a horseshoe-shaped desk in the newsroom on the third floor. On any given night, copy editors reclined in swivel-back ergonomic chairs around the rim and pecked away at computer consoles, trimming, rewriting, changing her work.

This was the moment of maximum danger. It was while her stories were still on the rim that Herb Smith would often wander back from dinner, have them sent to his computer, and tamper with her precious copy. Sometimes he rewrote her pieces. Sometimes he would meld them with an AP story and replace her byline with the words, *From staff and wire reports.*

Did Smith have it in for her because she was a woman bureau chief? Or was it that he just didn't trust stories from a suburban bureau? It always seemed as if Anne Carlson got bad placement, buried deep in the Metro section next to the car ads. She had never made every journalist's dream, "P-One," the front page.

Anne had befriended several of the copy editors, guys she partied with and helped out from time to time. She suspected that more than one of them had a crush on her. Her friends on the rim would send her e-mail reports, let her know how her story had come through the editorial gauntlet, where her piece was going to be placed.

There was no e-mail for her tonight.

So the guys are busy, she thought. The president of Russia was rumored to be "on the roof." If he died before midnight, they'd have to rip up the whole front page, bumping stories throughout the news section, which she knew was already overloaded. In the great daily record of America's second largest city, her little piece about corruption on a suburban city council was a minor footnote.

The phone rang. She expected Herb Smith to tell her not to get her hopes up, that this time she was getting pushed back to the comics.

It was her deputy, Jack Brauer, on a car phone.

"There's a dead guy at the Nixon Library. He was found in one of the archive rooms, reading microfiche or something. I caught it on the police radio."

"When?"

"Just after I picked up my date."

"You listen to police radios on your dates?"

"I was showing her how it works. I can go if you like. But we've got tickets to Los Lobos."

Brauer's car phone was on speaker. Anne heard the snapping of a compact case.

"I wouldn't want to tear you away from that. How'd he die?"

"Didn't hear. Probably a heart attack or something."

"Okay, I'll go this time." As if she didn't go every time. "Did you hear what they're doing with my city council story?"

"I heard just a few typos and a couple of fact checks. You'll run tonight, don't know which page."

Anne left the office grateful to have something to do.

She slipped her black Mazda RX-7 into fifth gear and cruised down the damp freeway, for her first visit to the Nixon Library—to see a corpse.

After months of drought, a dense marine fog had settled on the land like a soggy sweater. As she drove on, the fog lifted to reveal the immense blackness of the Santa Ana mountains to her left, jeweled at their base by the lights of prosperous, working class suburbs, the rest a forbidding wilderness of scrub, sage, and mountain lions. The flat horizon of lights to her right was Fullerton, a buffer between the suburbs of western Orange County and the inner-city L.A. County war zones of Downey and Compton, another kind of wilderness with a different kind of predator.

An ambulance, a fire truck, and a half-dozen Fullerton and Yorba Linda police cars sat parked before the terra cotta facade of the library entrance. At the other end of the parking lot, a broad-shouldered pilot in an FBI windbreaker stood guard in front of a helicopter. Anne Carlson walked past the security guard, who merely nodded at her *Times* identification, not noting that it lacked the required police brass. She kept walking, as if she knew exactly where she was going.

Brauer had mentioned microfiche. It shouldn't be hard to find the archives. But she didn't. She got lost in a maze of exhibits—letters, campaign buttons, video loops that kept the voices of Nixon and Kennedy echoing in the dark halls. There was a giant Woody station wagon, megaphone perched on its roof with a "Nixon for Senate" sign beside it. She saw Nixon on television, black and white, telling the nation about his children's dog, Checkers. She passed an illuminated narrative of Watergate, from break-in to resignation. Voices of Haldeman, Ehrlichman, Mitchell, and Dean. Then there was a large, dark room, cold, but full of people.

They stood in clusters as if engaged in cocktail party conversations. They ignored her, whispering to each other, but she could not quite make out what they were saying. She felt a slight rush of fear. Something was wrong.

Ambient light rose from the ceiling. The shadowy figures emerged as life-sized bronzes of world leaders: Chou En-lai sat in an overstuffed chair; Winston Churchill, a bowler hat smashed on his head, engaged in what seemed like friendly banter with Konrad Adenauer, while Charles de Gaulle looked down on both men from an imperious height. Golda Meir, Anwar Sadat, Leonid Brezhnev, and Nikita Krushchev stood in small, friendly groups like an afterlife welcoming committee for Nixon. The figures had presence. They looked real.

Anne felt another presence. Behind her. She turned— and gasped, as the figure moved. A security guard, hand resting lightly on his holster, studied her intently.

"Ma'am, we've been watching you from the first minute you got through the front door. Mind telling us who you are?"

She quickly caught her breath. "I'm Anne Carlson of the *Los Angeles Times*. Guess I got lost."

"I guess you did. Let me see your ID."

"I showed it when I came in."

"Let me see it."

The security guard watched her with the impassive

black eyes of a Doberman. She gave him her ID. He looked at it, mumbled into a walkie-talkie, handed the card back, mumbled some more, and then told her to follow him.

They retraced her steps to the front entrance, past the first security guard, glowering with anger, out the front door to the damp night air.

"You stay here," he said and walked away.

Talking to the press had never been Agent McGuire's favorite pastime. So J.D. took the job. He actually enjoyed the verbal sparring. Besides, if complaints were made to the FBI about J.D., not much would happen. If the Bureau got too pissy about it, Joe DeVine could tell them to stuff the contract. It was that simple.

This one was easy to size up: attractive woman, early thirties, good shape, quality knock-offs from the best career woman business attire, blonde hair a half-inch longer than a total butch. What was it, J.D. wondered, that caused perfectly good-looking, straight women to want to imitate *Ellen*? Was there some weird, secret self-flattery in attracting guys and lesbians too? He had quit trying to figure out L.A. women, especially the professional ones. It just wasn't possible.

J.D. spoke first. "I understand you had some excitement in the library."

"I understand you did too." She handed him her card. "Anne Carlson, *L.A. Times*."

He handed her his. "Joe DeVine, Special Consultant *to* the FBI, but not *of* the FBI, so I can go on background with you."

"I want to speak to the agent in charge."

"You can speak to Agent McGuire, but don't expect him to say anything."

"Uh huh." She stood with her weight on one foot, her lips tilting into a barely perceptible smile. "So, you gonna tell me why this parking lot looks like a plane just crashed?"

"Somebody had an overdue library book?"

"I can ask my editor to wake up your boss."

"Wake up the world if you like. I'm my own boss. I'm not like that poor fella over there. You put that guard in a world of trouble. Got it? All I can tell you for now is that we have a Caucasian male, age 36, found in a deceased condition in the research portion of the library. Basement microfiche room, to be exact."

"Who is he and how did he die?"

J.D. took a small notepad from his inside breast pocket, wrote a name and some other information on it, ripped off the page and handed it to her.

"Here's his full name, correct spelling. We're already getting to the next of kin, so you can go with the name. I honestly don't know how he died."

"Overdose? Suicide?"

"No known cause of death."

"How about an apparent cause of death?"

"No apparent cause of death. Call me tomorrow. I'll let you know what we find out."

Anne gestured to the parking lot. "Why all this heat?"

"It's a president's library."

She studied him. If he had been an L.A. detective, he would have taken her on deep background, earnestly trying to erase any suspicion of cover-up, incompetence, or mis-conduct, sucking up like a goldfish. But not this hotshot Joe DeVine.

"Let's talk tomorrow," J.D. said. His blue eyes flashed as he smiled a goodbye and walked away. Anne looked around and ground her heel in the pavement. She looked at her watch. All right, she thought, I'll retrieve a short bio from the on-line morgue, write a squib, and file it as a late bulletin by e-mail.

But this had better be all.

The Jetranger bucked and shook as it landed, against whip-ping sheets of rain, on the rooftop of the Wilshire federal building. J.D. and McGuire ran across the rain-slick helipad to the stairwell, where they shook their jackets and brushed water out of their hair.

"So much for your California weather," said J.D.

"Yeah, to hell with you too," replied McGuire, shoving him down the stairs. They stopped at the fourth floor, where they entered the plush office of the Los Angeles Special Agent in Charge, Carolyn Suarez. J.D. thought she didn't look half bad for a fifty-year-old gumshoe. She wore a low-cut, black evening dress, and seemed less than pleased to see him, as if it were somehow J.D.'s fault that she had to leave the awards portion of the United Way dinner.

"So what's all this Doctor Dirt business?"

McGuire took a seat, and waved J.D. to explain.

"I knew him. Name is Todd Thornburgh. He was a high-flyer in GOP circles, and a good source on political crime. Lived in Alexandria, Virginia. He was the sole proprietor of Clarity, what Washington calls a political opposition research firm, what you and I call professional dirt diggers. Twenty-one employees. I know his client list includes the California governor, both Texas senators, a county commissioner race in Cincinnati, congressional races in Florida and New York. He was a major consultant on the last two Republican presidential campaigns."

"Family?"

"Wife is Ruth Thornburgh. Never met her. She's a pediatric surgeon in D.C."

"What do the surveillance cameras show?"

"I haven't seen the tape, but I've been told nothing suspicious."

"How come no one heard it?" the SAC asked. "He had to put up a fight."

"Actually, he didn't," McGuire broke in. "No bruises, no abrasions, no blood that I could see. His shirt-tail was neatly tucked in, and his clothes hung on him like they're still on the rack."

J.D. finished the point. "None of the library staff heard anything because he was killed in a basement annex, well off the main research room, at least thirty minutes after the last visitor—a UCLA history prof—checked out."

Suarez sank in her chair. J.D. noticed silver-framed photos of two strapping teenaged boys in soccer uniforms, and was reminded that she was a widow. Her husband, working undercover for the DEA in Mexico, had been tortured to death more than a decade ago.

"You have nothing yet on cause of death?"

"No wound that I could see. But his neck was awfully stiff for a homicide just a few hours old."

"And next of kin?"

"The locals tracked down his wife at the Pasadena Sheraton," J.D. said. "They were about to leave for a Hawaiian vacation."

"Anything else?"

"Yeah. Thornburgh was doing more than just looking at microfiche. He had a bunch of old Nixon papers in front of him. When forensics is done, we should read those papers."

"Read them?" Suarez stood up. "You're gonna memorize them."

CHAPTER
3

Anne came to the downtown office as often as she could. It wasn't for the decor, which was futuristic and sterile, paneled in bright blue on one floor, bright yellow on another, with thick padded railings running the length of the hall. Only the newsroom reminded her of what a major daily should look like, with more than fifty people at small desks, some taking notes on the phone, others pecking at keyboards, with the wire editor yelling "hot copy" at least five times a day. But it seemed good politics to stay in touch with the boys on the rim.

She was leaving the cafeteria, a Styrofoam cup of coffee in her hand, when Nancy, the editor's wispy, nervous secretary, pecked at her arm.

"Ah, Anne, Jim would like to see you."

Jim Miller had been editor for two years, brought in from AP Moscow to shake up the staff, sharpen the reporting, and keep the paper competitive with the *Washington Post* and the *New York Times*. His signature slogan was "quality coverage." He always hammered his reporters to get "quality coverage."

His office was surprisingly small, hidden from the newsroom, and crammed with baseball memorabilia, family photos, and the usual bronze-on-walnut awards. He was reading a memo, from a large stack of memos, when he motioned her in.

Anne took a seat, wondering if she had screwed up the councilman story. It hadn't made P-One, but it did make page three, the next best placement. It ran above the fold, with a wide-angle photograph of the councilman walking out of city hall, looking befuddled. The story continued on page 26, totaling 42 column inches. She had been receiving congrats about it all morning. What now?

Jim Miller looked up. He was a big man, and his whole face took on the texture and color of a rooster's comb when he was angry.

He didn't have that angry look now. He looked concerned, inquisitive, and pale.

"Anne, how long have you been with us?"

"Three years this April."

"And how do you like it out there, in Pasadena?"

"Fine. I'd like it better here, in the newsroom."

"I don't see that happening any time soon."

She shifted in her chair. "Look, Jim, if I've screwed up, tell me what I did wrong."

"Okay." He stood up and walked around the desk, head down, face starting to redden and contort as if he were removing a particularly painful splinter. "Anne, I heard through a friend, a big donor to the Nixon Library, that Thornburgh didn't die of natural causes. He was murdered."

Anger and humiliation coursed through her veins like a warm liquid.

"Who did it? How?"

"I have no idea. The point is we blew an exclusive. We're likely to get scooped by one of the suburban rags."

"But the FBI's man at the scene—some kind of consultant to the Bureau—he assured me nothing like that happened."

"Did he? What did he say, exactly?"

Anne searched her memory, closing her eyes and placing her hand flat on her forehead. "He said, 'there's no known cause of death,' 'no apparent cause of death.' Known—apparent. Oh, God."

"Sister, you've been had. Didn't it strike you as strange that a routine death was being handled by the FBI? Was this so-called consultant based in L.A.?"

"Actually," she was now completely shame-faced, "Washington. He said something about working closely with the Justice Department."

Miller was now sitting on a corner of his desk. "Anne, don't you know this guy can't really speak for the Bureau? He can say anything he wants, and there's no comeback for him. It's not official unless a bona fide FBI agent says it. Tell me Anne, do you care about quality coverage?"

"I care about anything that bears the name of the *Times*."

"It's probably too late for you. But I'm not going to pull you off this, not yet. You made a solid hit on the developer story. I'm giving you a chance to see what you can do to turn this around."

"Thank you, sir."

She emerged into the bright and noisy newsroom knowing that her face was flushed, her eyes teary.

"There you are." Nancy ran after her with mincing steps. "Somebody's been trying to get through to you."

Nancy handed her a pink message slip from Joe DeVine. "You want to use my phone, sweetie?"

After three rings, Anne got a secretary who said DeVine had left for his hotel and would soon be flying to Washington. Damn the lying son-of-a-bitch.

"Tell him that this is Anne Carlson from the *L.A. Times.* We met last night at the Nixon Library. I'm leaving for the federal building. He'd better be there."

The drive took almost an hour in traffic. She parked in front of the federal building on Wilshire, signed her name on the visitor's log, and was directed to take the elevator to the seventh floor.

The door opened to one of the tallest men she had ever seen off a basketball court. His dark blue slacks covered a pair of black cowboy boots. He wore a western belt with a large silver buckle that pushed into his flat gut. She wondered if it hurt.

He extended a hand. "Hi, you must be Ms. Carlson. I'm Agent Mike McGuire."

So this was the other one. "Where's DeVine?"

"You mean J.D.? We caught him at his hotel. He'll join us here as soon as he can."

He led her down a corridor to a small office.

"Good. My boss just ripped me a new asshole. I'm ready to give him a matching set. Who is he? I mean, who is he exactly, if he's not an FBI agent?"

"He's a *retired* agent, a private investigator working on

retainer for us. Ms. Carlson, understand this, J.D. was a very fine law enforcement officer. Used to be one of our best, and he doesn't screw over reporters for fun."

"That's supposed to make me feel better?'"

McGuire laughed nervously.

The door swung open behind her. J.D.'s open windbreaker framed a black T-shirt emblazoned with the announcement, "Still Plays with Boats and Cars." He smiled.

"I called because I thought we ought to follow up on last night's conversation."

"You mean the part where you forgot to tell me that the guy was murdered?"

J.D. shut the door. "Who told you that?"

"It's starting to get around. I'll probably get fired, you lying asshole."

J.D. walked over to the window. "I didn't lie to you, you won't get fired, and no one in this room is an asshole." He leaned against the window frame and put his hands in his pockets. "We're going to hold a press conference tomorrow morning, when we know a little more and we've had time to let his wife prepare herself for the onslaught of publicity. So there's a good chance we can still offer you an exclusive."

Anne took out her notepad. "I doubt it. But you owe me. What happened?"

"The deceased was killed when a sharpened four-inch metal rod, about the diameter of an ice pick, was thrust into the tender spot at the base of the neck. It was stabbed upwards, into the mid-brain, then moved around a bit just to make sure. We believe he was killed instantly, and prior to that did not put up a struggle. From the angle of entry, the perpetrator probably snuck up on him from behind, as he was reading."

"That's great to know. *Now*."

"At the time we spoke, there was no blood, no visible wound. The way Thornburgh was leaning over, with the object lodged flush to his skin, all the bleeding was internal, mostly down the sinuses and throat. Until this morning, I wasn't absolutely sure it was murder."

"Do you know who did it?"

"We have no idea."

"Don't they have cameras in that place?"

McGuire spoke in a modulated tone, as if to effect a calm counterpoise. "The murder took place downstairs, in a microfiche room off the main library. The nearest camera doesn't actually cover the room. But we're in the process of interviewing the library staff and all the signed-in visitors for that day, and reconstructing their movements in the open area. None can be termed as currently under suspicion."

"So what happened?"

J.D. shrugged. "Don't know yet."

"So was this murder weapon really an ice-pick?"

"We've sent it off to the FBI lab to be ID'd."

"You said that at the time you weren't sure it was a murder. Was there anything else at the crime scene?"

"We've got to hold some details until we know more. I can tell you one thing about the murder scene." He looked to McGuire, who nodded. "I'm authorized to use the following phrase—*ritual mutilation*."

"What's that? Some kind of religious thing, voodoo, pentagrams carved in his chest?" The two men were impassive. They did not acknowledge her question, which only made Anne more anxious, more animated.

"Was it sexual? Was anything cut? His genitals? Any other blood?"

McGuire responded, "We cannot give you the exact details of what we mean by ritual mutilation, except to tell you that it was not sexual in nature, nor were there any signs of Satanic ritual. Anything more, and we could compromise the investigation."

"Is there some reason to believe that he knew the killer?"

McGuire's tone hardened. "Anything more, Ms. Carlson, *and we could compromise this investigation.*"

CHAPTER
4

The alarm went off at 7 AM. J.D. hit the snooze bar and fumbled around the bedside stand until he grasped the remote control. As if by braille, he hit the "on" button, and flipped to C-Span to ease himself awake. He was in the hotel airport at Dulles, but still operating on California time.

C-Span's call-in show was reviewing the newspapers. One article about Bosnia, more plutonium smugglers caught at a German airport, the president's continuing legal problems, and something about Todd Thornburgh.

"The *Los Angeles Times* is reporting that the dead man found in the Nixon Library in Yorba Linda, California, was murdered by a single stab wound to the head. Police say they have no suspects, but that some form of ritual mutilation was involved in the killing, which occurred in an isolated part of the library complex. The FBI is investigating."

He sat up, open-eyed. He always dreaded this part, when the press added the unpredictable element of its reporting to an ongoing case.

J.D. scanned to CNN, where a newswoman was speaking, a large photograph of a smiling Todd Thornburgh projected behind her. Lurid red letters spelled "Doctor Dirt."

"Police have cleared library staff, saying that the killer followed Thornburgh into the complex. Now a report on Thornburgh, famous in political circles as Doctor Dirt, master of political dirt-digging."

The screen cut to B-roll, with the camera showing Clarity Research offices. Then came footage of senators, governors, presidents, and presidential candidates, all former clients of Doctor Dirt. A male voice narrated the piece, detailing the major casualties of Thornburgh's research, including former Senator Michael Hughes, whose drive for the presidency was derailed by compromising photos.

The next shot was of the narrator, a correspondent in an overcoat standing in front of Clarity Research, ticking off other victims in senate races, mayoral contests.

Then there was footage of Thornburgh, a shock to see him alive, hands casually draped over a podium at a conference, a slight smirk at the corners of his mouth. He said, "The stark truth is that most elections are won or lost in the library."

CNN cut back to the correspondent. "At this point, the authorities are not willing to discuss who might be the murderer of the man who called himself Doctor Dirt."

J.D. took a cab to Andre Bodin's International Motor Cars in McLean, Virginia. The garage doors were closed. He fished Andre's business card from his wallet, read the keypad numbers penciled on the back, and soon had the motorized garage door moving up its steel track. He walked swiftly toward the partitioned office wall and disarmed the ADT alarm system. He switched on the overhead lights. The concrete floors, as usual, gleamed where grease stains should have been. The polished cars shined brilliantly. Andre was obsessed with cleanliness; his wealthy clientele expected it and paid for it.

Along the north wall were the real mistresses of executives who had lots of disposable income and a thirst to drive some of the most high-powered automobiles ever made. Porsche Turbos were preferred, but dark BMW sedans sporting V-8s, and other exotic European beasts made up the rest of the collection, all facing J.D., headlights staring straight ahead.

Perhaps two million dollars worth of exotic horsepower, in dazzling colors, waiting to be fired up.

Andre had personally made special adjustments to each one, occasionally adding horsepower or increasing stopping speed by drilling and venting the disks. These beauties could compete with the best European teams on any track in the world.

J.D. walked to the other part of the garage, where Andre kept his personal stable. Three identical Porsche Turbos, silver coats the sheen of liquid mercury, bearing the International Motorsports logo, were being prepared for the next high-speed match. One was on jack-stands in the middle of a brake change. Another had the engine out, awaiting reassembly. Every part was shiny, polished, perfect.

The sight always gave J.D. a sensory flashback to younger days of Sebring and Daytona, when he and his buddies spent their weekends watching cars and drivers from all over the world trying to break lap records without breaking their cars or their necks. The sounds, the smells of the burning fuels and exotic motor oils were something that, once installed in the memory banks, stayed with you forever.

You either loved cars and racing or you didn't.

J.D. did.

He walked to a fourth car and lifted the plush, lined cover. Andre had finished the transmission overhaul in record time, but J.D. didn't want to imagine what the bill would be. It was getting harder and harder to find original parts for this particular beaut.

He had found the tired, but complete, '64 Porsche 356 Super Cabriolet in Tucson, where rust is only a rumor. The car had been taken down to its frame, bolt by bolt, nut by nut. Each component had been cleaned, polished, renewed, or replaced. But the best thing about the car was the engine, which ran like a cheetah.

The subtle pale-yellow paint contrasted nicely with the navy-blue leather interior and deep jet-black carpet. The car had special add-ons—like a digital cell phone and fax—but most of all the car had what assembly-line jobs lacked: character.

This car had been hand built.

The engine coughed, then roared to life. J.D. watched the oil pressure surge. The car looked and ran like a car should. It was the best, and Andre was a great nursemaid for his baby.

He pulled the car out of the lineup, and then put it in neutral, letting the engine warm. He pulled the hand brake and got out to secure the alarm and the door. Funny how things turn out.

J.D. had acquired this expensive toy only because

Andre's kid had been kidnapped. J.D. had cracked the case, rescued Andre's boy, and in the process had taken out the kidnapper with a double tap from his service-issued .357 magnum. That double tap won him Andre's loyalty, but it had also cost him his career in the Bureau. No official reprimand, just special scrutiny for his every damn case that followed until he'd had enough of second-guessing Bureau-Crat managers. So he became a PI.

It was on his first assignment as a private investigator that J.D. found the car in Arizona and called Andre. He asked for Andre's help. Andre jumped at the chance, even offering to store and tune the car when J.D. traveled, which was often. Andre's first racer had been a 356, and he prized the old car as much as J.D. did. It was a fine arrangement.

Sometimes expensive, but fine.

J.D. put the tan canvas top down and headed in the direction of Washington. He caught surprisingly light traffic for a weekday morning down the George Washington Parkway, driving by the marshes of the Potomac, passing the dark, looming clocktower of Georgetown University across the river.

The Potomac, green in the summer, was now a river of pewter. On the city side of the Memorial Bridge, a thin film of watery, soot-black snow from a recent freak storm edged the curbs, the salt on the roads crackled under his tires.

This east coast weather was just fine by him. J.D. had his moods. He figured the weather should too.

The drive down Constitution was another reason why J.D. liked living within an hour of Washington. He loved the vast oblong of the Mall, ringed by museums that looked like Georgian mansions on a grotesque scale, the dome of the National Archives, the sharp elbows of the East Building of the National Gallery, the oddly out-of-place red towers and crenellated walls of the Kremlin-like Smithsonian.

It reminded him of his college years. An outsized campus for the middle-aged.

He drove between the Supreme Court and Library of Congress, making a left onto East Capitol Street, his favorite street in the city.

He passed the Folger Shakespeare Library—a New Deal version of a Greek temple. On the west lawn, a statue of Puck stared with an impish grin at the stump of his right arm. Several years ago a thief had chiseled off his hand. Puck's complaint was carved into the marble fountain below, "Lord, what fools these mortals be!"

J.D. had once lived on the Hill with his wife, not five blocks from this very street, but that was another life ago.

Many of the houses on East Capitol were pre-Civil War-era, three- and four-story brick mansions with gabled porches, porte-cocheres actually meant for carriages, top-story porticos ringed in balustrades. The vast gallery windows of several of the homes were framed in ancient, green copper. On the inside, many of these homes had drawing rooms and dumbwaiters, paneled libraries and immense wooden staircases.

J.D. navigated Washington by history and by landmark. The next landmark on this block was a three-story brick townhouse, home to a legendary political opposition research outfit: Clarity.

Time to make a turn to the right.

J.D. was led upstairs to the office of Ben Grossman, Clarity's managing director. J.D.'s first impression was of junk: thrown books, newspaper clippings, collector's Jim Beam bottles, a six-inch Pope doll, a ceramic Elvis head, a life-sized John Wayne cutout in the corner. There was the customary wall of fame, photos of Grossman shaking hands with Republican presidents, diplomas announcing that Judah P. Benjamin Grossman IV had earned a Ph.D. in American studies from Rice University and a Juris Doctorate from Tulane.

They had met before. Thornburgh had brought his deputy to meetings with J.D., at the Old Ebbitt Grill if the matter was a little sensitive, or to safe rooms in hotels if it was very sensitive. If it was really top secret, they walked ouside, perhaps slowly down a sidewalk so as to not be over-heard or recorded. The purpose in every case had been to share dirt on Democratic fundraising practices with the Justice Department.

In their meetings, Thornburgh had always shown a love for personal secrets, collected and labeled them with all the pride of an oenophile fussing over a first-class wine cellar. But Ben Grossman seemed to care little for gossip, preferring the hard, intellectual work of correlating facts from public sources into a tree of Aristotlean logic, inputing a single piece of information into as many as six or seven related categories, so that a pocket veto of parole reform by Michael Dukakis would lead a Clarity researcher inevitably to Willie Horton.

Grossman was standing, looking out his window at the courtyard, his belly button peeking through a part in his shirt just above his size 48 waist. He saw J.D. and said softly, "Come in."

They shook hands and sat on either side of the desk.

Grossman's large jowly face was still that of a man on the younger side of middle age. His large, black, Gypsy eyes were moist and searching as he looked at J.D. "You tell me who did it, and I'll jerk their damn lungs out."

"We don't know who did it. That's why I'm here. You'd know who would want to kill your boss."

"Yeah. Sure. Twenty to thirty people who didn't get to be senator or president 'cause of him. Know what's in those files, J.D.? Ain't pretty."

"I can imagine."

"Yeah, I guess you would," Grossman spoke almost with remorse. Then, as if to change the mood, he stood up, and said, "Follow me."

He led J.D. out of his office and walked him by another. Thornburgh's nameplate was still outside the door. J.D. caught a glimpse of a sparsely decorated room, a couple of modernistic paintings, a Japanese paper lantern, a large, ornately carved desk, but Grossman didn't stop. He led J.D. down to the second floor and waved a hand over a room sliced into a jigsaw by gray upholstered partitions. A dozen young people were staring into personal computers, earnestly manipulating mouse and keyboard, phones cradled under ears. A few more kept a constant stream of documents filing into copying machines.

J.D. could remember when these "fast-trackers" were crammed together in little rooms redolent of sweat and glue, cutting, pasting, filing and cross-filing newspapers, journals, periodicals. They were young men and women who worked long hours all week, earning just above minimum wage, compiling information that might become "a nasty"—a bad vote, an insensitive remark, a bribe, an illicit sexual encounter. Clarity was a private-sector FBI, the intelligence agency of the Republican Party.

"In three hours, Clarity will be nothing but voice mail and a sign that says 'Closed for Business.'"

"That's it? You'll just close shop?"

"That's Ruth's decision," Grossman said. "But I hope not for good."

"Ben, I want a complete list of your clients and targets."

Grossman leveled his sad-dog eyes at J.D. After a pause he said, "Yeah."

"And I want to see the house out back where you store everything."

"Not much to see, just a computer and a lot of disks in boxes."

"I want the nasties."

Grossman was silent.

"Well?" J.D. asked.

Grossman's head twitched. He wanted to say no.

"I need to know everything you've got," J.D. said testily.

"Uh huh. Look here, I'll get you an inventory and a synopsis, but you can't let this fall into the White House's hands like those nine hundred FBI files did. You got it, J.D.? That stuff's poison."

J.D. felt heat rise from under his shirt. The filegate scandal was one of the greatest embarrassments the FBI had ever endured—and all out of a misguided loyalty to a White House that was trampling on the law.

"Release them to me, and I personally guarantee a close

hold. But don't give them to the FBI, not even if the FBI director himself asks for them. Just leave the FBI to me."

"Deal."

J.D. saw a stocky young black man stand and check his watch. Then he looked at Grossman. Grossman nodded.

"Okay, everybody, it's time," the young man announced.

Grossman led J.D. through the young people, a buzz of PCs shutting down, scraping chairs, backpacks dragged on the ground. They came down another flight of stairs to the first floor reception area, where the fast-trackers were already gathering. Red plastic cups were passed around. Some fast-trackers started with cola, some pulled beer and wine out of a refrigerator, others had brought down scotch and bourbon from Thornburgh's office.

A wake was starting, though it wasn't lively. There wasn't even much conversation. Thick birch logs crackled and popped in the fireplace.

"Let me introduce you to someone you should know." Grossman led J.D. to the stocky young black man who had called the fast-trackers together. He wore khaki pants and an expensive, tailored shirt with a bright Armani tie. He had a firm handshake and made a point of direct eye contact.

His name was Roman Grice, and he had come to Clarity by way of Howard University and the U.S. Army, where he had served as a lieutenant in a tank battalion.

"Roman here runs the operation out back," Grossman said. "He's the one who will actually inventory everything you need to know."

Grice wiped the corner of his eye. "You should know,

sir, that I saw Todd that day. I was his advance man. I dropped Ruth off at the hotel. Then I went on to the airport. Todd wanted to drive himself to the Nixon Library. I can't believe—"

The young man's dignified demeanor broke. He wept without shame while Grossman put a bear grip around his shoulders. J.D. made a mental note to check the airlines, confirm the time Grice had left California, and to call him later to ensure he delivered all the nasties.

Grossman followed J.D. outside to the front steps. "I want everything," J.D. reiterated. "Every last nasty you've got."

"Uh huh."

"And who were your last big scalps?"

Grossman took a moment, seemed to be making internal calculations.

"Well, how about knockin' Michael Hughes out of the presidential race and beating Leonora Vasquez for the U.S. Senate—picture perfect Todd operations that had the press screamin'."

"Yeah, I remember. Two golden Democrats dismembered."

Grossman's eyes took on an even more hang-dog expression. "Hey, J.D., you can see us as vultures if you want to, but the world would smell to high heaven if we weren't there to clean off the bones."

"All I care about is if it was worth killing for."

Time to turn to the left.

"I thought you'd been fired." Leonardo Lindstrom hunched

over a desk littered with newspaper clippings and court documents. His greasy blond hair was uncombed. His distinctive, unwashed body odor hit J.D.'s nostrils like a bad memory.

"Stinky, get it down—I retired. Now I'm on my own."

"So you're here about Doctor Dirt's death. The mudraker raked back into mud, filth flung unto filth, shit sediments sinking to hell."

Lindstrom's strange habits of speech had only become more pronounced since the last time J.D. had interviewed him. He had a patois all his own, a linguistic halfway house between beatnik-poet haiku and schizophrenic raving.

"Tell me about your dealings with Thornburgh."

"He was Murder Incorporated. Todd was a demonizer who worked for demons."

Lindstrom, the Democratic Party's low-tech answer to Clarity, was also one of J.D.'s best informants on the Left. What he lacked in technology, Lindstrom made up for by being the city's most prolific character assassin whose deadly information bubbled up easily in the mainstream media.

J.D. had seen photos of a youthful, golden-haired Leonardo Lindstrom, clean of eye and limb, one of the finest wide receivers ever to play for West Point, a decorated soldier in Vietnam. But alcohol and drug abuse had driven him to near madness, and soon he was camping out on the paranoid fringes of the anti-war protest movement in the states. In 1971 he was still presentable enough to win a top job in the McGovern campaign. But over the years his erratic personality forced him out of job after job, until he became his own boss, running a one-man political research firm out of this tiny office in Georgetown. The leaders of the Democratic Party still found him useful, but only if he could be kept at arm's length.

His office was filthy, the floor a minefield of scattered trash, discarded pizza boxes, wadded up newspapers, old Coke cans. Along one wall hung photos of a young, shirtless Lindstrom with his platoon in Nam. Another wall was covered with several pieces of a camouflage tarp stitched together with a First Calvary Division patch sewn into the middle.

J.D. asked, "So do you have anything for me?"

Lindstrom smiled for no discernible reason. "I have nothing but love for the Federal Bureau of Infestations."

"What's Thornburgh been up to recently?"

"Tell me what they mean, the press, you know, by *ritual mutilation?*" Lindstrom's eyes burned bright and blue, grime filled the pores of his pale cheeks and nose, stubble poked out like weeds. "Weird stuff, want the details, the dead tales. FBI pulls you out of deep-freeze before the guy's even buried. Sounds like politics. Or is it personal?"

"Suppose for the sake of argument you're right. Who would do him in?"

Lindstrom closed his eyes and lowered his head.

"The wife. She a suspect?"

"No."

"She's a surgeon. Wound made by a scalpel, right? Could be her."

"How about a political suspect? Or a financial one?"

"First, what's ritual mutilation?"

"Can't give you that."

Lindstrom gave that eerie smile again, baring nicotine-stained teeth.

"Show me yours and I might flash you mine."

He scratched a cheek with a long, yellowed fingernail that encased a crescent of dirt. Lindstrom was not going to say another word. They were resuming a dance that had gone on for years.

"You repeat this and I'll personally burn your office, with you in it.... Someone sewed his lips shut."

Sharing the information was a serious violation of procedure, but J.D. had long since learned to take a risk to get a return.

The image of Doctor Dirt, with his lips sewn fast, seemed to fire Lindstrom's pornographic imagination. He had battled Clarity for years, convinced that it represented the forces of evil and darkness. Now the power of justice and light had made itself evident.

"What an ending," he said, eyes shining with hatred. "Eye of the needle, lip of a liar, pig squealing on the petard of its own suffices—"

"That's enough of that."

"—capir of a stuck tapir."

"Cut it out—*now*. Any ideas?"

Lindstrom jumped and danced a jig. "Follow the money."

"What does that mean?"

"Who winds up with Clarity? Who gets the money?"

"Come again?"

"It's obvious, isn't it? Ben Grossman had someone kill his boss."

Left turn complete.

CHAPTER

5

He drank his coffee and watched the morning traffic go by.

It was April Fool's Day in Annapolis—and it showed. A thirty-eight foot Bayliner crossed into the channel, bearing at about six knots into a thirty-six foot Grand Banks, with neither pilot willing to correct to the starboard.

They finally cut at the last second, passing port sides, a shaved whisker to spare between hulls. J.D. shook his head. The State of Maryland should give an intelligence test to anyone wanting to own boats that magnificent.

He sipped coffee, watched his sailboat rocking gently, tugging at the lines fastened to the Spa Creek pier, the morning sunlight cutting a golden arc across the gleaming deck.

J.D. loved his boat, but there was no Andre to help him here. Taking care of this demanding big piece of floating fiberglass took lots of time and money. It was a classic thirty foot Morgan Out Island, and he had managed to bring it back to new with sweat and quite a few barked, bloody knuckles of his own hand.

He got it to where finally everything worked.

In spite of much care and the best parts money could buy, about once a month something stopped working, just like that. Salt water had a way of doing that to boats. So far, at least, all the things that had gone wrong had nothing to do with floating. J.D.'s fear was that a seacock would let go while he was out of town. So he had double clamped through-hull fittings after installing new hardware and hoses. He doubled the number of bilge pumps and put in new batteries.

But he still worried. A rational sailor always worried because when you're fifty miles out to sea there's nobody to help, and rescue can be hours, if not days, away. There was danger even at dockside. There was no greater humiliation for a sailor than getting a phone call that your beauty has come to her final rest on the murky bottom because you forgot to change a hose or fix a pump.

J.D. had bought the Morgan cheap, used, and abused from a lawyer who said he never had time to take her out. The lawyer never had time to clean her either. But J.D. made time for it. He enjoyed his boat on mornings like this, even when just sitting dockside.

This was his favorite part of the day, watching that slice of sun warm the varnished wood and dark blue and yellow cushions. Across Spa Creek, first light glinted off the golden spire of the Navy Chapel, edged down to the waterside shops and coffee houses of Annapolis to the speedboats that cruised in and out of the little inlet to the city docks the locals had dubbed Ego Alley.

Sometimes he liked to bring his brass telescope out on the deck and do a little sightseeing across the way. Especially if there were an early morning regatta.

Back when he worked for the Bureau, J.D. would have been at the office hours ago—at first light. Now, as a PI, even under a government contract, Joe DeVine made time to enjoy a few good minutes with his coffee on the back porch of his waterfront townhouse.

It wasn't a big place. But he couldn't have used anything bigger. A two-story, two-bedroom townhouse of dark wood, a bar next to the kitchen, and a useful loft under a couple of slow-moving ceiling fans. It was enough for him and his one-man agency.

He used the second bedroom as the office for DeVine Investigations. Last night, he had logged on to the FBIHQ database and entered his special code. The computer fired back a series of questions for him. One wrong answer and the screen would have gone black. Then a carload of FBI agents would have come knocking on his door to arrest the hacker trying to gain illegal entry to the FBI's best files.

He'd have to remember to thank McGuire for keeping him up on the prompts.

J.D. was soon able to confirm that Roman Grice had boarded an American Airlines flight from California to Washington, D.C., several hours *after* Doctor Dirt had been killed. Count him as one suspect. Gentle Ben Grossman had to be counted as another. What subordinate didn't at least once dream of getting rid of his boss?

The FBI had analyzed the Nixon Library files beneath Thornburgh's sewn lips. The files detailed the itinerary of an unofficial trip Richard Nixon had made to Indonesia in 1963.

The trip had ended abruptly, a fact easily explained by Nixon's business or political needs back home. Nothing else jumped out at him. What possible interest could that trip have had to Doctor Dirt more than thirty-five years later?

J.D. had also received Clarity's "nasty" files on five standard PC disks, delivered to his home by Roman Grice. They made very interesting reading.

The redacted files contained enough sex-dirt, money-dirt, bribe-dirt to bury half the elected or appointed officials in Washington. The bad news was, that narrowed his list of potential suspects to a mere several hundred prominent men and women and their staffs. Quite a collection for the police lineup.

He sipped his coffee. It was more pleasant to think of another collection, the books on early America that he had acquired and treasured over the years, long stacks of cloth and leather binding that made his bookshelves sag. They kept him occupied when the weather was too foul for racing cars or boats.

Some guys collected stamps. J.D. had spent too much at antique book stores. There was the musty compendium of the letters of George Washington collected by Noah Webster in 1843. Then there was the mid-19th century reprint of David Ramsay's *The History of the American Revolution*, first published in 1789.

Even now, beckoning from the window of the Old Mariner Book Shoppe, where his only daughter Sarah worked resewing bindings on tattered classics, was a first-edition 1805 publication of Fisher Ames's *The Dangers of American Liberty*, rebound in leather.

Four thousand bucks.

It was a lot of money for a retired gumshoe with serious toys like a car and a boat. But the money from his FBI contract was good, and he was getting other work, too. The older he got and the more he saw of contemporary corrupt

Washington, D.C., the more he felt a need to reconnect with the original Washington and the other founding fathers.

He took another sip.

The Dangers of American Liberty. Smacks of Federalist pessimism. Still, not a bad title.

His FBI recruiters had worried he might be too intellectual for the Bureau. The Bureau hired lawyers, but distrusted intellectuals. To his surprise, he found the Marine Corps more accepting. The Corps just wanted his ass. The Bureau wanted his thinking too.

He finished his coffee and resolved, somehow, to buy that book.

J.D. had just loaded the hamper in the boat when he saw her jump over the door of her battered grey Mercedes 190 convertible. Had to like the girl's taste, even if it took her every penny to keep it up.

"Hey, daddy, wait for me."

J.D. held out his hand and helped Sarah aboard. Her brown hair was cut into a page boy look, something she'd adopted as a student at St. John's. He figured that's what came of reading too many medievalists—like St. Augustine, which for some reason had been her passion then. Now, for some reason, it was Anne Rice vampire novels. But she did keep a lookout for him when new arrivals showed up at the bookstore—like the Fisher Ames.

She sat down, drawing her knees up to her chin, the light reflected off the water and danced around her brown eyes. It wasn't for a father to say, but she was a good-looking girl. And Sarah knew her way around a boat.

He had hoped to meet his daughter in Los Angeles,

where she'd flown out for a rock concert while he did his investigation into the Buddhist temple. They would have spent a day or two in Catalina, but the Thornburgh murder had cut his trip short. This was to make up for it.

The boat eased out into the water. J.D. pulled out a thermos and poured himself another cup of coffee.

"So how was the concert? Who was it again?"

"Phish—with a ph."

"And how was Phish?"

"Oh, you know, they're kinda like the new Grateful Dead."

"Them again?"

"Oh Dad, you still worry too much. I'm 26. I'm not going to fall for drugs now. That's what you're thinking, isn't it?"

"You know I almost had an arrest warrant for Jerry Garcia."

"Yeah, dad, I know. You've told me that a million times."

"Jeeze. Sometimes I have to wonder about you."

She smiled at him. "Don't worry. Not any more."

J.D. slipped the 356 into fourth gear, hitting eighty. It was still cold, despite the spring sun, even colder with the top down. But he loved the feeling of wind ripping around him. His own personal wind tunnel.

He took the 356 on twisting, undulating roads that brought out the best of car and driver. The rearview mirror of the 356 kept picking up the stabbing rays of the setting sun. J.D. hunched over to avoid it. His cell phone trilled. He was surprised to hear Carol Suarez calling from her office in Los Angeles.

"As of today, you're officially on the Doctor Dirt case." Carol was never one to waste time on pleasantries. "You're the best we've got on the political beat."

"I'm glad to hear it." Always good to know that a whole day's work wasn't for free.

"You now report directly to me. McGuire is working the California angle out here—that it might be a local psycho. I want you to work the political side, the national side. You can start traveling immediately; don't worry about your travel budget. We'll take care of it."

Before first light would light the golden spire of the Navy chapel, J.D. would be on a plane, heading West.

6

The marine fog had burned off, and it was warm enough for Anne to open the roof. She looked around for any sign of the CHP, slid the stick shift into fifth gear, and took it to ninety. The RX-7's powerful rotary engine hummed like an angry bee.

The open feeling on the road matched her good feeling. Jim Miller had done a 180, relieved her of a burden of guilt, and given her carte blanche to track Doctor Dirt leads wherever she needed to go. He'd wanted "quality coverage." Well, he got it. An exclusive: *Murder in the Nixon Library*. "Ritual mutilation" was the kicker. And now that she had the story, she could run with it.

Anne exited left off Moraga and parked in front of a mock-tudor three-story office building. She double-checked her address. By the looks of it, you'd never guess that this was the world headquarters of IAI—Independent Artists International—the most powerful agency in the movie business, one of whose top executives was Hollywood attorney Mike Hughes, a former United States senator and failed presidential candidate, whom Doctor Dirt had knocked out of the Democratic primaries by revealing "the voice of a new generation" as the voice of a drunken adulterer.

Jim Miller had made the appointment. A security man checked his list, called upstairs, then led her to an elevator and pressed the button for the third floor.

When the doors opened, she was immediately greeted by a secretary who led her into a conference room, impressionist paintings on the walls, an oblong mahogany table filling the space.

Anne pulled out a chair, sat, and waited. She looked again at the paintings. Her jaw went slack as she recognized Sisleys, Chagalls—originals, not prints.

A smartly dressed middle-aged woman entered and extended her hand to Anne.

"I'm Evelyn, Mr. Hughes' assistant," she spoke with the precise articulation of the public-schooled British. "I'm so sorry, but Mr. Hughes had to leave unexpectedly. Please accept our apologies, both to yourself and to Mr. Miller."

"Do you know how hard it is to get around this city?" Anne shook her head and stood up to leave. Her exit was blocked by a man Anne recognized only because she had seen him countless times in magazine and television interviews.

Barry Newhouse, chairman and CEO of IAI, was taller than she imagined, balding but not bad looking, in a dark, subtle, pinstriped, tailored suit that cost more than a European vacation. He was tan, with a naturally out-thrust chin that seemed to dare you to take a swing at him.

"Anne, is it? Delighted to meet you. Evelyn, thank you."

Evelyn, dismissed, smiled graciously and left. Newhouse stood close to Anne, closer than a new acquaintance would normally stand.

"So, you're here to interview Mike, are you?"

"Yes, we're doing a political piece and thought that Michael Hughes could steer us in some helpful directions."

"But Mike isn't in politics any more. He's an attorney with an entertainment practice. Is this about that Doctor Dirt fellow?" He slipped the question in as if it were an innocent afterthought.

His cologne was not sweet, but musty, and the skin texture of his face seemed too even, like the shiny pores of a freshly scrubbed orange.

"Yes, we're doing a wrap-up piece on Thornburgh's career, and we are interviewing people who dealt with him from both sides. Did you know him?"

"Not personally. So you want a victim's perspective, is that it?"

"In a nutshell."

Newhouse took a step back. He looked down for a moment and pinched his lips between thumb and forefinger. He looked up, and looked into her eyes.

"Can I be candid with you? I mean off-the-record?"

Anne nodded.

"I worry about what you're up to for several reasons. First, this is becoming sensational. I don't want IAI to be part of a story. I also worry for Mike. We've been friends for years. I supported him as a U.S. senator. I was his liaison with Hollywood when he ran for president. I stood by him during the worst of times, when he was ambushed and humiliated by the likes of your Mr. Thornburgh.

"Mike was hounded out of politics because of that man. And since he left, he's declared himself a noncombatant. He wants to be a civilian again, and he wants to be treated like one. Let me ask you, do you see Michael Hughes as a central part of this story?"

"I can't say yet."

"Can I have your word that you won't take this any further than you have to?"

"I can only promise to be fair."

Newhouse stared long enough to make her uncomfortable. He walked out of the room, but returned in less than a minute.

He took one of his business cards from a small leather case in his front breast pocket, and, with an expensive gold pen, wrote something on the blank side of the card.

"Let Jim Miller know I'm putting my trust in the *Times* and its journalistic standards. This is Mike's address. He'll be happy to speak to you."

Anne Carlson thanked him and walked toward the elevator.

"Oh, and Anne," Newhouse said, his smile showing capped white teeth, "it was really a pleasure to meet you."

Anne did her best to smile back. But she didn't like this carefully choreographed set-up one bit.

Anne found Hughes in a conservatory-*cum*-swimming pool, part of a luxury condo complex in Westwood. The air was humid, rich with the lush smells of growing things. Lilies and tulips carpeted the flowerbeds, palm fronds lined the wall.

Steam rose from the modest pool, where no one swam. Hughes was wearing a thick, blue robe over his dry swimming trunks, and was carrying a plastic cooler.

"Hello there, you must be the lady from the *Times*." His famous face had aged noticeably. His bushy hair, long his political trademark, had gone half-gray. Blue veins had spread across his sharp nose. But his blue clear eyes conveyed the same air of ironical detachment.

"I'm Anne Carlson."

They shook hands and Hughes motioned to several plastic chairs and a table.

"Care for a midday pick-me-up?"

"Considering the climate, water."

"I'll doctor it a little. Let me guess, scotch?"

Hughes opened his cooler, and made her a scotch and himself a Bloody Mary.

"Cheers. Okay now, Barry gave me a hint. So why don't you just cut to the chase?"

"Well, as you know a political consultant by the name of Todd Thornburgh was murdered on Wednesday night. I'm doing a profile piece on his career, on the people whose lives he touched."

"Well, he certainly touched my life," Hughes said, his deep laugh edged with bitterness. "Let me get this straight. The guy was murdered, cut up or something, and you say you're doing a profile piece?"

"Why not? The police are holding onto the crime details. And he had a fascinating career, one that few people were aware of, but that shaped our politics in a major way."

Anne felt flush, sweat forming on her neck and forehead. She took a sip of the scotch.

Hughes laughed again, and his eyes drifted around the atrium as if looking for someone else. He spoke carefully.

"I did not know Mr. Thornburgh. As far as I'm concerned, my political life is a closed chapter. But I certainly harbor no bitterness, and I am genuinely saddened to hear that a young man has lost his life."

"But weren't you aware of who he was during the race?"

"I may have heard his name bandied about. But frankly I had bigger issues on my mind at the time."

"But senator—"

"Not senator, please."

"—now this was the guy who dug up the island photos on you, sent copies by overnight mail to every tabloid and daily in America, and then bragged about it. Looking back, do you have any thoughts to share about the role of opposition political research?"

"Nope. And call me Mike."

"Is that it, you're going to clam up?"

"Yep."

Anne slumped back in her chair. A strand of her thick blonde hair stuck to her forehead. She waved it back and took a deep swig of scotch.

Mike Hughes smiled at her. She realized that many women would forgive his rudeness for his smile alone, and that thought made her angry.

"Do you like your job, Anne?"

"Most of the time."

"Tell me, every reporter I've ever known has a screenplay in the back drawer. Is that the case with you?"

She didn't like where this was going.

"I mean, are you interested in me as a story, or as a prospect?"

"No, I'm just interested in becoming a movie star, Mr. Hughes."

Hughes laughed. "Okay, score a point for you. Look, I can see you're getting warm. It's, uh, hot in here. Would you like to join me? I can outfit you in a nice bikini." He leaned forward. "We could swim all day."

Their eyes locked for a moment.

"I'm swimming now. In bullshit." She snapped up her purse and walked toward the door. Hughes rose with a grunt and followed her outside.

"Come on, you can't blame me," Hughes said. "You come to my place when I'm half naked and into my Bloodies."

She stood in the doorway.

"The Michael Hughes I hoped to meet was a one-man focus group on West Coast politics."

"I can be that. Look, I'm sorry to have been true to my own lack of character," Hughes laughed amiably at himself. "Why don't you come over to my place. Don't give me that look again. I promise, no funny stuff. A real, straight-up interview."

"Why your place?"

"Because it's across the way and if we stay by this pool, you're gonna melt."

"You got a point there."

A colleague on the political beat had described Hughes to her as eager to give the inside story on politics, a man with a sardonic, almost philosophic élan in defeat. Perhaps it depended on how much he had to drink.

She followed him to a back door that led to a residential alley. On the other side, Hughes opened a door in a wooden fence that led to a backyard ringed with clusters of banana trees and eucalyptus. They walked toward a rambling, one-story ranch house of dark wood. The lot was at least two acres, half of it covered by the house.

"This is your condominium?"

"Yeah, hell of a unit, huh? I suppose you want the truth? I have a deal with the condo. I pay them, they front for me, take names. I use their pool a lot. That's where I meet visitors. Great way to screen out various nuisances, like political reporters."

Anne had to smile at his corny act.

"This place was originally the estate of some silent screen star. I rent the guest side of the house from the current owner, an investment banker who is usually in New York, although I would hardly know, with my separate entrance."

The inside of the guest wing appeared to have been last remodeled in the 1970s. It had redwood accents on off-white walls and a stone fireplace. A Berber rug had been thrown over the shag carpet. The living room and dining room were divided by a bar. The furnishings were spare and eclectic, a Danish modern black-leather chair sat next to an antique rocker. Anne guessed that Hughes was left with what little furniture his wife didn't take.

"You don't really like to drink during the day, do ya?"

"I can handle one more, make it a scotch rocks."

Hughes came back from the bar with two drinks and handed one to Anne.

"Every time I meet a young lady—you can count on it—these days it's usually bourbon and Coke." Hughes dropped into the black-leather chair. Anne took a seat in the rocker. "So here's to your taste and to my second interview of the day."

"Someone else is on this story?"

"Oh, no, don't worry about getting scooped. Not a reporter."

Anne smiled and tried to be her most pleasant self. She really wanted to know. "May I ask, is he one of the FBI agents working on this case?"

Hughes took a sip and appraised her interest. He pulled a card from the pocket of his robe.

"Says here his name is Joseph P. DeVine, Special Consultant to the FBI."

"What did he want to know?"

"Same things you do, I guess. Ask away."

"I really want to know how Thornburgh treated you—what you thought of him—how he influenced the process."

"Well, the first one, that's a simple question. He cut out my kidneys with a rusty key and stomped them to mush in public." Hughes didn't smile or pretend he was being funny. "We're still on the record now, huh?"

Anne nodded.

"All right. To be honest, I never thought much about him—Doctor Dirt, as they called him. During the campaign, it's like a war. You're running up and down the trenches, giving orders, keeping up morale. The only difference is, in war, when a general gives an order, everyone goes over the top. In politics, the only one who had to go over the top was me."

Hughes's robe slipped open, and Anne could see that his stomach had gone white and soft.

"So when I got slammed, I didn't have time to obsess over who was doing it to me. From my perspective, the world was doing it. Everywhere I went, people like you were on my case. There were microphones, klieg lights, questions. Every meeting at the campaign was a living death, as I saw the disappointment, dealt with the resentment, of my own people. I had let them down."

Hughes snorted and looked down at his drink. "And, well, it didn't exactly do wonders for my home life."

His eyes locked on hers. "I don't mind telling you this. I don't mind telling the world. I'm like a man whose face has been scalded, there's no use trying to hide my scar." He leaned over to make a point. "I do so in the hope that people will remember the rest, the important part. Who I was, what I did in the Senate."

Mike Hughes settled back, the soft leather curve of his chair creaking.

"Of course, I was bitter at first. I made a statement attacking the media. As I've said since, I now realize that what happened was a mistake, my mistake, and I take full responsibility for what my actions did to the campaign, to my marriage."

"But what about Doctor Dirt? Didn't he degrade the process, lower the terms of the debate?"

Hughes stiffened a little, as if he suspected a trap. "Since then, I've read a lot and heard a lot about what was going on in the other side. I may have outsmarted myself, but I guess you can credit Todd Thornburgh for putting it together."

"How did he put it together?"

"Is it okay if we go off the record here? Otherwise, I'm going to clam up again."

Anne nodded. Hughes reestablished eye contact for a moment, relaxed and then continued. He had decided to trust her.

"I've often wondered about Thornburgh going down to St. Martin, finding the right bar at the right marina, interviewing people in a sly way so as not to scare them—that couldn't have been easy. Believe me, I've had plenty of time to think about it.

"That crew at the marina, they're not the friendliest crowd to mainlanders. Somehow this Thornburgh guy got these old seabirds to open up to a stranger, an American, no less! I imagine that he walks in, poses as a tourist, buys people drinks, talks a blue streak, and then gets them to talk about me. That took finesse. This Thornburgh, I never met him, but it sounds to me that his real calling was with the CIA.

"Then, on top of all that, he scours the place with enough discretion to avoid getting kicked out, and hits the jackpot. He finds the pictures, old Polaroids tacked up with a lot of other pictures and stuff behind the bar."

Anne remembered the photographs, snapshots of an obviously inebriated Hughes doing the lambada on a stage with two island girls. In the picture, Hughes grinned idiotically at the camera, the flash rendering his eyes as red orbs.

Eyes of the damned.

It took only a little more probing and some money for the girls to confirm that much more than dancing had taken place that night. It all hit the tabloids and television the day before Super Tuesday, the Bible Belt primary.

The Hughes campaign had been crushed.

"This may surprise you, but I don't hold it against them. As I said, I did it to myself. What I can't forgive is the side stuff."

Anne rocked forward. "The side stuff?"

"Yeah, all of the little petty harassment, the pecking at my ankles that came before the big fall. That Clarity outfit called my favorite high school teacher and badgered her as if they were investigating the early life of Adolf Hitler. They interviewed old girlfriends from college. They tore through my financials, deeds, meager investments. They became bulls of Pamplona, chasing after anyone who had ever done any business with me."

Hughes stood up. "Let me show you something."

They walked into Hughes's study. On the wall hung several diplomas, a divinity degree from Harvard, a law degree from Yale. His classical CDs and tapes, his history books and biographies of great world leaders, were organized alphabetically.

Papers sat in a stack on a small work desk, to the side of a small personal computer. Years of wet drink glasses had left deep, discolored rings in the wooden top of the desk.

Anne saw a wall full of trophy pictures from a lifetime in politics, Senator Hughes with Margaret Thatcher, Helmut Kohl, and every U.S. president back to Ford. There were also other photos, one of a young Hughes with long hair shouting into a megaphone before the Lincoln Memorial. Another showed Hughes with slightly shorter hair and a rumpled tie during his first campaign. The photo next to it captured a candid moment of Hughes as a young senator laughing at something said by a black girl on a bicycle while he was inspecting a housing project in a big Eastern city.

Another wall was lined with pictures of Hughes with movie stars.

The political trophy pictures were primitive forms of identifying with the great and famous; but she had to admit, they had a universal currency. These pictures certified that Michael Hughes had once been somebody, a near-great man, an almost president.

"You like that stuff, huh?" Hughes asked. "I had to pack a lot of them away, or else every wall would be wallpapered with grinning idiots shakin' hands. Take a gander at this one."

It was a photo of Hughes caught in an animated moment of conversation, his hands waving in the air. The president who had beaten him for the nomination sat across a paneled table, open mouthed and smiling, seeming to laugh at what Senator Hughes was telling him. It appeared they were in a large hotel room. Then Anne noticed the distinctive oval windows of a 747.

"Lady, many people have their picture taken with a president. But not many are privileged to have an official Airplane Working Picture. That's at least worth the best seat at Spago."

"So what was it that you wanted to show me?"

Hughes opened a drawer crammed full of papers. "Let me see here," he sorted the papers with manic energy. Some papers looked like bills, some like invitations. There was at least one legal brief. Hughes kept sorting until he pulled up a newspaper, thick and folded, yellowed with age.

He spread it out on the desk. It was a New York tabloid.

The headline read "Hughes on the Take?" There was a picture of candidate Hughes, scowling in the midst of reporters, cameras, out-thrust microphones.

"During the worst part of the campaign, someone tried to make a big deal out of the fact that I dabble in California real estate." He was close to Anne now, breath bitter with alcohol and bile.

"No one—not a single reputable investigative journalist, not one investigator for the IRS or the FEC or any state agency—felt that my real estate investments were anything but kosher."

Hughes was working himself up into a rage.

"It wasn't enough for those punks to humiliate me before my wife, my kids, my mother. They had to make it look like I was on the pad."

Anne didn't want to gawk at the story. She noted the publication date so she could have a researcher dig up a copy.

Hughes was so angry he was shaking.

"Keep that in mind, Anne Carlson, when you do your profile piece. Doctor Dirt distorted his facts. No wonder someone finally shut him up for good."

She scheduled an interview with another prominent victim of Doctor Dirt.

The evening flight to Albuquerque was full, every seat taken. Anne was going to fly against the sun, grateful that late afternoon would advance quickly to twilight. The engines roared to life and the plane lifted, bounding and unsteady as it fought a stiff wind off the ocean. They banked over the Pacific and then cut east, over a solid film of brown smog, toward the desert.

CHAPTER

7

Doctor Dirt paid J.D. a visit that night.

His distorted face was like a medieval grotesque, eyes beady-black behind wizened lids, lips drawn in a rigor mortis smile. He had grown a bristly moustache, and his nose came to an even finer point, moist and dark.

He was on all fours, a rat human in a glistening coat of sweat, grubbing the darkest and flithiest corners of a back alley for secrets.

Doctor Dirt looked at him with impenetrable rat eyes. Then his rat lips moved, like some horrible computer-generated animal on a beer commercial.

"*You* killed me."

J.D. shook himself awake. He slipped a robe over his pajamas and stepped out onto the second-floor balcony of his hotel, a faux adobe job with cable and pool. He took in the pinion-pine scent of the dry, Western air. The sky was blue and cold, a blustery wind swept down the mountains to stir dust and old newspapers in the town plaza of Santa Fe.

He went back inside, disrobed, and took a shower. The white noise of the water jets somehow made it easier to think.

Neither he nor Sarah had mentioned Doctor Dirt on the boat trip. But his secret knowledge of the murder had hung over him like a monk's cowl.

Damn Thornburgh, damn him to hell.

From the moment his gloved fingers had lifted Thornburgh's lifeless head from that table in the Nixon Library, suppressed emotion had been scouring J.D.'s guts.

Thornburgh had been a friend, yes. But then it had gotten personal.

Sarah's politics might not have been exactly J.D.'s own, but they were close enough. Chuck Beaumont, the Republican congressman who represented Annapolis, and for whom she was a press secretary, had somehow managed to squeak by election after election. But however close the margins, his seat was considered safe.

But Doctor Dirt didn't think so. He was paid not to think so by a wealthy Republican primary challenger who wanted that seat and thought he could hold it easier.

First came the rumors.

"You know, Beaumont's gay."

"Can you prove it?"

"Everybody says so."

The rumors built in a deafening crescendo that finally had to be answered, at least obliquely, at a press conference. Congressman Beaumont standing with his wife and kids, testifying to his belief in family values, with the inevitable reporter, prompted by Doctor Dirt, throwing the hardball. "Congressman, do you condone homosexual acts as acceptable family values?"

"No, of course not. I'm not in favor of prejudice, mind you, but a homosexual couple is not a family. We need to keep our definitions straight. I'm for the traditional nuclear family. It's under threat everywhere. We need to support it, not undermine it."

"And to be blunt, sir, you're not a homosexual yourself?"

Beaumont shook his head and spread his arms around his family. "Are you kidding? Next question."

But soon there would be no "next questions" for Beaumont, except ones he didn't want to answer. Doctor Dirt had videotape of Beaumont entering a gay bar in Washington, emerging later, with the unsteady walk of a drunk, and thin men, with big mustaches and cropped haircuts supporting him on either side, nibbling his ears, laughing, running their tongues along his cheeks. Supposedly there was more, but this was enough.

After twenty-four hours of embarrassed denials, Beaumont made his confession to a .38 caliber revolver that splattered his brains over the stall of a public restroom.

Notch up another one for Doctor Dirt, or better yet, Doctor Death.

To be honest, J.D. hadn't cared about Beaumont. But he did care about Sarah. She was smart, computer smart, book smart, but still vulnerable, still hearing echoes of the illness, the trauma after the divorce that almost took her from him when she was a girl.

Getting such a bright girl admitted into St. John's had not been difficult. Getting her admitted into real life and responsibility was much harder.

As a young press secretary, Sarah had embraced her job with intensity; a vibrant enthusiasm that her colleagues had taken as youthful ambition. Only J.D. saw the dark side of her success—the manic edge to her energy.

When the crash came, she had fallen hard. Worse than the grief and shock of losing was being blamed by the press for holding back, for stupidly allowing her boss to set himself up.

Now no one on the Hill would touch her. Sarah had become radioactive.

Her depression after the suicide became crippling. Bouts of uncontrolled, red-faced anger, followed by crying jags. He took her in for a while, but it wasn't easy. Her tirades would come like some form of Tourette's syndrome, and then end in a flood of tears after she'd hurled his books to the floor, then shamefacedly returned them to the shelves.

But it was past. It was over. Her job in the antique book store was a way-station. Sarah would be fine. She'd be just fine.

I don't care if you haunt me, Todd Nathan Thornburgh, but to my daughter you'll stay dead and buried.

8

Anne leaned out her car window and pushed an intercom button at the entrance to Rancho Los Vaqueros.

"Hello," a man's voice said.

"I'm Anne Carlson of the *Los Angeles Times*," she shouted. "I have an appointment with Leonora Vasquez."

"*Hoy*, another visitor? Why didn't you come together? You could have had a convention! I'll be there in a minute."

In the distance, behind the gated iron fence, she could see a ranch house surrounded by an adobe wall. The door of the ranch house opened and an old man emerged. He wore an old, green windbreaker with blue jeans stained by axle grease and house paint, tucked into a pair of scruffy black cowboy boots. He crunched through the snow, unlocked the chain around the gate, and swung it wide.

Anne guessed the old man was a ranch hand.

"Hello, Ms. Carlson. I am Nacho."

Anne suddenly recognized him. He was the Alcalde, a legend in political circles, Ignacio Vasquez, patriarch of one of the wealthiest families in New Mexico, one of the most politically powerful dynasties in the United States. His older brother Manny, long dead, had served in the Truman cabinet. One son was a congressman, another had been Secretary of the Interior. Although the old man refused to hold public office himself, Nacho Vasquez had given orders to governors and senators as if they were hired help. Now this proud old man had watched his daughter publically humiliated, her political ascent foiled by Doctor Dirt.

The old man climbed into the passenger seat, pulled off his thick leather work gloves, and shook her hand. She felt rough, callused skin. They drove slowly toward the estate.

"I hope you don't take this too far with Leonora. It was her idea to talk about it. I would rather forget, but it's her life. I just hope you don't get her upset."

"I'll do my best." It was the most noncommittal reply Anne could muster. "Tell me, was another reporter here?"

"No."

So it had to be that Joe DeVine, that J.D. again, always one step ahead.

She parked and followed Ignacio through a snowy courtyard with several shiny-metal sculptures of abstract design. The house was two-story cream-colored adobe inlaid with massive mahogany beams. The tiled roof came to a crest, with a blue ceramic cross at the apex. Ignacio swung open a heavy wooden door of dark wood. Before stepping inside, Anne noticed a tall, shiny flagpole at the corner of the courtyard, an American flag snapping in the wind.

Their feet clicked on the tile floor. The family room was not large, but the ceiling rose to a full second story, making the room both cozy and magnificent. A massive hanging quilt of old patches of denim and colored fabric covered an entire wall. There were names in each square, some kind of elaborate family tree.

An elderly woman rose with difficulty from a comfortable chair by the massive stone hearth. She was more stooped than her husband, with a spine as crooked as her smile. The old woman was wrapped in a shawl, her thick hair straight and gray.

"Hello, I am Tita." Her searching eyes shined with compassion. Anne introduced herself. Ignacio walked away without saying a word.

"So you are here to interview Leonora? She'll be happy to see you. She just finished talking to a detective. Did you see him? No? You must have just missed him, maybe passed him on the road. Are you married?"

"No."

Tita smiled and nodded her head slowly, the way a doctor does when a patient offers a meaningful symptom. "You're on your own and you like it that way. Yes? Tita has an instinct for these things."

Then the old woman slipped her hand inside Anne's arm and led her down the hallway. "Did Nacho give you the speech? The one about his delicate daughter and her delicate condition?"

"More or less."

"You listen to me. If ever there was an overprotective father, it is Nacho. He didn't want Leonora to run for office, and he looked over her the whole time as if he were her chaperon, not chairman of her campaign. When the trouble hit, I think he took it harder than she did."

They slowly moved up a staircase of dark wood, a loud creak with each step. Tita stopped at the landing to catch her breath, and Anne noticed Tita's exquisite silver earrings,

66

each inset with a fat plug of turquoise. They started up the stairs again, to the second floor.

"I have a good feeling about you. I think you'll understand her."

"Why?" Anne asked in spite of herself.

"Because I see it in you, in the way you walk, the way you carry yourself with dignity, the way you look directly at me. You're simpatico. You and Leonora, you've both had to overcome a lot to shine. Not like me. No, I've raised three children and it seems as if I raised five grandkids, and I have no complaints. But you and Leonora, well, you're proving yourselves.

"I hope I haven't embarrassed you." The old woman withdrew her hand and opened a door to the second-floor study.

Leonora Vasquez was sitting at the end of a long couch reading *People* magazine. One wall of the room was lined to the ceiling with books, another served as a showcase for family pictures. A large color television was on, and a little boy, no older than three with an unruly mat of thick black hair, was sprawled in front of it on a thick Zuni rug. He watched a Power Rangers cartoon, the sound effects loud and violent.

Tita turned off the TV set. The little boy whined until Tita said something soothing in Spanish. She hit the eject button on the VCR and removed the tape.

"It's okay, Mannito, you can watch downstairs again, just like you did when the policeman was here." Tita led the boy out of the room. Leonora stood to greet Anne.

"Call me Lee," she said. "Little Manny, he's actually pretty good about this stuff. So many visitors."

It looked as if Leonora Vasquez had acquired twenty pounds since her Senate campaign. But she was still beautiful, her long black hair lustrous and shiny, her liquid eyes almost as black as her hair. She wore jeans, a blue workshirt, and an ornate silver bracelet. Anne guessed that the heart-shaped silver amulet drooping from her necklace kept a photo of her son close to her breast.

Anne sat in a reading chair with a Thunderbird design stitched into its back. Leonora took off a pair of house shoes and curled up on the couch opposite, drawing in her bare feet for warmth.

"So what brings you to Los Vaqueros?"

"Just wanted to ask a couple of questions about Todd Thornburgh. My interest in this is rather straightforward. I believe that opposition political research—"

"You mean dirt. That's what Thornburgh's Clarity outfit is all about—digging dirt."

"Okay, digging dirt, if you will, has become an important, but little understood part of our system. Few people know how it works and how it shapes our democracy. That's why I think your story is important."

"Well, this can't be any worse than being grilled by someone from the FBI for an hour."

"What did DeVine want?"

"Did I mention his name?" Leonora sat up, alert and suspicious.

"Just a lucky guess. He crossed my path on my last interview."

"If you have to know, he just asked questions a lot like yours, wanting to know all about my experience with Doctor Dirt."

"If it makes you more comfortable, I don't see your part in this as a victim story," Anne said. "After all, you've had something of a personal comeback since you ran for the Senate. You've had a little boy and started a charitable foundation for children with HIV."

"My husband left me. I gained weight and moved back in with my parents."

Anne watched her for a moment. Her words sounded bitter, but her tone wasn't bitter at all. It was a morbid, self-deprecating humor that spoke of an inner confidence.

Anne said, "So perhaps it *is* a victim story after all?"

"A victim? Certainly. I feel like a three-ton rig ran me over, stopped, backed up, and ran me over again. But I refuse to remain a victim. I've got Mannito. I have my charities. And I've just been invited to sit on a hospital board in Albuquerque. Not quite the most august deliberative body on earth, but at least it's nice to be allowed to show your face again."

Anne settled back in her chair. "Did you have your heart set on being a senator?"

"No. But I did have my heart set on being a Vasquez. Ignacio doesn't understand why his little girl would want to join in the rough and tumble of politics. He compares it to a Mexican rodeo, you know, where they trip the horses. In this case, it is the politician who is the horse." She smiled at the old family joke. "The truth is, I always wanted to serve, just like my brothers. I've wanted it ever since daddy took me to an event in the White House and I got to shake hands with President Johnson."

Anne wondered how realistic a view Leonora had of her father.

In the 1950s and 1960s, it was widely believed that Ignacio Vasquez bartered blocks of votes like cattle futures. There were dark rumors from those days, stories of smuggling, undercover customs agents found dead in the desert, a Vasquez mafia running New Mexico barrios. Anne was tempted to probe that past, but didn't.

It was Leonora who broke the pause. "Let me ask you a question. Have you ever gotten into something where you felt way over your head?"

"Yes," Anne said without hesitation. "I am now. Up until last week, I covered the suburban beat from a little office in Pasadena. This is my first national piece, and only the second really big investigative story I've ever worked on. I worry about getting this story right."

"And if you don't?"

"I'll lose my job and wind up as a proofreader for a second-rate ad agency."

Leonora laughed, looking pleased. She went back to her half recline and drew in her feet again.

Anne asked, "So you always wanted to run for office?"

"Yes, or at least I thought I did. Even in college, I was actively preparing for a political career. I was deeply involved in Stanford's student government. I served as president of the campus Democrats, as student coordinator for the Carter campaign. I did everything but what, in hindsight, I should have done—graduate. And Doctor Dirt found that out."

"What happened?"

Lee grasped her feet and began to knead them. "You have to understand how it all started. The truth is, I was accepted into Stanford. I did make the dean's list my first quarter. I did do all those political things while in college. So when I'd give a speech, the Rotarian or Lions Club busybody who would introduce me would take my first little bio—which clearly said I attended Stanford University—and he would invariably introduce me as a graduate of Stanford. After awhile, the difference seemed to become insignificant, a minor matter. I did have some Stanford education. Who cared about the sheepskin?"

"It seems a lot of people did care."

"That's because of the way I let it unfold. You see, the staffers who wrote my literature for the campaign really emphasized my academic background. I was young. I had never started a business or held office. We were sensitive to the charge that I was just trading on the Vasquez name. So they embellished a little. They wrote that I had been in student government. Absolutely true. They wrote that I had graduated from Stanford. Absolutely not true, but I had started to lie to myself. I remembered being a few credits short. Who gave a damn anyway? And they wrote that I had been on the dean's list. True, but now I acknowledge that was misleading."

"Why?"

"I had made straight 'A's', heading for honors in my first quarter. But after I got wrapped up in student politics, my grades took a nosedive.

"So here I am, the Democratic nominee in a state that has a tradition of electing liberal Democrats to the Senate. We're two months out from the election, and I am twenty points ahead. I think I can't lose. I'm already deciding who is going to be my chief of staff, my press secretary, my legislative director.

"Then on a Monday, after speaking to the Gallup Chamber, I find out Doctor Dirt blast-faxes a press release to state editors and political reporters that made fun of me for claiming to have graduated from Stanford on the dean's list. I acknowledge that I didn't graduate on the dean's list, just made it one quarter.

"That was my last opportunity to come clean.

"On Tuesday, Doctor Dirt sends out another fax, noting that I had made a string of 'D's' in one quarter—that was when I had been so busy in student government. I don't know how he got a copy of my transcript, but by then I am embarrassed and for the first time, running scared. I gave a speech publicly attacking my opponent and his dirt dealers for spending so much time worrying about report cards.

"Then comes Wednesday, and he sends out a one-page fax. It says, 'Oh, and by the way, Lee Vasquez isn't a Stanford graduate. In fact, she doesn't have a college degree at all.'

"That makes it a national story. I am forced to apologize, first to my campaign and supporters for not being up front with them from the start. And then to the entire state. I explained that I was just a few credits short of graduation, which was my recollection.

"On Thursday, Doctor Dirt lets it be known that I was actually twenty credits short of graduation. My press secretary quit on Friday. My campaign manager went fishing for the weekend, and never really came back to work. The money dried up. I took a thirty-point drop in the polls. Nacho, poor Nacho, he was fit to be tied. He hated that man, that Doctor Dirt. I have never seen him that angry."

Anne heard a burst of Spanish invective from the other side of the door. She could make out the word *pendejo* in Nacho's swearing, almost a growl.

"Daddy, have you been eavesdropping on us?"

"No, I was just walking down the hall when I heard you talking about a little man who mouthed off a lot of lies. It was a natural reaction."

"Daddy, you were listening to us, admit it."

Ignacio half entered the room, his hands in the back pockets of his blue jeans. "Remember, I was your campaign chairman."

"Hell, Nacho, in the last few weeks you *were* the campaign."

"Okay, that is true. But as your campaign advisor, I am interested only in how the story turns out." The old man bowed with elaborate courtesy, his arm across his waist the way waiters do in television comedy skits.

"It will turn out fine," Leonora said. "And besides, let's have a little Christian charity. The man is dead, after all."

"Yes, you are right. After all, the man is dead. Well, I need to change clothes. I have been invited to have a late lunch with the mayor of Santa Fe."

"That is quite an honor," Leonora said as the old man left. "For the mayor of Santa Fe."

Anne said, "You seem to have recovered quickly."

"Listen, I have a strong family life, a great home, and the most meaningful work I could do. Yeah, I have recovered. I forgave Doctor Dirt in my heart."

"And have you forgiven yourself for screwing up?"

Leonora looked back at her for a long time. "I suspect we all have a lot to forgive ourselves for. I'm working on it. How about you?"

Anne felt flustered under her gaze. She thanked her and left.

Tita met Anne at the landing, and took her arm to escort her to the door. "So how did it go?"

"You were right," Anne said. "Your daughter is strong, a survivor."

Tita patted her arm. "We are more proud of her today than ever. You print that, okay?"

Anne smiled and said "okay." She instantly regretted it. She never made solid promises about how her stories would turn out.

"This is a young woman who has lost her husband, her career," Tita spoke with firmness. "But she is doing well because she has family. She has faith. And she has something else."

"What is that?"

Tita laughed. "Needlework. You know, Leonora never was allowed to do any kind of physical labor. Not that there wasn't plenty to be done around here, but Nacho would never let a daughter of his clean the barns or shoe the horses. That was for his sons. But after the election, I suggested she go back to sewing, which she was so good at as a girl. The many quiet hours of humble work have been good for her soul. You know what I mean?"

Tita led Anne to the family room. She got one last look at the massive quilt displayed like a priceless tapestry. The light from outside was very bright, reflecting off the snowy

Sangre de Christos, transmuted by a stained glass window into a blood red that splashed across the entire quilt.

"Can you imagine? There is the entire Vasquez family tree. And she put all of that together in fourteen days with needle and thread."

CHAPTER
9

She stood at the shallow end of the pool, calculating her dive, knowing the old man was judging her every move.

Shannon Crocker sprang forward. With one deft motion, she cut, torpedo-like, just below the surface. By contracting her ribs, she forced her wind down to the bottom of her lungs, conserving it for the twenty-yard underwater swim to the shallow end. She pulled herself up on the metal railing at the deep end, barely out of breath.

The old man said nothing. He remained impassive, reclined in his beach chair. The pool had the classic rectangle and symmetrically spaced Ionic columns of a Greek temple.

She toweled down in front of him, grateful for a little sun. Looking out over the San Marcos cliffs above the sea, she could see a curtain of mist beginning to blur the horizon. In a few hours, the fog would be back and it would be as cold as it ever got on the San Marcos Peninsula.

"It is a good thing that you swim," Franklin Manoulian said. "You were on the USC swim team, I was on the USC track team. That was long ago, and I don't run anymore. But it's important to do things to stay in shape, especially as you get older."

He often spoke like that to her. He was the seventh richest man in the world, but he sounded like her swimming coach, or even her dad.

Manoulian, at seventy, looked two decades younger. Despite his broken nose, his pockmarks and large pores, he reminded Shannon a little of Paul Newman. His short salt-and-pepper hair swept back in waves. His face was deeply lined and deeply tanned, setting off pale blue eyes that were so hard to read.

"How often do you work out, Frank?" She was the only one of his employees who could call him by his first name.

"Three times a week in the gym, mostly free weights. I spent a fortune on the machines, but I find that I absolutely hate being tethered to one of those things."

Despite his spreading middle, his arms and shoulders were well conditioned. A thick mat of hair covered his chest and spread out to his shoulders. Liver spots speckled the backs of his hands.

"And of course there's golf. You're too young for that. A woman your age should play tennis. I did until just last year. Should take it up again."

"Can I get you anything?"

"No, thank you, Shannon. It's too early for a drink and too late for coffee."

She took the chair next to him, slinging her wet blonde hair behind her. Her face was at first glance pretty, but at second glance a little hard, as if petrified by the sun. Her body, revealed by a wet, single-piece bathing suit, was athletic—more angles than curves.

In truth, Manoulian was glad she wasn't a knockout. He

knew most of his people thought they were sleeping together. But the truth was, if he were to have sex with Shannon Crocker, it would be like having sex with one of his daughters. Unimaginable.

After all, he had held Shannon in his arms when she was an infant, twenty-eight years ago.

Lincoln Crocker, her father, had been his lawyer and best friend. She had grown up playing with the Manoulian girls. Shannon was family.

Now Linc was several years dead from a heart attack, and his daughter had become Frank Manoulian's right hand man.

"Did you read the story about the rates coming down again?" Manoulian asked.

"Don't believe it. The Fed's not going to budge."

Her answers were usually like that, firm and to the point, just like they teach in business school, though Manoulian sometimes doubted how deep her knowledge really went. Business school was one thing. Business reality was another.

A long time passed in comfortable silence. The low sun was disappearing in the approaching fog. The cliffs were momentarily inflamed with golden light.

"Shannon, I need to talk to you about something. If any of this makes you uncomfortable, stop me. And above all, I don't want to be misinterpreted."

Frank Manoulian spoke without looking at her, his eyes on the steps that led from the pool, back to the great house at the top of the hill.

"This deal on the San Marcos Presidio. We had to get

it through a lot of committees, through Interior, Public Works, Armed Services. We had to rely on friends in the California delegation, the governor's office, the speaker of the assembly. Above all, we worked closely with someone in the West Wing of the White House. We had to call in a lot of chits, all of them. When the EPA started to make trouble over the clean-up around the artillery range, we couldn't do anything about it. Too public. Even the White House couldn't help us. We got a great deal on the land, but we've still got to eat the clean-up cost.

"So as you might well imagine, I'm risking a lot on this development. And Shannon, my exposure is not just financial. It's not just personal, with the movie stars flocking to live here and the president himself building his retirement home. It's legal. You follow?"

"I follow."

"Promise you'll stop me if I say anything that makes you uncomfortable. If I say something that you don't quite understand, or don't want to hear, just raise your hand and I'll shut up. Okay?"

"Okay." She was starting to get cold, and hoped he wouldn't mistake the gooseflesh on her legs and arms for apprehension.

"Mike Hughes—you know he's now hooked up with Independent Artists—called me last night. He was very drunk, and when he drinks, which is about every night, he starts picking at old scabs. He tells me he's still pissed off about the way he was treated in the campaign. Then he tells me he's pissed off because he doesn't feel like he's getting his fair share from us.

"He tells me he's sick and tired of being ignored by me, as if he can't wait a few years for our arrangement to be completely fulfilled. He tells me he's been talking to the *L.A. Times*. He even talked to someone involved with the FBI. God knows what about. Then he says he wants to hold a press conference. I'm not sure what he meant. I'm not sure he knew what he meant. But I took it as a threat."

He paused a moment, letting his last word hang heavy.

"Barry Newhouse has two jobs these days, head of IAI, and Mike's keeper. Barry tells me that Mike is becoming unreliable, that he's blabbing all sorts of bitter, untrue things to friends, maybe even to other reporters, trying to even old scores over losing the nomination.

"If he keeps picking at this old scab, it's going to open up a very old and deep wound. It could lead back to an arrangement set up not just for Hughes, but for several other members of the U.S. Senate, the California assembly speaker, a lot of friends in Hollywood. And, of course, the ultimate power couple and their glorious retirement amongst us."

Manoulian sighed and stared at the sea for a moment. "Let me tell you something you probably don't know. I've known Barry and Mike half my life. More than that. And what Barry says is true. You can't depend on Mike to act rationally. To think before he talks. He's old and forgotten, and he's getting bitter about it. He'll say anything to anybody. You get the picture?"

"Yes, Frank."

"So Barry is getting nervous about his old friend. And as Barry becomes nervous, he too might become... unreliable. Do you follow?"

"Yes, I follow."

Frank Manoulian reached down and pulled up a long, chocolate-brown Cuban cigar, put it in his mouth, and started chewing on it.

The old man's shoulders were high, tense around the neck.

"Shannon, I'm going to ask you something I had to ask your father only once. Will you do anything for me?"

"Yes, Frank, I will."

The old man's shoulders relaxed a notch. He flicked a shred of tobacco from his lips.

"Don't worry, I won't ask you to do anything beyond your level of comfort. I just want you to call somebody. Make a contact. Pass along some material."

"I'll do it, Frank."

"Let's go inside, it's getting cold."

Halfway to the house, he turned and faced her. For an uncomfortable instant, she thought he was going to get romantic. Instead, with slow dignity, he put his hands on her shoulders and kissed her chastely on the cheek.

Frank's eyes bore into her soul.

"I'm counting on you kid."

CHAPTER
10

"Dee-me-tree," one of the whores said. "Where didya get a name like that?"

He looked at her in a way that made her shut up. "If you don't know me, you don't know my name."

"No, sir, I don't." She wasn't bad looking, more black than Puerto Rican, no older than eighteen, perhaps as young as... sixteen? But he could tell she read the look he was giving her, probably the same look her business manager shot if he thought she was holding out on him. Dmitri wondered if she knew how much worse it could get.

For a moment, her manner grew reserved and respectful, as if she were a little girl and back in church.

"All I meant was, I liked partying with you. Remember me, I'm Jasmine. Maybe again sometime?"

"Maybe."

Dmitri Popova relaxed, slumped nude onto a dingy mattress as hard as a palette on the floor. He must have talked when he was drunk. Dmitri rarely made mistakes like that on a job. Cleaning up after such errors could be ugly.

"Yeah, don't forget me either," said the other whore, the one who looked more Puerto Rican, squatting on the other side of the mattress, smoothing out her hose.

"Nice to be with you," Dmitri said. "Both."

Nice wasn't quite the word. He lit a Marlboro and pulled a drag to the bottom of his lungs. He had paid them extra, a lot in fact, and then talked them into doing the kinds of porno-movie moves with him and each other no woman would imagine on her own, acts that existed only to flatter and satiate male lust. Now the room stank of smoke, sex, and stale beer ground into the musty carpet.

For a moment, he felt ashamed. Not over what he did, but over the fact he had to pay to get it. Back home, he could call any one of a dozen women. Some of them good-looking, classy, the wife of a submarine captain, a woman who anchored the news in Volgograd, a girl with Intourist.

But here, this was okay. He told himself this time it was necessary. He was on a job and if he had to have sex, absolutely had to have it, then it would have to be anonymous. He convinced himself that it was a risk, but not a big one.

The girls stood over him, getting a little bolder, smiling slightly, contemptuous of the pale, naked man sitting below them. For an instant, he thought they were going to ask for more money. Then he gave them that look again. The one who called herself Jasmine nodded, a defensive gesture of respect. They both left.

He locked the door after them and swore in Russian. He looked into the mirror over the sink to confirm that the large bandage on his left arm was secure. He stripped off the tape and rolled up the square of gauze to reveal an old Soviet Army tattoo, the sword thrust across a shield bearing a hammer and sickle, a pretension of the *spetznaz*, the elite special forces of forty thousand attached to the old Soviet KGB specializing in counterinsurgency, counterterrorism, and special operations behind enemy lines.

The tattoo was useful to flash before a client in a private sauna. It was decidedly inconvenient elsewhere.

He pulled on a robe, lit another Marlboro, and walked down the hall to the public bathroom, taking a shower in a bathtub marbleized with scum.

Even though he had worn condoms, Dmitri always scrubbed himself down after being with whores, an old habit he had picked up as a soldier. Once, when he couldn't get to a bath in Kabul, he went back to the soldiers' bar and soaked his penis in a glass of vodka. How his company roared over that one.

He remembered Andrei Samolovich, his commander, lips scrunched with suppressed laughter, face ruddy as a beet, "Tell us, Dmitri! Are you thirsty?"

What are you doing now, Samolovich? After saving our lives from an ambush in the Khyber Pass, leading us on secret missions in the birch forests of Poland, along the stony banks of the Amur River, what is it that you do now? Do you still wear a uniform? Are you a security man at McDonald's? A streetsweeper in Tomsk? A hotel doorman for rich Jews?

And what about me, Samolovich, you-son-of-a-bitch, would you be horrified or proud, or perhaps even envious, to know that I am making lots of money—stacks of dollars— more money than the KGB paid us in ten years? All to kill a man in Chicago. For what, I don't even know.

Dmitri Popova dried himself with his towel, and wrapped it around his waist.

The only remnant of the night's orgy was a slight hangover feeling, dull pressure behind his temples, dryness in his mouth, and weakness about the knees.

He regarded himself in the mirror. Dmitri's badly discolored front teeth detracted from his handsome smile. His arms were still hard, muscles like knots in a thick rope. His body was lean, legs in splendid shape. Only his belly had gone a little soft, and that was so slight it would take only a week in the gym to make it flat as a washboard.

Once his dark-blond hair was combed straight back, Dmitri looked almost handsome, his pale face long, his eyes mournful. Women found that sullen look of his to be either adorable or threatening, sometimes both in a single day.

Dmitri pulled on a pair of long underwear and a pair of blue jeans. He had paid cash for them the other day. They were the jeans kids wore, two sizes too baggy, with thick cuffs at the ankles. He slipped on a shirt he had acquired in a sports store, and over that, a jacket with a Chicago Bull's emblem. Into the generous cut of his jacket's front right pocket, Dmitri stuffed a Chicago Bull's cap and a blue winter face mask.

He slipped on a pair of white socks and expensive basketball shoes. In the closet he picked up a soft leather case, unzipped it and pulled out a 9 mm Glock-17 with the serial numbers filed off the handle and the barrel.

Kneeling over the stinking mattress, he double checked to make sure the chamber was empty, disassembled the hammer and the firing pin, oiled the metalworks in the plastic interior, and scoured it with a barrel brush.

He reassembled the gun and slipped it into his left jacket

pocket. He also pocketed several clips, each of them holding seventeen rounds. Then he wadded up his dirty clothes from the previous few days and stuffed them into the bag.

Dmitri flushed the bandage down the toilet. He searched the room looking for any other trace of himself. Everything else, essentials like his passport, visa, and cash, were stored in an airport locker.

He put the leather bag in a backpack, which he slipped over his arms. He put the blue mask over his face. Then he strapped on a Swatch wristwatch and checked the time, 6:45 AM. He was almost too late.

A half hour later, the American businessman emerged from his apartment on Michigan Avenue. Dmitri called his victim "Lucky." He was a stocky man in his mid-forties, his gray-flecked brown hair well styled, his thick arms and torso filling out a tan Chesterfield coat with a dark-brown lapel. Three days ago, on Dmitri's first day of surveillance, he'd been close enough to see Lucky's round face, brown-eyes, an expression that was an odd combination of cunning and unfeigned innocence.

Dmitri studied him now from a bus stop across the street.

He began to follow the businessman. This would be the day. He didn't quite know when or exactly how he would do it, but he knew the man's schedule well enough to improvise. It could be ten minutes from now. It could be after work.

But this would be Lucky's last day.

Dmitri felt a tingle and an urgency in his lower gut. It was always like this, no matter how many times he did a job—a mixture of fear and excitement that impinged on his professionalism. This time, he didn't mind that feeling. It kept him warm, kept him going in the bitter cold wind that sliced across the lake like a blue razor, on this freakishly cold spring morning in Chicago. He followed Lucky down the Miracle Mile, past bookstores and toy stores, wading through crowds of people shuffling to work. He followed Lucky past Gumps and Neiman Marcus, past an old water tower of limestone, a sign said it had been streaked black by the Great Fire of Chicago.

Lucky walked into the first floor of an apartment tower. Dmitri checked his Swatch, 7:30 AM, right on time. He watched the businessman inside the plate-glass reception area. Even at one hundred feet, he could see the apartment day manager look up from behind the desk, see Lucky, smile with recognition, and place a phone call upstairs.

Two minutes later, a smartly dressed girl of about twelve years emerged from an elevator and hugged her father, just like yesterday and the day before. The businessman opened the door for his daughter and they walked side by side down the sidewalk, toward the lake.

Dmitri began to follow from the other side of the street. The clouds parted, and the low sun brought out the dull colors of the city.

The girl had a round face like her father, with straight brown hair that she pulled back into a ponytail. She wore a pink overcoat and black shoes. Yesterday morning, they did not talk. Perhaps Lucky had an argument with his daughter. Or maybe they had been just barely awake, sleepwalking.

This morning they were wide awake, animated. The

father said something with a straight face that made his daughter laugh. Her laughter made him smile.

They kept a brisk pace. Dmitri maintained an even stride with him. You poor fool, you have made enemies from Grozny.

They came to the entrance of the private school and Lucky gave his daughter a hug. Dmitri looked away, to the lake, cold and deep blue like the Gulf of Finland. He could actually see faint ridges on the other side. Where would that be? Michigan? Ohio? He wasn't sure; his knowledge of American geography was still not what it should be.

But he had been certain for some time that he wanted to live in this country, that he belonged here. He would have to go to a lot of trouble and expense to disguise his past in the special services. After all, he didn't want to spend the rest of his life answering questions from the FBI or the CIA. But he could get in, become a U.S. citizen. Others had done it.

And if he could do that, he could find another line of work. He could start a business. Or become an actor. He would be a rich man. And there would be no one, no Push-kinskaya street punk or hood-eyed Chechen *taip* boss to ask for protection money. No one to tell him how to live.

All he needed to make the transition was a lot of money. And that meant he needed to finish a few more jobs like this one.

He followed Lucky down the street, down North Michigan Avenue, where he disappeared into a thirty-story office tower for the morning.

Dmitri stepped into the vastness of the biggest McDonald's in Chicago, pulled off his mask, grateful for the warm air that circulated from the blowers. He ordered a muffin sandwich with ham and egg and a Styrofoam cup of coffee. He picked up a newspaper from an empty table and took his station at a window-side table, the best vantage point for the entrance into the office building.

The greasy meal and coffee after a long walk in the cold seemed to work on his hangover. He was starting to feel very... with it? Yes, with it, very much alive.

Dmitri set down his paper and went to the pay phone next to the men's room. He used a long-distance credit card issued to a phony name, an account which he scrupulously paid months in advance every time he was in the United States.

He called his voice-mail service. He heard his own voice, his accented English sounding quite professional. "Hello, you have reached the offices of Eastern Enterprises, please...."

Dmitri depressed the star symbol, and a synthetic voice told him that he had two messages.

After the first beep, he heard the hysterical voice of Iriana, the Intourist guide. She must have blown a week's wages to make that call. It was hard to make her out, with the voices of her children and her old father in the background. She was crying, demanding to know where he was, when he would be back in Moscow, and if he didn't call soon they were through....

The message ended abruptly and Dmitri made a mental note to change his drop number and never again give it to a woman.

A moment of weakness.

Such moments were becoming all too common. Until last night, he had hired prostitutes only while waiting for instructions or while in transit. But last night, for the first time since he left the special services to go professional, he had hired prostitutes while actually on a job. He wondered if this relaxation of his professional code, taking an unnecessary risk like this, was a sign that he was getting tired of this business.

Keep this up, Dmitri, and you will wind up dead.

He felt a stab of self-recrimination, the whores knew his first name. And now he had a woman from Russia calling his secret American business number.

He pressed the star key again.

The second beep brought another woman's voice, this one speaking English. "My name is Shannon. We have a serious problem requiring possible action soon."

She left a number.

Shannon? Who?

He had never slept with a Shannon, as best as he knew. From the flat tone of her voice, it had to be business. He replayed the message, memorized the number—he had no idea where in the United States the 415 area code would be—and called.

After four rings, the receiver on the other end fell to the floor, someone groaned and fumbled around for it. "Hello," a woman said, a voice raspy with sleep.

"This is Eastern Enterprises."

After a half beat, the woman asked him to hold. He heard water running for a full minute.

"You'll have to excuse me, it's still early here in California. My alarm doesn't go off for another fifteen minutes."

"I see. And do you have some specific problem in the arena of international trade?"

"Yes," she said, "we need advice on exporting California wine."

So she works for Manoulian, you old Armenian cutthroat. Who is this woman to you? Wine was the code word he had given to Manoulian. If she had said pasta, it would have been the New Orleans mob. Vodka was given as a sign for a group of his fellow countrymen, now expatriates doing a thriving business out of Brighton Beach.

"So you work for the San Marcos Group?" he asked.

"Yes, I'm vice president of administration and I report directly to Mr. Manoulian. As you know, in addition to real estate, we grow grapes in the valley, and we're starting to produce several strong vintages."

"Great, well, perhaps we should talk about this sometime soon."

"Timing is critical. Are you in the country? I'd like to see you here."

"That would be difficult. I'm just about to shake on a deal. I intend to return to Moscow first thing tomorrow."

A long silence.

"Can you work me in this afternoon?"

"I don't see how."

"Can you see me at 4:30 PM? An hour is all the time I need to pick your brain."

He cradled the receiver, twisting it in his hand. This was unorthodox, against the rules, mixing clients and jobs like this. But Manoulian, the Armenian—he could pay. Maybe enough to make up for all the remaining jobs he had to do.

"That could be... awkward for me." He looked at the

entrance to the businessman's office across the street. "If you can possibly get here in time...."

"I can, flight schedules and weather permitting."

"...and I mean be here right on time, not a minute later than 4:30 PM, I can break away from my negotiations and give you no more than twenty minutes."

"Deal."

Dmitri liked the way she said that, so American.

"What is your whole name?"

A slight pause. "Shannon Crocker."

"All right, Ms. Crocker. I'll meet you at the DeWitt's ice cream parlor in downtown Chicago. Don't be late." He hung up.

At 10:30 AM, he called 415 information, got the number for the San Marcos Group, called it, and asked the receptionist for Ms. Crocker. The phone rang three times. Her voice mail clicked on, and he heard her voice saying she would be out of the office today.

Dmitri was satisfied. If the San Marcos Group had no such woman, or the voice was different, he would have dropped the job he was on, even though he was on the verge of finishing it, and he would have taken the first international flight out of O'Hare to Moscow, Mexico City, anywhere. The FBI, they loved to use set-up jobs, especially attractive women. They called them honey traps.

But this woman, this Shannon, had used the code word Dmitri had personally given to Manoulian over wine in a dark cellar of a restaurant, a little Armenian dive in an alley off Tverskaya. She worked for him all right.

She had to be okay.

Imagine that, trusting a woman with such a job. And she sounded young. Dmitri wondered what she would look like.

He resumed his place at a plastic seat by the window. A few minutes after noon, Dmitri watched Lucky stroll out for lunch, his hands resting in the deep pockets of his brown Chesterfield. The man wouldn't need to be followed. A creature of habit, he would wander down the street and descend a set of old-fashioned metal stairs to a steakhouse decorated in red velvet, where he would have lunch with other businessmen.

Lucky would be back around 2 PM, walking slowly after a big lunch and perhaps a few martinis. Dmitri wondered if Lucky took a nap in his office after that.

He didn't feel so wide awake himself, the effects of the morning's coffee wearing off. Dmitri remembered a snippet of poetry from his childhood English classes. Yes, he thought, I do have miles to go before I sleep. Thankfully, the fast-food restaurant was huge and busy. As long as he stirred a drink, none of the teenagers behind the counter would even notice him, much less kick him out as a vagrant.

He thought of last night, the long exertions, the booze, the lack of sleep. He still felt raw, tired. In such a state, sleep was best, but food would keep him going.

He went to the counter and ordered the largest burger meal, and took the tray to his table. Even after all his time abroad, he was still astonished to see a forest of french fries, a burger as big and round as a field canteen, enough cola to fill a helmet.

Dmitri ate slowly, savoring the heavy, salty food, washing it down with the icy sweet cola.

After lunch, he ordered a large cup of black coffee to keep awake. While nursing the brew, he saw Lucky return to his office. This time he couldn't see his face, but he had no doubt the man was returning from another heavy lunch, wearing an expression of near stupor.

Dmitri wondered if Lucky turned to his secretary before closing the office door and said something like, "Please hold my calls." Dmitri would like to have a job like that someday, one where you had an office and could tell a secretary to do things like that.

And to have such a job, and not to fear someone like himself, a killer for hire sent from some Mafioso or moneylender. That would be success.

For the next hour Dmitri pretended to read a newspaper. After that, the caffeine began wearing off again, he finally permitted himself a fitful nap. No one bothered him.

At 4 PM, he jerked awake, downed another coffee, and went into the bathroom to wash his face and comb his hair.

DeWitt's ice cream shop next door was a replica of a 1950s diner, with posters of Elvis and Marilyn Monroe, neon lights, and old Coca-Cola signs. He slid into a red-cushioned booth in the smoking section and ordered a chocolate malt.

At 4:15 he saw a short, broad-shouldered woman enter the parlor, her eyes heavy-lidded, her complexion dark and her hair curly. She was thick, like a wrestler, just the kind of woman who looked like she could hire a killer.

Her hand enveloped that of a five-year-old boy.

He slumped back and read the song titles in the little jukebox by the wall. Then he finished his malt, using a long spoon to pick at the last vestiges of ice cream at the bottom of the cold metal container. Dmitri could eat like that and never be more than ten pounds over his optimum weight. When on assignment, sheer anxiety alone seemed to burn off the food.

The glass door opened again and he saw a young woman in a dark overcoat enter. She was blonde, probably natural, with a face just a little too hard to be beautiful. She hung her coat on a metal rack, and Dmitri could see beneath her dark suit that she was firm, athletic in build, a tall young woman of no more than twenty-eight years.

She brushed back her hair and looked around the parlor with a feigned casualness that Dmitri found comic. They made eye contact, and she came to the table.

"Are you from Eastern Enterprises?" she asked, looking him over, taking in his Chicago Bulls outfit.

"I am Dmitri, Shannon."

She slid her leather case into the booth and took a seat facing him. By the uneven way she moved, Dmitri could tell she was nervous. He could also tell she was fighting to suppress it.

"I want to thank you for taking this visit," she said. "As you know, the San Marcos Group is concentrating on real estate although we do have some international interests."

"Yes, you're interested in selling wine, red wine."

She blushed. He could see she was breathing faster.

"If Manoulian sent you to me, he must have a great deal of trust in you."

"He does. His only son is dead, and his daughters— well, they're not interested in business."

"I know. And you are… interested in business?"

She met his eyes. "I am."

Dmitri lit a Marlboro, took a deep drag. "Tell me about it."

"We have a potential issue. Let me stress, there is no problem as of yet. But there could be, soon, unpredictably, depending on the direction of certain inquiries."

Dmitri was enjoying this, admiring her composure, watching her struggle to bring her strong professionalism to the situation. Her lipstick was smeared; she must have only had time to apply her makeup in a cab or airplane bathroom.

"And you want me to handle this problem?"

"We would like to put you on retainer and ask you to stay in the United States for a while."

"That I can do for three months. I'll need to extend my visa."

"And we would pay you to stay loose, to be ready when we need you. If we need you." She leaned forward conspiratorially. "The bottom line is that we might not have a problem here. We might pay you for not having to do anything."

Dmitri was amused by her professional woman approach to this dirty business. "So tell me, in your polite way, what kind of job would we be considering?"

She looked down at the formica top. "It would be at least two, possibly more. And they would have to be like accidents."

"Okay," he said. "I accept your project if you accept my terms. I want three things. One, a thousand dollars a day, from which I pay all expenses. Two, fifty thousand dollars to start, and final bonus of fifty thousand dollars per job. And this is not like hotel room, Shannon—there is no discount for doubles."

Shannon Crocker didn't see that he had made a little joke. "And three?" She was very serious about all of this.

Dmitri chewed his bottom lip and thought about it.

The codes and phone check with the San Marcos Group confirmed that she was Manoulian's agent. He knew that the old man himself would never consent to meet him in the United States. This was the right time to make his request, make it to the old man through this woman.

"I want help to become lawful citizen of the United States."

"Three surprises me. I have the authority to agree to the first two. I'll bring up the third point with Mister M."

"Call me. You know my number." He patted her long fingers and rested his hand on hers.

"Yes, although I must tell you, while I was in a hurry to get in touch with you, I'll be changing mine soon." She withdrew her hand. "Let me give you a folder that tells you all about our current operations."

Dmitri ripped open the manila envelope. He peeked inside and saw that it contained photographs of two men. There was writing on the back of the photos. He also saw a thick wad of cash. He set the packet next to him, removed the money, and thumbed it under the table to get an idea of how much was there.

"That's fifty thousand dollars," she said.

Dmitri mocked her severity with a frown. "Manoulian

knows me well." He put the cash in his front pants pocket and zipped the packet into his backpack. She grabbed the handle of her briefcase and got up to leave.

"Tell me one more thing. Where is this job?"

"California."

She left, not looking back, as if she wanted to forget his face.

After she had been gone for ten minutes, Dmitri returned to the hamburger joint. He walked into the men's room and took a seat on a toilet in a stall. There was that feeling again, that anxiousness, a churning excitement, a flutter in his stomach and tightness in his sphincter.

It was not a bad feeling. In fact, Dmitri felt somewhat aroused.

Lucky's time was coming.

He pulled off the backpack, removed the leather case, and drew from the bottom of it a small compact case and a vial of black mascara. Looking into the small mirror with all the concentration of a Bolshoi star applying makeup, Dmitri blackened his nose and the flesh around his eyes, mouth, and ears with mascara.

He unscrewed a case of "Afro All-Black Eyeliner," swabbing tiny portions onto a Q-tip, and delicately applied it on his eyelashes and, with even greater delicacy, on the crimson strip of skin between his eyelashes and eyeball.

He carefully swabbed the part of his wrist that would be revealed between his glove and his sleeve.

Dmitri churned the contents of the backpack, looking for a can of hair spray, closed his eyes tightly and pursed his lips while he sprayed it directly onto his face, and even on his eyelids. He coughed a few times and then sprayed each wrist.

The chemistry of the mascara and the hairspray combined to create a professional quality makeup, a natural look. The makeup would not rub off or streak with sweat. Only a hard scrub with an astringent would clean it off.

He pulled on the face mask and pulled the Bull's cap down over his head. He studied himself in the mirror. Dmitri liked to watch American action movies on his VCR back in Moscow, especially movies about gang violence. What did they call themselves? American homeboys?

Yes, he was now a homie.

An American black man for the day.

No one in the busy hamburger restaurant noticed him, much less his transformation. Outside, the clouds had returned, the sky looking like a runny watercolor of gray. The occasional snowflake drifted by, twirling almost vertically in the wind. People streamed out of offices, walking to the elevated trains or cars that would take them home. They seemed to be walking much faster toward home than they had to work in the morning.

He had to be vigilant now. It would be easy to miss Lucky in all this commotion.

For a moment, a bus stopped on the curb, obscuring his line of sight. He was ready to cross the street when the bus door hissed to a close. The bus left a cloud of dark exhaust that was slow to dissipate in the cold.

When the smoke cleared Dmitri saw him.

Lucky looked neither happy nor sad, just the bland expression of a man coping with his daily routine.

Dmitri knew he wouldn't have to worry about the little girl. The mother picks her up from school, a little mercy that would make his job easier.

The man walked down the sidewalk. Dmitri crossed the street and followed him.

I know you, kind sir. You will turn right at the next intersection.

The man turned right.

You will stop with everyone else at the next crossing, cross, and then make another right.

The man made another right. The streetlights came on, night falling hard.

Next came the first of several opportunities for what Dmitri called an improvisation. It all depended on what Lucky would do for dinner. If he was going out, Dmitri would get him later like a mugger on the street.

If he was making a bachelor dinner at home, he would duck into the little store on the corner.

Lucky went into the convenience store on the little side street. The nearest people were commuters heading for the El, crossing the major intersection a half block away.

He walked by the storefront and saw a wiry little man manning the counter, a Cambodian or perhaps a Thai. Everything looked sickly and unappetizing under the harsh florescent lights, even the open racks of apples and pears. With a few more steps, he saw that the businessman was picking out a package of spaghetti and a jar of sauce. Cradling those in the crook of his arm, Lucky picked out a bottle of red wine.

Dmitri would have to be quick. That little man behind the counter, those types could be dangerous.

Dmitri stepped into the little store. He could feel the eyes of the storeclerk on him. With one fluid motion, Dmitri pulled the Glock, aimed the long, fat barrel of the gun directly at the bridge of the clerk's nose and fired.

The clerk's head snapped back as the back of his skull splattered against the rack of cigarettes behind him. He softly sank to his knees and then pitched forward, his head banging against the hard wooden counter.

It didn't matter. He didn't feel a thing.

Dmitri stepped behind the counter. The man's nose bent against the floor tiles; twin pools of blood ran from his ears, making donut-sized circles on the floor. Dmitri smiled. It looked like he was wearing mouse ears.

Dmitri turned to the businessman standing in frozen terror. Lucky dropped his armload, the wine and spaghetti sauce bursting at his feet, creating more gore than the splattered brain matter of the store clerk. Yellow strands of spaghetti clattered and rolled across the floor.

Lucky started to shout something, to offer money, but Dmitri didn't want to hear him beg. He fired four shots in a tight semicircular pattern around the front breast pocket of the man's Chesterfield coat. The glass behind the target went as opaque as ice as it shattered. A thick plastic jug of milk exploded on the shelf.

Lucky crumpled and fell back.

The smell of burnt cordite rose to Dmitri's nostrils. He walked over to deliver a coup de grâce. Then he remembered he was playing for a camera, likely installed in the ceiling, or above the counter.

So he looked up and mouthed the words he had learned from an American movie. "Fuckin' honkey," he said, making sure his lips moved with enough exaggeration to be read later on security cam photos.

Dmitri reached behind the counter, pushed the release button with his gloved finger, and opened the register.

He leaned over and grabbed wads of cash and Food Stamp coupons, stuffing them into the pockets of his jacket. On his way out, he grabbed a bottle of vodka. He kicked open a metal door into the back of the store, holding the vodka bottle in one hand, his drawn gun in the other, ready for the shopkeeper's wife. There was no one, just a little cold storage room full of boxes.

Dmitri ripped off his mask, took off his Chicago Bulls jacket and shirt. Then he doused the shirt in vodka, and used it to rub the black coating from his face, wadded the blackened shirt into a tight ball around his mask, and stuffed it all into his backpack.

He slipped back into his jacket and kicked open the locked back door that led to the cold alley.

The evaporating vodka on his skin gave a strange sensation of burning cold. The whole operation had taken less than two minutes. He disposed of the gun by casually flipping it over the side of a bridge above the Chicago River.

He couldn't care less if the police found it. It had no fingerprints, no serial number, and Glocks were very widespread here—inexpensive enough to almost be considered common apparel in American cities.

Besides, it would be easy enough to get another one in California. Almost as easy as buying a newspaper.

Within an hour, Dmitri Popova checked into an airport hotel, showered, and settled in for room service and the ten o'clock news. He watched impassively as the anchors kidded each other, told stupid jokes, and then read the news from Washington, then Moscow, where it turned out that the nation's inebriated president was not going to die after all. In both capitals the leaders looked more ridiculous than ever before.

Ever since Gorbachev, Dmitri had had enough of politicians.

Then came the "area news."

"A prominent Chicago accounting executive was gunned down tonight along with a—" Dmitri plugged his ears and hummed. He did not want to hear the man's name again. That's why he thought of him only as Lucky. He never liked to remember the names of people he killed.

See, I have forgotten you already.

He took his fingers out of his ears, quit humming, and looked at the television screen. There he was, in jerky, black-and-white frames, in his Bull's jacket, his face hidden behind the mask, his hand clutching a gun, moving toward the cash register.

His nose, ears, and the skin around his eyes were convincingly dark. The eyeliner did its job, preventing him from taking on that look of an American white minstrel singer of the 1920s.

"The suspect is a black male, between twenty-five and forty years of age, six feet tall and 180 pounds."

Dmitri turned off the television. He debated with himself whether to stay another day and kill the whores.

The girls had been a stupid and unnecessary risk, he had to admit that to himself now. But the risk wasn't too great. After all, this job for Manoulian was going to be his last. And besides, work hard, play harder.

The only remaining chore was to stuff his homie clothes, the stolen money, and the food stamps into the plastic liner from the bathroom and toss it into the dumpster behind the hotel restaurant.

By morning, he would be on his way to California.

Another job, likely the last and biggest of his career.

11

The instant the seatbelt light went off, Anne stood up, smoothed her blouse and walked down the aisle. As she approached his seat, J.D. put down his paper and faced her directly.

"What now?" he asked.

Anne's mouth hung open. "You've shadowed me across Los Angeles, all the way to Albuquerque, and now to Washington, and you ask me, 'what now'?"

"Wouldn't be a bad start."

An older Japanese businessman in the window seat, face half-buried in a pillow, moaned in irritation at having his nap disturbed.

Anne spoke again. "We're not starting anything."

J.D. grinned. "I thought you were shadowing me."

The man in the window seat looked up, his eyes rheumy with interrupted sleep. He offered to trade seats.

Anne looked to J.D., who shrugged. The man left and J.D. slid over to the window seat, while Anne tentatively took the seat next to him.

"So you're doing the same thing I'm doing?" she asked. "Interviewing the victims of Doctor Dirt?"

"Look," J.D. said, "since we're covering the same ground, why don't you tell me about your interview with Hughes? You might have something I don't. Or I might have something you need. Could get you another exclusive."

"Hey, you talked to him before I did—how could you know I saw him later?"

"He told me you were coming." Actually, J.D. had glanced at a small yellow pad in Hughes's study. Her name had been scrawled under "appts."

J.D. leaned forward. "You know, you shouldn't jump to any conclusions without talking to me. I might have info that could blow all your theories. Todd's business could connect to a lot of different angles."

He caught his slip and regretted it instantly. Her eyes lit up. She had noticed.

"Todd? You *knew* him!"

J.D. chewed the inside of his cheek.

Anne pressed him. "You still owe me. So tell me, how did you know him?"

"I assist the Political Crimes Unit at FBI Headquarters. Todd was a good source for political crimes."

The seatbelt light came back on as the plane started to rock and list in turbulence. Anne buckled in and looked squarely at J.D.

"Then you know how Clarity works. I want to see them in action."

"Clarity's boarded up."

"I want to see Ben Grossman. I want to see the dirt business from the inside; see how they justify wrecking people's lives."

J.D. reached into his jacket pocket, pulled out a notepad, and found Grossman's unlisted home number.

"Now you owe me," he said.

As she copied it down, Anne bit the tip of her tongue at the corner of her mouth, an eccentric gesture that struck J.D. as endearing, even a little appealing.

"Now," Anne said, turning to J.D. "What else do you know?"

"I know I need a nap."

Like the Japanese man before him, he curled up against the window.

He heard the pop of the airphone. "Hello? Ben Grossman? This is Anne Carlson of the *Los Angeles Times*...."

Roman Grice was waiting for them outside the luggage concourse.

He wore a natty charcoal-gray suit, perfect as a Sunday supplement model, grinning broadly. "So, Miss Carlson, you're eager to see Cyclops?"

She gave him a blank look.

"Clarity's secret weapon," J.D. interjected. "Yes, she is. We both are."

Anne turned on him, her eyes narrowing, lips tight. "I'm not about to do an interview with a gumshoe peering over my shoulder."

"Good. Neither am I. I'm a consultant, remember? Let's go."

She whispered under her breath. "Quit screwing with my frigging sources."

"Just remember where you got 'em from, baby."

"Don't call me, 'baby.'"

"Then don't call me gumshoe."

The windows of the old Capitol Hill townhouse, once warm with the light of desk lamps, were shuttered and dark.

Ben Grossman greeted them at the door, dressed in a cardigan and bow tie, looking to J.D. like a Louisiana Santa Claus. "Come on in. It's colder than an Eskimo Pie out there. J.D., I didn't know you were comin' along."

He led them through to the back door of the townhouse. "I'm going to show both of you one of my company's deepest and most closely held secrets. No one else has anything even remotely like what we've got."

"So why are you doing this?" Anne asked.

"I'm showing the FBI consultant because I figure I have to. I'm showing you because a few awe-stricken paragraphs on the power of Cyclops just might inspire someone to buy this place."

"Aren't you thinking of buying it yourself?" J.D. asked.

"Sure. But I'd need a loan bigger than a trucker's underwear for that."

Anne wrinkled her nose. "A trucker's underwear?"

J.D. explained Grossman's colorful use of language. "Take a side glance when one of them's changing a tire." She looked as if someone had waved rotten cheese under her nose.

J.D., Anne, and Grice followed Grossman out the door and over cold, stiff grass that crackled and crunched under their shoes.

Plaster had crumbled around the exterior corners of the converted carriage house, revealing ancient brick. The inside was all brick, painted institutional white. One window faced the townhouse. Another cast the dying sunlight on white carpet. A huge, saucer-shaped lamp hung from the ceiling. A war-time poster of Winston Churchill, index finger thrust forward, challenged Britons to "Deserve Victory!"

Against the wall sat a featureless computer the size of a freezer. An operator's chair, its casters on a hard, plastic mat, was pulled up to the computer's Radius computer monitor, one huge green screen like the oculus of a monster. A laser printer rested like a huge paw alongside. The adjoining wall was obscured by shelves, floor to ceiling, filled with black plastic boxes topped by covers of smoked, translucent glass.

The little building's single room was almost as chilly as the open yard.

Grossman punched in a security code in a wall-mounted keypad to deactivate the security system, then led Anne and J.D. to the shelves. He opened a plastic box from a shelf, revealing what at first appeared to be a CD. When Anne held it up to the lamp, a ray of light cast through translucent glass, streaking the white carpet with the iridescent colors of a dragonfly wing.

"Optical Disks, incredible storage capacity," Grossman smiled, as if he were still lecturing a class of graduate students at Rice. "Years of data you can't find just on the Internet. Its real power is in a trademark software we've adapted just for Cyclops."

He returned the disk to its case, and patted Cyclops. "I

won't bore you with all the technical details, but Cyclops is the ultimate fast-tracker. It uses Boolean logic, negation, conjunction, affirmation, to find secret relationships. It gives us nasties in a mathematical form called a 'truth table.'"

"But where does it get all the information?" Anne asked.

"Cyclops, here, Todd's dream machine. It took one helluva investment from big donors who don't like their candidates to lose, and one helluva investment in programming time. It took us a year, but we put fifteen million stories dating back to 1960 on these disks. We've also got the entire database of the FEC, the SEC, the FCC, the Census Bureau, and other neat stuff. It also has a powerful search engine to roam the Internet. But that's not the key, and neither for that matter is Cyclops here. It's the software. In the heat of a campaign, you need stuff in a nanosecond, before your opponent or a live, twenty-four-hour CNN shoots you dead with a story.

"Our software can organize words, phrases, ideas, in seconds. It can simultaneously sort through congressional votes, FEC reports, lists of financially owned subsidiaries, directories with names and addresses of corporate officials, and a hundred other things to draw relationships of who paid what to whom to vote how.

"Hell, this thing's even got digital optics. It doesn't just analyze words, it can analyze pictures, it can analyze voices. It's a giant brain prowling for facts. It's a cybernetic FBI."

"Enough already," said J.D. "How about a test drive?"

Grossman walked over to the far wall and pulled a plastic box down from the shelf. He sorted through the optical disks. "This will just take a minute to set up. What would you like to see? The real story of Chappaquiddick? Newt Gingrich's book contract?"

Anne had another idea. "How about the real estate investments of Michael Hughes and Barry Newhouse?"

Grossman looked surprised. "That's a very interesting choice." He selected another set of disks. "Roman, fire these up."

Grice rolled his chair a little closer to the computer console. The large Radius screen came to life and an animated character appeared. J.D. chuckled, Anne gasped. It was a vivid cartoon version of Lee Atwater, the late Republican political operative, dressed in the robe and armor of a samurai warrior.

"Todd had his own sense of humor," Grossman said. "Lee had been a mentor, and this was his way of paying respect. Samurai Atwater is basically a search engine that pulls some of this information off our disks, some off of Web sites."

After the prompt, Roman typed in a command. "Samurai: relate\michaelhughes\barrynewman**realestate."

"Geographic specificity would help narrow the field," Grice said.

"California," said Anne.

Grice tapped it in.

Samurai Atwater bowed, drew a sword in a jerky cartoon motion, and attacked a row of icons at the right hand side of the screen. One icon represented a television, another a satellite, another a newspaper, another a radio. Several others represented government and public databases.

The Samurai Atwater slid his sword back in its sheath.

He spoke, "First datum."

Grice clicked an icon and a picture popped on the screen of an old New York tabloid article, front-page, seventy-two-point headline, "Hughes on the Take?" The subhead read, "The Shady Friends of the Man Who Would Be President."

"Can I have a hard copy of that?" J.D. asked.

"Make it two," Anne said.

Grice hit a button and it printed.

The samurai continued to search, bowing again, drawing a sword and attacking more icons. The modum screeched, Cyclops accessed the Internet in search of more information. It returned to center screen.

"Second datum."

The screen filled with a deed filed in San Marcos County, California, for possession of 1,240 acres of land, referred to as "Presidio," from possession of the U.S. Department of Defense to Franklin Manoulian.

"The billionaire?" Anne asked.

"Who else could afford a military base?" J.D. said.

"Dad used to own a cabin near San Marcos. It's beautiful out there," she said wistfully, almost to herself.

Grice jerked back in his chair. "What the hell! We've got ourselves a hacker!"

"What?" Grossman bent closer.

They all saw it now, a green blob monster slowly oozing right to left across the screen.

"Well, I'll be damned. Let him have it, Roman."

Grice typed a series of commands and Samurai Atwater

crouched, pulled a ninja star from his collar, and hurled it at the green blob monster. The green ooze reversed course from the screen.

"That won't just keep him out," Grossman said, "it'll cripple his computer with a virus, trace his address, and print it on hard copy."

The blob gone, another deed popped onto the screen showing the transfer of 604 acres from the Department of Defense to Barry Newhouse. There were more deeds for more parcels, none larger than five acres, in the names of major Hollywood movie stars, producers, directors. The only full, five-acre residential parcel was deeded to the soon-to-be-retired president and his first lady, with a major Los Angeles bank as an underwriter.

Grice kept the printer humming, as Cyclops pulled up more files on Manoulian, his many businesses, his longtime financial support of Senator Mike Hughes, and his role as chief fundraiser for his presidential campaign. J.D. kept pulling the papers off the printer, handing copies to Anne, organizing his own. Among the papers spit out by the printer was the address of the hacker Cyclops had traced. J.D. looked at it and palmed it into his pile.

"Now you know what it feels like to strike oil in your own backyard," Grossman said, slapping J.D. on the back.

J.D. looked across the room. No one had noticed.

As Cyclops pulled together more deeds and papers, the door opened to the chill outside. J.D. turned to see an attractive, well-dressed woman.

"Excuse me," she said to Grossman. "I looked for you all over the house when I realized you had to be out here. Please don't let me interrupt."

"No interruption at all. Anne, J.D., I'd like you to meet Ruth Thornburgh. Anne's from the *L.A. Times,* and J.D.'s a detective."

"It's my fault for the imposition," Ruth said, "but Ben and I need to meet with the lawyers to sign some papers tonight, and I have to be back in the hospital at nine."

"That's fine," Grossman said. "Don't want to spoil these buckaroos anyway."

Grossman bumped Grice off the computer, his fingers gliding over the keyboard, making liquid clicking sounds.

J.D. stepped forward. "Ruth, it's a pleasure to finally meet you, even under these circumstances. I dealt with Todd professionally—"

"I know. He mentioned you."

She held his hand firmly for a moment. Ruth Thornburgh had the radiance of plain beauty and health, enhanced by subtle makeup and large earrings of burnished gold sculpted into an abstract design. Her overcoat was open, her body lean under the navy-blue dress.

On the way out, Grossman turned off the lights and punched in a code for a keypad alarm on the door. Then he keyed in more commands to activate motion detectors, laser sensors.

"Time to seal the bat cave," Grossman said. "You don't want to try to get in here without Roman or me. We got booby-traps that'll bust your balls."

"Thanks for the warning," J.D. said.

That night, J.D. uncrumpled the paper he had taken from Cyclops with the hacker's address, and picked up the phone.

"Sarah, it's your dad."

She gave a plaintive, "hi."

"Just wondering if I could borrow your computer for a little work tonight. Mine's on the fritz."

There was a long silence.

"That's weird. Small world. My system crashed this afternoon. I'm gonna have to take it in to be repaired."

"It is a small world, isn't it?"

12

Pennsylvania Avenue is a deep canyon running through dull-gray government. On one side, the Archives Building is crowned by a dome, suggesting a monument to balding bureaucrats. On the other, the massive J. Edgar Hoover FBI Building looks like an impenetrable fortress, which it is.

For the first time in her life, Anne took a cab past the FBI Building, down Pennsylvania Avenue, then up Fourteenth Street, and arrived at the National Press Building. She waited in the marble foyer for a sluggish elevator to appear behind massive brass doors. It was 8:10 AM, already ten minutes late to meet her new boss.

Henry Jacobs, the Washington bureau chief of the *Los Angeles Times*, welcomed Anne with a mix of wariness and feigned enthusiasm.

Jacobs's drooping black mustache and thick black hair reminded her of old clips from fifties television, what Ernie Kovaks would have looked like if he had put on weight and lived to be sixty-two.

He led her into his small, eighth-story office. The walls were lined with framed news photos and editorial cartoons dating from the Reagan Administration.

"Now just so we're clear," Jacobs said, "you do know

that you're supposed to stick to the Doctor Dirt story. The rest of the national beat isn't your concern."

"Oh yes, absolutely."

"Good. Now, here's your office." He escorted her to a little cubicle with a phone and a personal computer.

"Thank you."

"Make yourself at home."

"Actually, I need to go. I'm scheduled for a nine o'clock breakfast with the Geoffrey Group."

Jacobs could not disguise his astonishment. "You're having breakfast with the Geoffrey Group?"

"Jim Miller lined it up for me."

He stared at her for the longest time. Henry Jacobs had spent four years covering Capitol Hill, four years covering the White House, six years as bureau chief, and he'd been invited to the group three times in those fourteen years.

Anne Carlson got invited on her first morning on the job.

Jacobs spoke in the deadpan voice of the congenitally disappointed. "Okay, Anne. Just check in with me from time to time."

The invitation to breakfast had surprised her no less than it did her new boss. To tell the truth, before Jim Miller scheduled the breakfast she had never heard of Geoffrey Peters and his group. Every profile piece she found on the Internet referred to Geoffrey as "the dean of Washington journalists." He had started his career in New York, but had worked in Washington for forty years, first as a *Washington Star* correspondent covering the Eisenhower White House, and then on to the *Post*. Geoffrey had retired in the late Reagan years, when Anne was still in Columbia journalism school.

Anne's cab dropped her at the Monocle, a "Senate-side" hangout, where the invitation-only group met every Thursday to dine on eggs benedict and coffee—no substitutions and no vegetarians, a Geoffrey rule, though one could imbibe alcohol if one chose.

Anne recognized Geoffrey from the photos she'd pulled off the net, clean, thick-rimmed glasses, a crown of white hair set off against a choleric complexion, and a long, thin face. He welcomed her to her seat and made the introductions.

Facing Geoffrey across the table, as always, was Sid Sherman, former journalist, long-time Geoffrey Group member and now the president's Deputy Chief of Staff, chief spinmeister, and speechwriter.

Sherman was in his mid-fifties, but his bushy hair had already gone a shock-white, a Mark Twain look that he seemed to cultivate. In truth, though, Sid Sherman looked more like the haggard campaign aide and New York weekly news columnist he had once been. He was a slight man with a reddish complexion and a smart-ass, wise-guy look about the eyes.

Around the table she saw an infamously opinionated national correspondent and Sunday-morning commentator from ABC; a dark, intense thirty-something Hill reporter for *Newsweek*; the deeply tanned, grandfatherly editor of *Human Events*; and the senior Senator from Nevada, a longstanding fixture of the Republican party. Geoffrey, presiding at the end of the table, tossed questions like a soccer coach kicking out a ball, content to watch the toddlers chase after it.

Geoffrey looked from side to side, following the ball, smiling or grimacing, depending on whether or not he agreed with each of the discussants. Whenever an issue evolved into a set speech, it was time to change the subject.

Geoffrey leaned forward, smiling slightly, "So what do we make of the fact that Doctor Dirt has been swept away by history?"

For the first time that morning, silence reigned around the table.

"Sad, sad day," the Republican senator from Nevada said finally. He looked genuinely stricken.

"Well I'm going to miss him," the *Newsweek* reporter said. "He always gave me the inside skinny, and I wouldn't be at all surprised if, when all is said and done, he wasn't the one who flushed out the president's fondness for interns in berets."

The editor from *Human Events* waved a commanding hand to suggest a better epitaph. "Beneath all the razzmatazz, he was one of the best strategists the Republicans had."

"He was a good leaker," said the ABC correspondent and commentator, slurping coffee.

"He was a friggin' leach who finally got burned off the asshole of history," said Sherman, his eyes as red-rimmed as the Bloody Mary he whisked with a fat celery stick.

Anne asked, "Senator, what did Todd Thornburgh do for you?"

"Opposition research. Of course, he was a bit redundant, since I never faced any serious opposition in those races." The senator smiled. "Seventy-two percent both times."

Geoffrey straightened his back. "You never had any serious opposition. Of course, rumor had it that Thornburgh still collected dirt on everyone in the state, in every cathouse and casino, from the governor to the guards at Hoover Dam."

The senator shifted uncomfortably in his chair.

"Doctor Dirt's real value to you wasn't what he did to your lightweight opponents on the ballot, but what he did to keep your heavyweight opponents off the ballot."

"I wish you wouldn't call him that. His name was Todd," the senator said.

"His name might as well have been Doctor Mudd." Geoffrey was having a good morning. They evaluated the torrent of press coverage. There had been a *Washington Post* "Style" section feature on Doctor Dirt; articles in *Time*, *Newsweek*, and *U.S. News and World Report*; a wry column in the *Economist*; and an ironic farewell in the *New Republic*.

While the senator from Nevada launched into a red-faced tirade against what Geoffrey had said, the ABC correspondent came to Geoffrey's defense. Apparently bored, Geoffrey took Anne's right hand into his, massaging her knuckles white. He turned to her. "Miller told me that a big story brings you to Washington."

She looked around the table, Geoffrey got the hint. He led her to a nearby empty table. The Group was too busy arguing to take much notice. She told him her story as Geoffrey nervously fiddled with a fork. They were almost whispering now, eliciting a look of curiosity from Sherman at the other table.

"You want to know what I think?"

"Yes, Mr. Peters, I do."

"I think," he now twirled a spoon as if divining something in its reflections, "that you don't yet have a story. All you've got is another profile piece. And this city needs another one of those like the president needs another girlfriend."

"So what should I do?"

Geoffrey set down the cutlery. "You started out on the police beat or some such, am I right?"

She nodded.

"Very well, then, it's not so much what I think as what you know. This is a murder story, pure and simple. Pursue the evidence, find the suspects. Go for it."

Go for it. She couldn't help but smile at those words from Geoffrey's octogenarian lips. She would go for it. She'd go for the widow.

"You want an interview?" It was hard to tell if Ruth Thornburgh's tone was one of resentment or astonishment.

"Well, perhaps for background."

There was a long pause.

Anne added, "It would help me understand his achievements, and get the story right."

"Maybe," Ruth sighed. "If you promise it's strictly background, no attribution. Then, I'll say okay."

"If I break my word on that, I'm not a journalist. Can I see you sometime this week?"

"God, the funeral was just the other day."

"We could do the interview over the phone."

"No, make it lunch. When you ask questions, I want to see your eyes. Today's best."

They met at a French bistro with a stunning view of

the north side of the Capitol. Ruth Thornburgh was seated and waiting when Anne arrived.

They made small talk and ordered salads with strips of marinated chicken. Anne sipped chilled white wine. Ruth declined.

"I'm doing a skin graft this afternoon. Poor child, burned over forty percent of his body, another latch-key kid left at home to fend for himself."

"It must be hard," was all Anne could think to say.

"There's something about my work that aids the grieving process. In the last day, I've felt like patient and physician were healing together."

Their salads arrived, and they ate in silence. Anne took a sip of wine for courage and began the interview.

"The side of your husband that the media sees—I know you must hate this—is the Doctor Dirt image."

"I do hate it. Todd was tough, but he was in a tough business. The bottom line is that he cared about the people who worked for him. Ask Ben. Ask any of the kids who worked for him."

"So what do you plan to do with Clarity?"

"Ben and I closed on a deal. He practically had to mortgage his children, but now he's the 100 percent owner. I'm free of it."

Anne took another sip of wine and felt almost ashamed for wondering how much Ruth Thornburgh cleared on the sale. She looked out the restaurant's plate-glass windows as she contemplated her next question. The Capitol looked as white as a wedding cake topped with a single figurine, The Statue of Freedom, in full armor.

"Do you think there was anything political to your husband's death?"

"The FBI followed the same line."

"J.D.?"

"Yes, he asked about Todd's files, his schedules, his list of current clients and their opponents. Nothing seemed even remotely plausible. It must have been a random thing. Someone broke in, followed him and…. It was terrible, that someone could do… could do that to him." It looked as though her composure were about to break. She forced herself back by anger. "I just hope they catch the son-of-a-bitch, the freak, who did that to him."

J.D. sat in the Dilbert-type cubicle he'd been given inside the Hoover building and stared out the window. Four stories below, the lunchtime crowd poured out of office buildings and into McDonalds, or Planet Hollywood, or did their shopping in the grungy stores nearby.

On his computer screen, flying toasters came down in a torrent, a screensaver long since activated by an absence of keystrokes. He had been working from his notes until he could no longer stand to look at them.

But he suspected he might be onto something. He had also convinced himself that something wasn't his daughter.

She was smart as a whip, that girl. If he hadn't made her that way, St. John's had, or maybe the two of them together. Now here she was, a bright kid, time on her hands, free time spent jerking around on a computer like a lot of bright kids. Her curiosity is on fire about Doctor Dirt. She wants the inside scoop, to tap into Clarity and find out what the fast-trackers are saying on their e-mails. And like a kid in Paducah who accidently hacks into the computers at the Strategic Air Command, she stumbled into the jackpot—before she got fried. A one-in-a-million thing. But that was the end of it. Had to be. One conclusion was that he ought to consider hiring her as his own computer fast-tracker.

Another was that Doctor Dirt had something to do with Hughes, and what Anne and Cyclops had found.

He sat in his chair, swiveled back and forth, put his feet up on the gray steel desk that so many others had abused, and basked in the warmth of the spring sun through the window. He touched a key and the screensaver disappeared.

J.D. looked at notes he'd taken on the interview with Hughes. Though he denied it, Hughes was still trying to get even with Thornburgh. He still seethed about the real estate corruption charge that everyone else had forgotten.

J.D. clicked onto a gossipy, old story from the *New York Observer* about California real estate mogul Franklin Manoulian. The writer had adopted an appropriately objective stance, but the headline screamed in your face like the beer and pretzel man at a baseball game.

Manoulian was a big financial donor to then-Senator Hughes. How interesting, the *Observer* smirked, that Hughes helped push through the sale of a deactivated military base on the picturesque central California coast. Manoulian's deal with the government included relaxed federal rules on cleaning up toxic wastes from the oil pans and fuel tanks of thousands of Army trucks and helicopters. While other bases had been turned into colleges or turned to other civic uses, Manoulian's plan called for building large mansions overlooking the ocean. More than 120 lots had been sold, including some to Hollywood stars, and one to become the retirement home of the first couple.

J.D. clicked the story off the screen. A lot of speculation, nothing solid. Most likely, Doctor Dirt had been the source.

J.D. clicked open Manoulian's FBI file, which, at his request, had been put on the FBI's classified main frame. He clicked on the "summary," a two-page synthesis of the most credible information gleaned from the "raw" file that would be more than fifty pages long.

Franklin Manoulian and his sidekick, Lincoln Crocker, were still legends in the Central Valley. Both had been born poor in a shanty town outside Fresno.

As teenagers, the two had worked side by side in the vineyards east of the city, their callused fingers raw and bloody by the end of each day. Vowing they would never have to work that hard again, they teamed up, moved to Los Angeles in the late 1940s, and did odd jobs, earning enough to put themselves through USC. Then they were drafted.

Manoulian knew how to type, so he was stationed as a Navy clerk in San Diego. He was still in uniform when he made his first real estate deals. Within a few decades, while San Diego was adding as many as ninety thousand residents a year, Manoulian was well on his way to becoming the seventh richest man in the world. Joining him as sidekick and attorney was Lincoln Crocker, who had earned a law degree at Boalt Hall after surviving Korea.

The FBI believed that Manoulian made his original fortune as a commercial front man for various mafias. But in the California population explosion of the 1960s, legitimate real estate had become more lucrative than crime.

By the 1970s, Manoulian was buying respectability with large charitable donations and influence with big political contributions. He delivered briefcases full of cash to CREEP, the Committee to Reelect the President. He had once hosted a dinner for Nixon and Brezhnev at his San Marcos estate, described by the FBI agent who compiled the report as a "Mediterranean palace." J.D. downloaded an image of a mansion and pool, a residential Parthenon overlooking the sea.

Recently, Manoulian had served as the counsel-general of Armenia. He had bankrolled hospitals throughout the Caucasus and had been instrumental in organizing earthquake relief. He had many import–export dealings, his enterprises dotted the old Soviet map, thriving in old nations reborn as corrupt, new republics, Sicily across a dozen time zones. Here the Bureau cited CIA intercepts showing that Manoulian was in deep with the Russian mob.

The file speculated that Franklin Manoulian, for all his wealth, was now a painfully lonely man. Lincoln Crocker had died in 1987 from a heart attack. Manoulian's wife died from cancer in 1995. That same year, his only son had crashed his one-engine plane into the San Marcos mountain range. There would be no one to carry on the Manoulian name, to build a dynasty from his fortune.

J.D. did a word search for "political" and found a few pertinent paragraphs in the "raw" file. It seems Manoulian had changed with the times. After Nixon's fall, Manoulian had supported Jimmy Carter, and after Carter, other Democratic candidates. Manoulian had become especially close to Mike Hughes, a New Ideas Democrat running for president.

The FBI report confirmed that it was Hughes who at the eleventh hour had rammed through the special environmental concessions for the San Marcos deal, but there was no evidence that Hughes was paid off by Manoulian.

A voice broke J.D.'s concentration.

"Mr. DeVine?"

He looked up to see a young girl, she looked to him like a child, must be an intern. "Yes."

"The director wishes to see you."

The director's secretary chaperoned J.D. into the FBI's sanctum sanctorum on the seventh floor. While the office retained some of the old touches J.D. remembered—the dark paneling, the U.S. Criminal Code as wallpaper, the most recent crime bill encased in glass, with the signature pens of the president lined up in a row—it definitely bore the mark of the new director. There were clusters of chairs for his now-famous weekly seminars to which he invited White House officials and staff, breaking them into "work groups" to discuss broad topics like "New Trends in Law Enforcement." And there were far too many blown up "candids" of the director with the president hanging on the walls for J.D.'s taste. It could have been the office of a senior partner in a politically powerful law firm. It all seemed a long way from law enforcement on the street.

Director Louis J. Firelli sat at his desk, eating a salad and reading a report. Firelli rose, walked around, and shook his hand. The director's grip was firm, a product of weekend tennis games and spade work around the flowerbed. He was a lean and athletic man of forty-five.

"Let me say how pleased I am that we've got someone with your experience to agree to come back and work on this case."

"Thank you."

"Carol Suarez surprised me by making this move on her own. I believe it will turn out to have been the right decision."

"Sir?"

"I just called you up here to impress upon you the extraordinary sensitivity of this investigation. With an election under way, and the president pinning his hopes on being succeeded by his vice president, the White House is in an understandably fragile mood."

"Of course."

"They have only one legitimate concern in this investigation. The Bureau should not weigh in on information damaging to one side or the other until we fully understand the implications."

"Right, sir, the implications."

"We don't want to be a part of this election, to politicize the FBI in any way."

"Of course not."

"Will you do me a favor, J.D.?"

He nodded.

"Will you see someone at the White House, just to give them an idea of our parameters, just to set them at ease? If you can do it without in any way compromising the investigation, it would mean a lot to me."

"Sure."

"And one other thing. I'm told this Doctor Dirt may

have kept files on people all over town. Have you come across any copies of such files?"

"No, sir."

"Will you deliver them to me personally the instant you do?"

"Instantly."

"Something this sensitive must be secured, if you know what I mean. They have to be handled with extreme care, like plutonium, lest they fall into the wrong hands."

"I couldn't agree more. If I *ever* come across *any* such files I assure you we will keep them out of the wrong hands."

"Your friends have told me you're a good, honest man, a man who keeps his country first in his mind. I think they are right. Good to see you, J.D. Call me as soon as you get possession of those files."

J.D. had never been to the White House in all his years in Washington, not on business or on a tour. Before he left for his late morning appointment, he had logged onto the official White House Web site and taken a cyber-tour of the West Wing. It always paid to know the lay of the land.

At a distance, the White House reminded him of a wedding cake. Up close, behind the black, twelve-foot high wrought iron gate, the old mansion was solid, foreboding. Down to the last block and line of mortar, it was an impregnable palace of stone and steel. A white palace for government employees, some of whom just happened to rank among the most powerful people on earth.

J.D. checked in at the guardhouse posted at the west

entrance. Despite his FBI credentials and appointment, it took five minutes for the guards to clear him through.

A Secret Service agent led J.D. into the West Wing reception area. It almost took his breath away to see Eastman Johnson's painting of *Washington Crossing the Delaware*, with its heroic figures and absurd icebergs. He noted the huge, rounded gallery clock made in 1810, its works of gilded wood still keeping time to the second. The agent led him down a hallway, past several agents standing in front of a large white-paneled door.

J.D. realized that he was walking by the Oval Office, and he was surprised that proximity to the president—even one he privately had little respect for—made his pulse race slightly. To his right he looked into the Roosevelt Room, with its large, polished mahogany table and American battle flags.

J.D. followed the agent to the end of the hall, past an array of small offices. One of them, at the right side of the White House chief of staff, would belong to Sidney Bartholomew Sherman. J.D. was surprised to see that a West Wing office for a deputy chief of staff and chief speechwriter to the president was smaller than some of the cubicles he had been assigned in the FBI.

"Just a minute, a minute," Sherman muttered. He was standing, chin down, a shank of white hair hanging over his forehead, eyes locked on the speech draft in his hands. He seemed to be going over one sentence, again and again.

J.D. looked around the tiny office. Lights, tastefully recessed into the molding, reflected evenly off the ceiling and gave the room a uniform illumination. On the wall behind Sherman's credenza hung a landscape from the National

Gallery, a George Catlin depicting an Indian village along the primeval Mississippi.

When he looked up, Sherman seemed startled that the person he had seen out of the corner of his eye was J.D. Sherman had a question ready, just the same.

"I've got a speech here on gangs. Tell me honestly, if you like this line: 'It's high time we understood it's high noon for a generation of young Americans who are on a highway to despair.' Whaddya think?"

"Sounds like a lot of 'highs' to me."

"That's it! That's the point! High, high, high—don't get high, it's high time, it's high noon! Get it?"

"I suppose."

"You suppose. You're from the FBI and you suppose," Sherman looked down at the script and struck the line with a pen. "You had lunch?"

The White House Mess was a small affair, tucked into the basement next to the Situation Room. Anywhere else, the brass railings and captain's instruments along the wall, the paintings of men-of-war and brigantines, would have been kitsch, no different than seafood restaurants back on the Annapolis waterfront.

But this was the real thing, where the waiters were uniformed navel personnel.

Looking around the small room, J.D. saw White House aides sitting with what he assumed to be a mixture of journalists and corporate lobbyists.

"We're in luck," Sherman said, taking a seat at a small table with two chairs. "This is Mex Day. Try the guacamole."

Instead J.D. ordered coffee and a tuna sandwich on toast. Sherman ordered beef and chili tacos. It arrived minutes later with tortilla chips and salsa.

Sherman bit into a taco, pushing the chili oil across his lips before he spoke. "I asked you here to tell you the president is concerned that the FBI avoid even the appearance of interfering in politics."

"We can investigate political matters without being political ourselves."

"I'm glad to hear that. Point is, I asked you here to underscore another message. This is an election year. It's no secret that this president has his hopes and dreams invested in his designated successor, the vice president. While we understand you have a job to do, we do not want to see the FBI tilt the playing field."

"I'm not sure I follow you."

"Doctor Dirt's dirty laundry has to be kept in a good, safe place. His files, his disks, all his slanderous stuff."

"What's a 'good, safe place'?"

Sherman looked around the Mess as if to say, where on earth could be more secure than the White House?

"The safe of the National Security Agency down the hall there, for example. There could easily be national security implications. Or Lou Firelli's office. The point is that any loose files need to be protected."

"I couldn't agree more."

"Look, DeVine, as you unravel this case, you're likely to trip over skeletons. On behalf of your ultimate boss, I'm ordering you to keep me informed—"

J.D. cut in. "No one orders me to obstruct justice."

Sherman sat back, more astonished than angry, as if he had just witnessed an act of defiance by a bug. He reached into his breast pocket and took a hit off an asthma inhaler.

"All I'm asking is that you be very careful not to go public with any unfounded accusations that could get mixed up in election year politics. I'm sure that your boss doesn't want to take the FBI back to the Hoover days of blackmail and playing favorites."

"No, sir, we do not. This is a murder investigation, pure and simple."

"So tell me, what have we learned from this little meeting?"

J.D. slapped a ten-dollar bill down on the table. "I've learned that the Navy still makes good sandwiches."

Sherman pushed the bill back at him.

13

Dmitri stood in the warm California sun, tapping a large manilla envelope against his head. Shannon had thought of everything, except his car. That should have been easy. In America, so many to choose from.

But one needed ID, even if paying cash. It was a problem. Talking to the whores had been a mistake. He couldn't afford another.

It would have to be improvisation. Pure *spetznaz*.

He stood on the street corner, the sleeves of his T-shirt rolled up to catch the baking rays of the sun. Sun glasses, T-shirt, Levis, dangling cigarette—he was James Dean, a cool American. Yes, he could do this. He twisted his thumb to the street, trying to hitch a ride. Twenty minutes, half an hour, no takers.

Dmitri flicked his third cigarette into the gutter and watched it sputter, then disappear under a mass of orange metal. A big orange car.

"Hey, want a ride?"

Dmitri looked into the eyes of a fleshy, freckled, slack-jawed girl, maybe twenty, long dirty-blonde hair, vacant brown eyes, a plunging tank top that showed she wasn't wearing a bra. She sounded drunk.

Dmitri glanced at the driver. He saw acne, peach-fuzz beard, frizzy hair like a golden nuclear cloud, arms as skinny and white as a fish belly, a thin bumpy neck disappearing into a T-shirt of swirling green and purple and yellow and orange.

"Want a ride?" she repeated.

"Yes," he said hurriedly opening the back door and jumping in.

"Hey, man," said the driver, "welcome 'board the Texas Traveler." The driver hit the horn, and Dmitri was surprised to hear a cheerful tune, a brass bugle sound, come from the car. "Yee-hah!" the driver shouted, laughing. The girl laughed too. It was their little joke.

"Thank you." Dmitri looked over the front seats, out the front window, down the burnt orange hood of the enormous car, and saw an ivory-like set of long horns springing from the radiator.

"Say that again," said the girl.

Dmitri looked at her questioningly. Was something wrong? "What? Thank you?"

"You're foreign!"

"Ah, yes, immigrant, from Poland."

"What's your name?"

"I am… Jerzy."

"Hey, Jerzy, like a toke of this?" She passed him a joint.

"Ah, thank you, but no. I want no trouble with immigration authorities."

"No trouble with us." She sucked on it. "Hey, where are you going?"

"Where are you going? I am traveling America."

"Cool, but where's your bags?"

"Bags?" He really was slipping. No fake ID, no good story. But that was all right. The whole car stank of the sickly sweet smell of marijuana. These kids were stoned. They would believe anything. "They are still flying over from Poland. I came ahead."

"Spiritual traveler, man, you're a spiritual traveler," the driver said nodding. "Let's hear it for the spiritual traveler." He hit the horn and the cheeful tune sounded again, and again they burst out laughing.

"We're going to crash," the girl said. "Hotel, in Encino. That okay? Want to come along?"

"Oh yeah, great," Dmitri nodded.

"You drink? We can drink there and chill awhile. We're takin' off tomorrow, though, followin' Phish. Wanna come along, Jerzy? Wanna become a Phish head?" she laughed.

"We'll see," he said, smiling, and leaned back into the cracked leather seat, picking at the duct tape that held it together.

In his imagination, he could feel the driver's neck cracking under his fingers, cracking like the neck of a goose.

But no. It had to be an accident.

The driver reached under his seat. "Hey, dude, want a beer now?" He flipped a can into the back seat.

Dmitri held the beer in his hand. It was still cool.

He had paced himself well, stretched full length on the sofa, its coarse, stained, off-white fabric redolent of smoke and sweat. Nine o'clock. Only four beers, no hits of the marijuana. He had passed on what they called "shrooms" (he told them he got very sick eating them in Poland, and they laughed), and he had dropped no LSD. Now the two of them lay curled up like dogs on the floor near the television.

Dmitri snapped to his feet. Peach Fuzz pulled his head up and squinted at him. "You okay, man?"

"Yes, just a little drunk. Can you help me to the bathroom?"

"Fuck, man. I'm messed up."

"Maybe you need a shower too. Come on. Be good for you."

Peach Fuzz rose like a zombie and staggered into the bathroom. Dmitri ran the bath.

"Go ahead, take off your clothes."

"No, come on, man. I don't want to."

"I think you should do it."

"No, man, I'm going to go back and crash."

In one swift move Dmitri simultaneously swung his right boot, scything Peach Fuzz's ankles, while the butt of Dmtri's left hand crashed against the back of Peach Fuzz's head. His acne-covered forehead rebounded off the tub.

"Tiles, so slippery," Dmitri said shaking his head. Covering his hands in towels, he undressed him, and lifted him into the bath. Water sloshed onto the floor. "So, so messy." His toweled hands seized Peach Fuzz's ugly face and shoved it underwater. "*Das vadoyna*, Peach Fuzz," he said through clenched teeth. There was no resistance.

When it was surely over, Dmitri lifted the sopping towels out of the water and dropped them on the tiles. He snapped to his feet again. *Very spetznaz.*

He looked at himself in the bathroom mirror. Yes, he could be an action hero in films, in Hollywood, as a citizen,

after this one job. He touched up his hair with his finger-
tips. *Looking good.*

Now, time for Fatty.

He strode to her curled up body and nudged her with
his boot. Nothing. He kicked her before he got a response.

"What is it?"

"Your boyfriend's in the bathroom, he needs you."

"Fuck him."

"No, it's serious. Hurry."

She couldn't stand, or she wouldn't try. She crawled on
all fours like a slow, stubborn donkey. Dmitri had an over-
powering desire to ride on her back. Instead, he stood in her
path.

"Why don't you just get undressed?"

"Huh?"

"Undressed."

"Oh."

Somehow, something clicked. She stood up, pulled off
her tank top, and took her large breasts in her hands, shaking them at him, smiling stupidly.

"Take off everything."

When she was naked, he waved for her to follow him to
the bathroom. "Peach Fuzz is waiting for you."

She looked at him. "Is he asleep?"

"Very much asleep. Take a look in the water, a very
close look, you can see things, very interesting things."

She bent over the tub and twirled the water with a finger. He stood staring at her for a moment. It would be like
drowning a kitten. A big, fat kitten, with big, messy breasts.
He took the sodden towels in his hands, pushed her forward,

seized her head, and shoved it to the bottom of the tub. He was flush against her, her fat legs kicking hard, slapping the tiles like trophy fish hurled on a deck. She was trying to squeal, every silent scream a rush of water into the lungs. When the legs stopped, he used the sopping towels to tilt her fully into the tub. Another big splash and her body docked on Peach Fuzz, as though she were performing a porno move on him.

Dmitri laughed. *Perfect.*

He collected his beer cans, the only things with his fingerprints, picked up the car keys, and with a washcloth over his hand turned out the lights and locked the door from the inside.

The car was his. He moved quickly, dumping the cans on the passenger seat with the wash cloth, and drove carefully out of the hotel parking lot.

It was an insane risk, but necessary. Dmitri decided to give himself no more than three days in L.A., no more than five days total with the car. He would have to park somewhere dark and remove the horns, change the license plates, and steal new plates every day until then.

But somehow this felt right. It was his last job. He could afford to take risks, to relax his standards slightly. This big car was a talisman, an engine of success, the battle tank that would complete his last job.

Soon he'd be back at his hotel. There'd be another envelope under his door, with orders that would either be "Go," "Hold," or "Job Canceled."

He knew Manoulian. If the old Armenian were behind this, it would be a "Go."

"Manoulian!" Geoffrey almost shrieked. "Manoulian, that old rug merchant, that whoreson, thieving back-stabber of a back-stabber, that creep of the Caucasus! You think that human switchblade might actually be innocent of something!"

"Look," Anne held her ground, but just barely. "I'm not making him out to be a total innocent. But murder?"

Geoffrey leaned forward, speaking in a conspiratorial whisper that left it unclear if he were serious or mocking. Probably both, Anne decided.

"You think he and Hughes were making money off each other?"

"Yes."

"If Doctor Dirt leaked it to the tabloids, as you say he did, you've already established a motive for murder."

They were sitting on crushed velour chairs in the dining room of the Hay Adams Hotel, almost hidden from the other diners by a red velvet curtain, barely parted. The little anteroom had a Victorian drawing room feel, broken by the arrival of Sid Sherman.

Sherman took a seat. "So what's tonight's lesson? Is Geoffrey sharing with you his tedious fourteen-point plan to fix Social Security, or is he telling you old war stories?"

"At least I've been in a war, Sid," Geoffrey said. "The only incoming you've ever dodged were press calls and draft board notices."

"So what is it tonight?" Sherman repeated. "And pour me a glass of wine."

To Anne's alarm, Geoffrey told Sherman her entire conspiracy theory.

"So, Sidney," Geoffrey concluded, "what do you think? Is the barbarous billionaire of the Barbary Coast our man?"

"I'll tell you what I think. Nothing happened by chance. Do you really think it was a coincidence that Lee Harvey Oswald set up shop in the same building as Jack Ruby's mafia boss? Or that a man who looked like E. Howard Hunt was prowling around the Grassy Knoll that fateful morning? Anybody who thinks Doctor Dirt's murder was just a freak thing when people like Manoulian are involved is indulging a Kennedy reaction."

"A Kennedy reaction?" Geoffrey asked incredulously.

"Yeah," Sherman waved back a lock of white hair with a jerk of his head. "Of course no one is more adamantly anti-conspiracy than the Kennedys, because they don't want people digging up personal and family skeletons. It's almost instinctual."

"Oh, Sidney, you're getting insipid as well as impotent in your old age." Geoffrey often taunted men thirty years his junior about their age. His age was irrelevant, since he considered himself immortal.

"Tell me, Geoffrey, do you ever confuse your teeth on the beside nightstand for a scotch and water?"

Geoffrey's cheeks and forehead colored. "At least I never

quit respectable journalism to write speeches for someone who buys his own crock of shit."

"America should be so lucky to have another president like this one. In fact, I think we will be."

"You mean your vice president—a man as wooden as the erection on your satyritic oval office demagogue!"

"Guys! You're destroying my last illusions about sophisticated Washington."

The combatants settled back in their chairs. Geoffrey spoke first.

"Okay, Sidney, let's cool it. We're starting to upset the children."

To Anne's disbelief, Sherman raised his glass in a toast, looked at Geoffrey with undisguised affection and said, "You ancient fart." They clinked their glasses and drank.

They talked politics over a steak dinner. It was obvious that the two men were rivals, but close in a way that surprised her. It was equally obvious that having a novice like Anne around gave them both a lift. They liked having an audience for their belligerent antics.

After dinner, Sherman visited with Anne in the lobby while Geoffrey waited outside for the valet to bring his car.

For a moment, he turned away from her, fumbled in his jacket pocket, pulled out a pocket-sized aerosol tube and sprayed it into his mouth.

"Asthma," he explained. "My cross to bear."

As Sherman waited to regain his breath, a strange look passed across his face. He turned, clasped her forearm in his hand tightly, then painfully.

"Do your instincts really tell you that Thornburgh's murder was part of a political conspiracy?"

She felt violated by his intense stare. He had no right to ask what she felt or didn't feel about her story. He had no right to know anything. She wished Geoffrey had never broken her confidence.

She felt as if he were twisting the skin off her arm.

"Yes," she answered.

"Then follow your instincts. Check out Manoulian. My money's on him." He released her arm.

"Your money should be on a therapist."

Sherman pretended not to hear. He stepped outside to join Geoffrey. She watched him through the glass as he said good night to the old man.

Anne looked at her arm. There were no bruises, but the pressure from Sherman's fingers had left red stripes. She almost went outside to tell Geoffrey what had happened, but decided against it. The marks would fade away in a minute.

She could fend for herself.

Her next appointment was for drinks with Ben Grossman, that night, outside the entrance of the Old Ebbitt Grill.

Ben's wife had obviously persuaded him to go for a total remake. The new proprietor of Clarity wore a dark, pinstriped suit cut generously to cover his girth. His hair was neatly cut, clean, combed, and sprayed in place. A black, mesh briefcase sat at his right ankle.

To her surprise, J.D. emerged from a cab and joined them.

"I thought it made sense for both of you to hear this," Grossman said. "Improve the odds that either exposure or indictment will eventually happen."

They took a booth, their privacy protected by glass partitions. Anne was amused by the masculine decor, the paintings of nude goddesses, stuffed animals, dark paneling, and flickering gaslight. They even ordered vodka martinis.

"I got to tell you both," Anne blurted, "that Geoffrey spilled the beans for me. He told Sid Sherman everything we've found out."

"So the White House knows we know that Mike Hughes pushed through the Presidio deal," Grossman said. "Big deal. Or that Manoulian helped establish Hughes in Hollywood through Barry Newhouse. Any putz with a library card can find that out. But did you know they were all fraternity brothers at USC? Not at the same time, of course. Newhouse and Hughes didn't get to college until the late 1950s. But here, let me show just some of what I got."

Grossman pulled a laptop computer from his briefcase. He entered a few keystrokes and brought up a newspaper story from the society page of the *Los Angeles Times*, 1964. "'Greeks Fight for Charity,'" he read. "'USC fraternity raises $5,000 for children's hospital.'" He scrolled down. "And here's our picture of Franklin Manoulian promising to match the fraternity's money three times over."

Manoulian looked bright and handsome in a well-tailored suit. He radiated success and confidence.

Standing next to him were the fraternity's vice president Michael Hughes and president Barry Newhouse. Neither looked old enough to drive. They had flat-top haircuts, slicked back on the sides.

"Anything else?" Anne was not impressed.

"Well, did you know Manoulian provided the seed money for Newhouse's Hollywood agency? And take a look here."

Grossman pulled up files that showed a fat stream of donations coming into the coffers of the presidential campaign of Michael Hughes from Hollywood and from Manoulian's company, the San Marcos Group.

"Now the thing here," said Grossman, "is timing. This money's comin' in just weeks before Hughes pushes the Presidio deal through the House-Senate conference committee. You could call it the deal of the century if you look at this." He pulled up an EPA contract and searched for a clause buried in the boilerplate paragraphs. "'The final cost of all contaminated land will be one dollar.'"

"What?" Anne exclaimed. "How'd he get away with that?"

"Privately, Hughes had leverage, and he used it all," Grossman said. "Publically, he argued the land was so contaminated, the feds actually saved money by getting rid of it. Ain't true, of course. But there you have it."

"And that's where the first couple comes in," J.D. said.

"Yeah. They saw low hanging fruit in the form of golden apples, and decided to pick a few for themselves. And, of course, one other thing that's protected the Presidio deal is all its friends, aside from Mike Hughes."

"What's the property value once it's cleaned up?" Anne asked.

"Well," Grossman said, "the California Department of Finance estimates $200 million."

"But how does all this tie into the Nixon library?" Anne asked.

Grossman shut off the laptop and downed the last of his drink in one gulp. "Don't know. Haven't cracked that one yet. I'm hopin' you might be able to do *somethin'*."

That night, after Grossman left, Anne and J.D. walked down the street. The ice had melted from the sidewalks, the night merely cool. "Now tell me something, Agent DeVine, are you always going to be in my way?"

"I'm not getting in your way, I'm conducting a murder investigation. And if you get in my way, I'll have you arrested."

She put her hands together in front of her waist. "Oh would you please? I like the way handcuffs feel, and besides, I could use the promotion."

She was probably right, it would get her promoted.

"So what do you suggest?"

Anne tilted her head, looked at him from the corner of her eyes. "We could work Manoulian from different angles, then trade information. Which works for me, as long as I get a story ahead of everyone else."

"And you'll give the Bureau time to work before going to press?"

She changed the subject. "So what are you doing this weekend?"

"Seeing which one of us gets back to California first."

"You're on." Anne kissed him on the lips, just a beat longer than a purely social gesture, then went after a cab, leaving him standing there with his hands in his pockets.

CHAPTER
15

He remembered that some French philosopher once said that three o'clock in the afternoon is either too early or too late to get anything done. Mike Hughes felt that way, as he rose a bit wobbly from an afternoon nap. He had been out late the night before, gorging on sea urchin, salmon, and Asahi beer, with two of the best entertainment lawyers in L.A. The night had ended embarrassingly, at a karaoke bar, that much he could remember.

He'd got home at five and slept till eight. He had his customary breakfast of coffee ice cream, downed a Bloody Mary, and took four aspirin.

Throughout the morning, he felt that familiar ache behind his eye sockets and in the joints of his knees, mouth dry as old newspaper. All of this only reminded him of how much he liked working through a hangover. And he did work, negotiating the financing for a movie that would probably be the hottest action film in two summers. After lunch in Westwood, he swung home, stretched out to rest his eyes, and wound up sleeping for the better part of an hour.

He padded into his study to check his phone messages. Nothing. He rubbed his scalp, and felt where sleep had shaped his hair into a rooster's comb. He rubbed the side of his face where a little corduroy pillow had left deep furrows. He looked down. Feet, shirt, pants—wrinkled.

He realized there was nothing to do tonight, no date, no dinner, no evening engagement. That would have to change. He showered, shaved, and doused himself with cologne. He put on a pair of khaki pants and a dark shirt with a Navajo pattern. Over that, he pulled his best cashmere sweater, slipped into boot socks, and hitched his feet into his pair of ostrich-skin boots, the gray skin mottled by pimple-like quills.

It was still too early to go out, so he ate a sandwich and sipped a vodka tonic. He read magazines and watched the news.

Finally at eight, he was in his new silver Jaguar purring along the streets of West L.A. He found a space almost directly in front of the entrance of his favorite bar, O'Shaunesseys, the place he always went when he had nothing better to do.

With its brass rails, brick walls, cherry wood bar, and framed pictures of Irish gentlemen on their steeds, it was mail-order decor. But it attracted just the right crowd—the secretaries, the stews, the little rich girl art majors, the girls who might appreciate him as a vaguely remembered celebrity.

The music pulsed, the crowd jostled around the bar and under palms and slow-moving ceiling fans. Hughes made his way to the bar and ordered a Bloody Mary with half a jigger of vodka. He knew he would have to pace himself. After all, the hunt could go on until two in the morning.

He tried talking to a little honey-blonde at the end of

the bar, a sweet-looking thing with a freckled nose. His approach was always gentle, soft, almost avuncular. He introduced himself and asked her all kinds of questions about her life—making her laugh with an occasional quip or slightly off-color observation.

She told him her parents in Tula, Mississippi, had sent her to L.A. to go to a private girl's school. She had dropped out and was now working in a record store. She could be no older than seventeen.

Mike Hughes didn't leave immediately. He listened some more, wondering if she was a friend of the bartender or had purchased a fake ID. After a discrete interval, he took her hand in his, and told her it was great meeting her.

Perhaps they would meet again. In about seven years.

As he made his way down the bar he saw another woman looking directly at him. She was smartly dressed in a woman's business suit. Her short, black hair was combed forward, the strands gently splayed on her pallid face.

Hughes smiled at her and ordered another Bloody. This time he ordered it with a double shot of vodka. When he got his drink, he looked back and pointed at her, as if to ask "Can I get you one?"

She shook her head but kept eye contact. He made his way through the crowd and introduced himself.

"Senator," she said, "I'd know you anywhere. It's great to meet you."

She transferred a white wine spritzer to her left hand and shook firmly with her right. Her name was Melinda King.

"You must be into politics?"

"I know who you are and some of the ideas you had for the country. You were a good senator."

"I'm flattered." And he was.

He asked her a lot about herself. While she spoke, he took in her full red lips, her pert nose, the dark makeup around her baby-blue eyes. He guessed that her eyes were colored by contacts, her breasts accentuated by a plastic surgeon.

She said that she worked for an accounting firm on Sunset. Never been married, no family nearby. Perfect.

"And if I may ask, what was it about my politics that you liked?"

She seemed momentarily at a loss. "I guess it was your commitment to people, your caring."

Obviously her enthusiasm was part put-on. It could have been worse. People often mistook him for a game show host.

A tall, athletic-looking man in a leather jacket walked over and put his arm around Melinda's chair. He looked at Hughes for a moment in mock wonderment and then put out his hand.

"I am Jerzy, from Poland."

The man's greasy dark-blond hair was brushed straight back. His eyes were intense, his handsome face looked weathered, singed, as if he had been staring into a furnace.

They shook, and Hughes started to make a polite exit. "Leaving so soon?" Melinda King sat forward in a slouch. "We were just getting to know you."

"That's right...."

"Senator Hughes," Melinda said to Jerzy.

"I'm not a citizen of this country for a month and I meet a senator."

She touched Hughes lightly, her fingers lingering on his forearm. "Stay with us. Let us buy you a drink."

Hughes looked up and down the bar, seeing no inviting prospects. "Sure."

After an awkward moment, he asked, "Are you two married?"

They looked at each other, laughed, as if the idea were utterly preposterous.

"No," she said, "we're just buds, right?"

"We are buds, party friends."

"So you two are a pair?"

Something about that phrase made Jerzy break into unrestrained laughter. Melinda laughed and snorted, wiping tears from the corners of her eyes. Hughes wondered if they were coked up.

With visible effort Jerzy straightened up, raked a knuckle along the bottom of his eye, coughed and, still smiling, said, "No, my friend, we are not lovers. I have a wife and daughter in Warsaw. Sometime soon I hope to bring them here."

"So how did you two meet?"

They looked at each other and laughed. "It's a crazy story," Melinda said.

"You are not going to believe," Jerzy added.

"It was my birthday. I was at the office."

"You must understand, my friend, I need money."

"So the girls chipped in and got me a singing stripper."

"Me, the singing Polish stripper," he said. For another moment they were racked again by convulsions of hysterics, like two children desperately trying not to laugh at a funeral. After a few false starts, they composed themselves.

"So I come here that very night, after work, with a few of my friends. And guess who's standing at the bar?"

They looked at each other, smiling, and said in unison, "Your singing Polish stripper!"

Hughes had long ago reconciled himself to the fact that a middle-aged man cannot sleep with a great many young women without developing a high tolerance for juvenile antics. But this was getting to be too much for him.

Perhaps sensing Hughes's irritation, Jerzy had gone in an instant from party animal to maudlin family man.

"When you come to America, you have to be willing to do what it takes to make money—to get your wife and kids over here."

Hughes felt a slight annoyance, as if there was something not quite right with Jerzy, something put on. "I thought you had just one daughter?"

"Uh? 'Kids' is just figure of speech."

"Why L.A., why now?" Hughes pressed on. "Didn't you see the riots on TV? You know how hard and expensive it is to live here."

A fierce look crossed Jerzy's face. "Listen to me, I am telling you this, life in this country on its worst day is a thousand times better than the best day in Poland."

Hughes relaxed. This guy was all right, the genuine article. He reached for his glass and clinked it against the beer stein Jerzy grasped in one hand.

"So what are you into now?" Melinda turned to Hughes. She reclined in the small, wooden bar chair, her back slightly arched, her legs crossed.

"Well, I'm into meeting new people and working in the movies."

She bolted forward. "You're in the movies?"

"Well, I'm not in them exactly, but what I do I find a lot more interesting, even glamorous. I work with the big agents, the studios, the actors, and the financial community to put together deals, to make the movies happen."

"Wow! Do you know Tom Cruise?"

"Know him? We went deep sea fishing down in Cabo."

Melinda was still wide-eyed and open-mouthed. Having been a United States senator on the fast track to the White House was nothing compared to fishing with Tom Cruise.

"If you like, maybe sometime we can meet Tom and Nicole for brunch." Mike Hughes was often simultaneously ashamed and amused by himself. He took in her big, believing baby-blues, her lips, her breasts, her legs. Could he pull it off in one night? He wasn't sure but he was warming to the task.

Jerzy, visibly bored with their flirting, was having a conversation with a couple at the bar about the relative merits of the Los Angeles Kings over the San Jose Sharks. "You're not pulling my leg are you?" She suddenly looked hurt and vulnerable.

"No, but I'd like to." That made her laugh.

They talked awhile, about L.A., about recent movies.

"I'm glad I met you." Hughes affected his most sincere manner, a way that even now, still came across as boyish. "You're very... nice."

She stared at him. "I'm glad I met you." Her voice had become thick and throaty.

"Would you like to continue this conversation somewhere else? I mean back at my place. If you stay too long, you can take the bed, I'll take the couch." Hughes knew only two techniques when it came to women. Take a sincere interest in them. And always make them comfortable, always give them an out.

"Sure, why not. I'd love to see your place. Do you have pictures of movie stars?"

He smiled and made a little joke. "Well, I have a great picture of me as a Congressman shaking hands with Golda Meir."

"Is she as pretty as she looks on television?"

"Come again?"

"I mean how she used to look in those old '60s movies."

Mike Hughes let the air out of his lungs slowly, as if he were a deflating tire. He looked her over again, one more time, just to remind himself what he had to look forward to.

She stood up with him, took a twenty out of her purse and walked over to the bar. "Jerzy, we're going to head out. Would you be a dear and add this to our bill?"

Jerzy gave her a strange, quizzical look. They spoke to each other heatedly, but the bartender had the music cranked so loud that Hughes couldn't hear them. For a moment, he thought the man was jealous. But he looked more embarrassed than angry.

He could just make out a little of what she was saying. "You tell him yourself."

Jerzy picked up a small, white shopping bag from under the bar and turned, his eyes on the floor. He looked up at Hughes. "Listen, I hate to ask this of someone I can admire. As you go back to your place, I was wondering if I could go along too? Just to crash."

Jerzy looked down again and shuffled his feet.

"You see, I've been living in a place where you rent by the day. Not very good, all hookers and drug sellers. Tomorrow I'm putting down a deposit for an apartment down by airport. Is nice. But I need somewhere to crash tonight."

Mike Hughes shook his head. "I don't know."

"Jerzy's fine, he's cool, I know him," Melinda rubbed Hughes' arm, part come on, part pleading.

"I promise, you two have a great time without me. I'll crash somewhere on my own. Just give me a pillow and a blanket."

"Well, there is a fold-out couch in the guest room." Hughes wondered if his judgment had been compromised more by vodka or by lust.

Jerzy threw his bag into the Jaguar and had to slide sideways into the backseat, drawing his long legs to his chest. No sooner had Hughes turned the ignition than Melinda King reached into her purse, pulled out a small, hand-rolled joint, and lit it with the cigarette lighter from the dash.

"I wish you wouldn't do that," Hughes said, taking the top down.

"Don't fret. It looks like a cigarette." Under the harsh copper street lights, her skin looked sallow, small pockmarks showing.

"What the hell." Hughes took the doobie with one hand as he steered out to Santa Monica Boulevard with the other. He drew in a deep, satisfying hit that filled his lungs, saturated his blood, rose to calm his restless brain.

He checked in the rearview mirror and saw that Jerzy

was already slumped back, his eyes closed, jaw slack. With any luck, Hughes could let him sleep in the car.

Hughes and Melinda shared the joint until there was nothing left to suck. He flicked the roach onto the street.

"I'm hungry," she said. Hughes wasn't sure if it was a statement or a command. But he was hungry too, so he turned east and twenty minutes later pulled into the parking lot of Musso and Franks.

Leaving Jerzy in the car, they went inside and shared the same side of a booth. Hughes had not been stoned since he first got serious about the White House twenty years ago, and was surprised by the potency of what he had just smoked.

Melinda caressed the inside of his thigh while they ordered, a rubber hand on his rubber leg. Hughes felt slightly apart from what was going on around him, as if the scene around him were mere reflections, five mirrors away from reality.

They ate omelettes and toast with silent greed. They slurped coffee. Hughes felt himself coming around by the time he paid the bill.

"I wonder how Jerzy's doing?" she said.

"With any luck, he's hit the road."

But Jerzy was still there, curled up, his face flush against the backseat.

"Take me home," she said as Hughes started the car again.

"Where do you live?"

"I mean to your place. That's where we're going, isn't it?" She was looking directly into his eyes. They drove without speaking, arriving at Hughes' home in under fifteen minutes, pulling into the dark driveway. Hughes had left no houselights burning.

Jerzy woke up. "My friend, please show me to couch, that's all I need." He sounded drunk and dazed. After some fumbling with his keys, Hughes opened the door and let them in.

"Right this way." He led Jerzy to the guest room beneath the stairwell, across the house from his own bedroom. "The guest bathroom's to the left."

"Thank you, my friend. I will buy you breakfast in the morning." Jerzy disappeared with his bag. Hughes wondered if it contained all he owned.

Melinda was already in the master bathroom, so Hughes busied himself pouring two cognacs at the bar.

After more than ten minutes, long enough for Hughes to almost fall asleep, Melinda King came into his bedroom wearing nothing but a black bra and panties. He was still feeling a little high, feeling as if he could drink the sight of her, her concave stomach between the rise of her pelvis, breasts that pressed hard against her bra.

She grabbed the stem of the snifter as if it were a beer stein. "Listen, it's getting late, if we're going to do anything, I want it to happen now."

Hughes let her have a sip, then grabbed her drink and set it down with his by the bed. Sometimes when he made love to a woman, he started slowly and cautiously, beginning with kisses that were almost chaste. He grabbed Melinda by the shoulders and kissed her openly.

They slid over to the bed and fell down. She pulled at his belt until he stopped her and unbuckled it himself. He could see in the dim lighting that she had already taken off her panties.

"Wait, wait," he said, piteously. "I've got to get my protection." He fumbled in the drawer of his nightstand and pulled out a condom, awkwardly tearing at it, slipping it on. "There." She shoved him back and straddled him, weaving and rocking.

A few moments later, it was over and Mike Hughes was surprised to see that she had sprung up from the bed, retrieved her dress from the bathroom and was already getting dressed.

"I usually don't like to kiss."

"Really?" he said, lying sideways, naked in the bed, amused at what he took to be her masculine temperament.

"Well, I mean it's usually not part of the deal, it's extra." She had fully dressed in under a minute.

"Extra? Extra what?"

"Extra money. What else?"

"Money, what money?"

"To do it like that, a lot. Don't ask me, ask your friend from Poland. He's the one who drops a thousand like it's a tip."

Hughes was sitting up in bed now. "Wait a minute, I don't get this. You're an accountant, right?"

"Sugar, the only money I can count is what I keep in this purse. And thanks to your friend, this has been a good night."

He started to stand.

"Don't bother getting up. I'll go see Jerzy, and we'll let ourselves out. We can get a cab at the hotel down the street."

"Melinda!" he cried out.

"Take it easy, I'll come back any time you want. Your Polish friend has my number." She left the room.

For the next five minutes, Hughes sat at the edge of his bed, staring at the illuminated numbers of his digital clock, trying to figure out what had happened.

His condom started to peel off, making him feel cold and sticky, so he walked to the bathroom, threw the rubber into the toilet, and took a hot shower.

That would sober him up, draw some of the alcohol poison and marijuana out of his system. If they were still in his house by the time he toweled and dressed, he would throw them out. If they wouldn't leave, he would call the police.

Melinda was surprised to find the man she knew as Jerzy naked, waiting for her on the fold-out bed.

"How did it go?" Dmitri asked.

"How does it always go?" She was always like this, blasé when not paid to playact. And besides, she was really ready for sleep.

"Well, Melinda, or whatever your name is, you did a real good job tonight. Even I thought you were an accountant."

"Yeah, I'd still like to know what this is really about. It doesn't seem like a practical joke. You don't even know this guy."

Dmitri looked straight at her, making a request with his eyes.

"Well, well, we never talked about this." She leaned in the doorway.

"Why not? I am certainly paying you enough."

"I don't care what you paid me, this will be more." She was tired and really not interested in making more money.

"How about another five hundred, just to end the job?"

"Okay," she said wearily, starting to take off her top, "just to end the job."

Melinda disrobed, took off her slip and underwear and started to straddle Dmitri Popova's sinuous, scarred body.

"You've been in a lot of fights. And that tattoo, is that some kind of like biker thing?"

"We did get off on wearing black leather jackets."

"Cool," she said, sliding down on him, waiting, waiting, nothing. "You're not even hard."

"Check this out," Dmitri said. He reached down and pulled up a plastic sandwich bag from under the covers. It was filled with a quarter-pound of thick, damp, grainy paste with little crystals that refracted colors like tiny beads of glass.

Dmitri stuck his finger into the crack cocaine and spooned it into her mouth. She sucked his finger and made a throaty sound of satisfaction. He pulled his finger out of her sucking mouth with a pop.

"Good shit."

"It's part meth, part coke. Very pure." He caked his wet finger with the paste, and began to rub her gum, all the way around the top of her mouth. She sucked and swallowed, her face and the skin over her flat breastbone flushed. Her eyes narrowed to dim slits.

"Try this," he said, taking another clump and rubbing more into her gums just above her front teeth.

"Oh wow, that's like, good, I mean...."

Dmitri led her to lie next to him, took some more paste on his fingers and began to rub her with it.

"Hey, that's not, I mean you're a John, you shouldn't…."

But she didn't stop him. He gave her more, a lot more. Her eyes were glassy now, as dark and featureless as the black-marble eyes of a mounted deer.

"That's so, so…." Her voice was weak and sleepy.

"Now try this." Dmitri forced her mouth wide open. He dumped more than half the bag into her mouth.

She sprang up, gagging. Dmitri grabbed an open bottle of beer he had by the bed and thrust it in to her mouth. "Drink!" he shouted. She drank the entire beer without stopping, couldn't taste the twenty muscle relaxants Dmitri had crumbled into it. The empty bottle fell out of her hand, and she slowly sank to the bed.

He waited a minute to make sure she wasn't going to vomit. And while he waited, an old feeling stirred in him, an anticipation of death, yes, but also of sex.

The two seemed to go together so often in his life.

But no, no, it would not do. He could not have sex with this whore. He could not leave traces of himself on this woman, sperm and hair for an FB78I microscope.

Dmitri pinched her nose tightly with one hand, sealed her mouth with the other, and jerked her head toward the bed. She struggled, but with her eyes closed, unconscious. Dmitri knew he had only to fight the dumb resistance of her body.

She clutched and scratched at her chest. The onset of a coronary artery spasm. From this point, it usually took less than a minute, but she was young and strong and lasted longer than that. At the end, she fought so hard that Dmitri's arms were getting bruised and sore. Finally, her body jerked violently, she convulsed and slumped. It was over. He rolled her onto her right side.

A minute later, Mike Hughes entered the room wearing slippers, gym shorts, and a Yale T-shirt, his hair slicked back, wet from a shower. Dmitri reached under the sheet to slip a single black glove over his right hand. He reached down and retrieved something from the floor.

Hughes looked surprised and disgusted to see both of them naked. "Now she's passed out? Wake her up. Get out. Both of you."

Dmitri stood up and with one panther-like movement crossed the room. He slammed his fist underneath Hughes' left elbow, forcing his arm to extend straight out.

With his gloved hand, Dmitri jammed a long needle into a fat blue vein in the white flesh of the older man's inner arm.

Hughes tried to move his arm, but Dmitri pushed inward, holding it fast to inject a full vial of liquid black-tar heroin.

Hughes screamed. "Stop it! Stop! Like fire!"

"It's over. There." He pulled out the needle and threw it on the bed. "And by the way, my name's not Jerzy. I am Dmitri."

Hughes was crouched over, rubbing the inside of his arm. "What was that? Who are you? Why are you doing this?"

"That was a little something to make you high."

"Jerzy, you crazy shit, you hurt my arm. What was that stuff? I'm calling 911."

"It's Dmitri. Let me show you one thing first."

"No." Hughes followed his assailant into the living room, looking for the portable phone. His head started to feel light, as if it might lift off his shoulders. But his legs were heavy, disconnected. It was getting hard to walk.

Dmitri, naked save for the black glove, awkwardly unscrewed the top of a scotch bottle with his one gloved hand. "Do you drink with ice?"

"I don't want a fucking scotch. I'm calling the police." Despite himself, Hughes fell backwards onto the living room couch.

"How many cubes?"

"Three," he said, wasted, resigned. "You'd better let me call the police."

Hughes took the drink and sipped it without taking his eyes off Dmitri. For the first time, the glove, the strange tattoo, registered.

"Who the hell are you really?"

"I told you, I am Dmitri. I planned this whole evening for you."

"And the girl, she works for you?"

"She did." The past tense. It sounded like some kind of private joke.

"So who are you?"

"I work for people who are concerned about your behavior. They are worried that you've allowed things to become confused, that you are talking to people about business."

"What was that stuff? I want to go to the hospital." Hughes slipped into a half-crouch, trying to stand.

"Don't worry, it's just truth serum. Now, do you really want police to be here, with prostitute and drugs all over the place?"

"Why don't you put on some clothes and get the hell out." Hughes was unsteady, but he was finally standing. He defiantly slugged back the scotch.

"Okay, but first hear me out. Your friends are concerned about the way you've been shooting off your mouth. My friend, you deceive yourself. You are so sick with drink and lies that you've forgotten that you actually have some things to hide."

"I have nothing to hide." Hughes rubbed his cheeks, starting to feel as if a mask of dead flesh were grafted onto his face.

"Others may not see it that way. You talked, to an *L.A. Times* reporter, then some guy with FBI connections. You talked to them about the San Marcos deal. If they find out about the holding company, it will not be pretty. Anyone else?"

"So Barry's behind this, that bastard."

"Right now, Mr. Newhouse is not your problem," Dmitri said. "I am. Tell me who you discussed it with."

"Just her, just that reporter woman named... named... Anne Carlsbad, Carlton, son."

"That's it? That's all, just her?"

"And the guy with the FBI. D.J., J.D. something. Now will you please go so I can call for help? And take the whore with you."

"Certainly," Dmitri said, but he was fixing another scotch. Hughes took it blindly as his eyes closed, weaving while he stood. He sipped on the drink almost unconsciously, by habit.

"What are you doing to me?"

"I am killing you."

Hughes opened his eyes, looked into Dmitri's hard gaze, and shook his head slowly, then violently. He threw the drink onto the floor and staggered toward the phone in his bedroom.

In no particular hurry, Dmitri walked ahead of him, bent over and unplugged the phone jack with his gloved hand.

Hughes slid a bookend off a shelf. He tried to throw it, but it slipped from his hand and shattered on the floor.

Hughes began to sob. "Okay, I'm sorry, I'm sorry. Tell Frank I'll shut my mouth."

"Frank knows you will shut your mouth."

Hughes turned and staggered again, his heels sliding awkwardly out of his slippers. He hit the hallway wall, fell to his knees, and crawled to the study. But Dmitri was ahead of him again, denying him the phone on his desk.

Hughes looked up and grabbed at his desk, raking off framed photos of himself with Cher, Madonna, Warren Beatty. "Please, please," he was whispering now, chin sinking slowly to his chest, eyes too heavy to keep open. "Don't let me die like this."

Dmitri took him by the hand. He led Hughes, eyes closed and staggering, to the guest bedroom, where he pushed him down on the foldout bed with the needle at one side, dead Melinda at the other.

"Please," Hughes whispered, almost asleep. "It's not like they say."

"You're right. It's not like they say." Dmitri dressed and then sat by the bed, watching the once great man sleep, his breathing becoming more and more shallow, until he blew out a few deep breaths and his chest ceased to move altogether.

The two of them looked intimate in death, Hughes flat on his back with an expression of stoned peace, Melinda curled up next to him. They looked comfortable and close, like an old married couple.

Dmitri walked down the empty back alley to an all-night diner. He ordered a huge American meal of flapjacks, eggs, and bacon, drank a lot of coffee. He had more orders of his own to fill.

CHAPTER
16

J.D. never left lights on. Then he noticed the curled corner of his screen window. He saw it all before he stopped his 356.

Someone had broken into his office and had stupidly left a light on.

J.D. stopped the car and pulled the Walther from his ankle holster. He checked out the cars in the parking lot. The seats were vacant. Hoods cool.

He felt the edges of the screen, bent five inches or more, most likely by a screwdriver. He lifted the screen, it was loose. He put an ear to the glass, listened for a minute or two, heard nothing but the automatic hummings of an empty house.

He crept behind the townhouse to the back door, letting himself into the kitchen. He swept each room, elbow slightly bent, pistol a steady extension of his arm. Then the shower, then the closets.

No one home.

The safe looked the same, the tumblers clicked in just the right way. But that didn't mean anything. A good safe man can slip in and out like the Tooth Fairy.

J.D. went to the closet, pushed aside heavy winter coats,

and found the place in the back where he kept his camping equipment. His old, beat up Coleman lantern was where he'd left it.

The safe stored his will, his deed, and a collection of silver dollars his granddad had given him. Secret material always went into the Coleman.

He unthreaded the stainless steel bottom. It was meant to be filled with white gas, but had been retooled by an old informant who had designed it for drug deals. He took the disks from the hollow compartment.

The Coleman, J.D. knew, was clever, but wouldn't hold. They'd be back, and when they returned they'd tear the walls apart. There was only one way to go. J.D. slipped the disks into a Rubbermaid sandwich container, sealed it, and put the plastic bag inside a small beer cooler. He sealed the cooler with a glue gun, bound it with waterproof duct tape.

J.D. set the alarm for three thirty in the morning.

He rose, washed his face, threw on a blue work shirt and some denims.

The stars were eerily brilliant that morning, bright pinpricks of light.

J.D. loaded the cooler and a fishing pole into the boat, and gently, almost without a sound, pushed the Morgan off the dock into the inky, black water.

He let the drift of the boat take him as far as he could before firing up the Atomic 4 Diesel.

J.D. cut the engine well out into Spa Creek. He put up the sail, wound the winch, tailed the sheet, and beat against the wind. He tacked into a steady breeze, an easterly dawn wind, and sliced north toward the tall shadows of vast radio towers.

He was at the mouth of the Severn, almost in the Chesapeake.

J.D. navigated in the dim morning light by the tall shadows of ungainly monsters, Navy long-frequency radio towers, erected in 1917 for submarine communications. Like so much military hardware, they would soon be gone, dismantled for scrap.

He sailed for a good half-hour. By the time the sky reddened against the contours of Kent Island on the other side of the Bay, he was as close as he could get to shore without scraping bottom. His depth finder reassured him that even with an outgoing tide, the Morgan would not get stranded. J.D. heaved a plough-shaped CQR anchor in the shallow water. He reeled in the inflatable dinghy he had towed behind, loaded the cooler into it, and brought along a small collapsible shovel.

He took the plastic oars of the dinghy, and quietly rowed to shore. The rubber prow crunched headfirst into a sandbar just off of Greenbury Point.

Government land.

Well, he had promised Lou Firelli that he would turn over any disks he found to the federal authorities.

Here it is, Lou. X-marks the spot.

He stepped out as close to shore as he could get, knee-deep in frigid water. *Colder than a brass cod piece in December.*

He floated the cooler, shovel on top, to the beach. He dug a three-foot hole under a coastal elm a good twenty feet from the lapping shore. He turned back, saw that the anchor had slipped, grateful that the CQR did what it was designed to do and dug back into the sand.

He had to hurry. After all, it wouldn't be easy explaining to M.P.s exactly what he was doing on land adjacent to the U.S. Navy Warfare Center and Laboratory.

As he finished, J.D. surveyed the scene, made a mental photograph of the shoreline and the tree. It was gnarled, distinctive, a good marker. In an hour or so, he'd be back home, taking a shower and getting ready for the airport.

J.D. had Andre go on-line to find a five-liter Mustang in a dull color. He wanted horsepower with style, but in subdued hues to keep the ticket-happy California Highway Patrol from taking a special interest in him. The 'Stang was waiting at the San Jose airport. But first he had to return McGuire's page.

J.D. got him on the first ring. "Tell me the story."

"Hughes is dead. Here's what's public—which is all we know. Double overdose, Hughes and a prostitute. Crack cocaine and a needle with several narcotics, including heroin, were on the scene. President's already been on camera at a golf course, saying what a great primary opponent Hughes was. His business partner Barry Newhouse denies he ever saw Hughes on drugs before running off to Rome on what he said was urgent business, but other Hollywood sources say Hughes lived in the fast lane. How's that?"

"Listen," J.D. said, "that's bullshit. I've read Hughes' FBI file. He ran from sharp objects. The man did everything but wear lipstick to get out of serving in Vietnam. He had to be sedated to have his hernia fixed at Bethesda. He asked for Secret Service from his first day in the campaign."

"What are you sayin'? That it's a setup?"

"I'm saying he wouldn't jam a needle into his arm and pump liquid crap into his brain," J.D. said.

"Uh huh."

"What did you find on Vasquez?"

"Leonora Vasquez and Ignacio Vasquez, no recorded travel to California. But get this. They've got their own Gulfstream. We checked. No record of it flying to L.A."

"What about across the border?"

"Always possible."

"Okay. Thanks. I'll call you later. Got a date."

"Now there's a miracle."

J.D. stepped out to find his Mustang.

The direct heat of the California sun felt good, and the faded interior of the Mustang looked as good as a pair of used jeans. He loaded his bag. The inside of the Mustang was hot, but the a/c kicked in as soon as J.D. left the parking lot.

At least he didn't need a map. Just go south on the state highway into the Central Valley, then cut west to the coast.

In twenty minutes J.D. was out of the city and rising into the cool shadows of coastal mountains thick with redwood and dense undergrowth. The car's wide-track tires and beefy suspension handled the winding road well. A steep road like this was a walk in the park for the souped-up Ford V-8.

J.D. cracked a window to let in some of the ocean air, clean and cold off northern waters. The air and the car's smooth ride helped him think. Ex-Senator Hughes had been murdered. That was the only explanation. But there was a problem with the m.o. It wasn't easy to fake an overdose. He caught a glimpse of ocean as he rounded a bend.

The coastal forests receded behind him. Ahead steep mountain country rolled into ridges of brown, scrubby grassland. After another twenty minutes, it rose again to a high pass that looked down on miles of elevated savanna, stalks of dry grass bleached to a wheat color under the relentless sun.

J.D. fished his cell phone from his pocket. Dialing with one hand, driving with the other, he got Washington, D.C., information and had the operator put him through to Leo Lindstrom.

"Stinky? It's been a few days. Got anything for me?"

"I've got two pounds of meat and glands aswinging. That's two pounds more than you got."

Oh Stinky, God bless the raving loony.

"I'm giving you a chance to inflict a wound on the opposition."

"You are the opposition, Agent Hoover."

"Anything at all?"

"All right, I found something in Ruth Thornburgh's garbage."

"Lay it on me."

"A month-old hotel receipt. She checked into the Hilton in Alexandria, her own hometown. But the room was under a credit card issued to Ben Grossman."

"You think they're lovers?"

"No, I think they meet for Trivial Pursuit in the middle of the afternoon."

"I got to tell you, it's a little hard to imagine."

"Want the truth about Ruth? Ben's smart, brusque. Must be her type."

"This is evidence," J.D. said. "Keep the original. It's mine."

He punched "off," and took in the scene ahead. In the distance, windsurfers cut across an enormous, twinkling lake contained in a high reservoir. Beyond that, on the other side of what had to be an immense dam, the land dropped steeply. The valley beyond was a flat landscape of green rectangles transected by dusty roads, farmland sustained only by the millions of cubic acres of water held in the reservoir above it.

The display panel registered an outside temperature of 90 degrees. J.D. turned the air to full blast. He was heading back down from the mountains and into the valley.

He noticed wide, chalky stripes above the edge of the water in the vast reservoir, showing how low it was. He couldn't get used to such a place, where rainwater came in torrents for a few months and then had to be captured and husbanded with great care, where you could drive an hour in either direction and change your climate from moist, foggy coastline to a blazing, dry valley of irrigated farms.

The road leveled off at foothills patchworked with vineyards. The road dipped lower and was soon bordered by fields, then rows of peach trees.

J.D. turned west back toward the coast and its river beds, cool forests, thick with redwood, hilltops obscured by pine and eucalyptus, nourished by the occasional sea cloud drifting into the coastal mountains. As soon as it was cool enough, J.D. turned off the air and cracked the window again.

In a moment, he passed the San Marcos Presidio, a rambling military suburb of small, plank-wood ranch houses surrounded by concrete office buildings. On the hill were the officers' homes, white Victorian two-story mansions with generous porches and thick columns. Near the empty sentry box was a sign.

Coming Soon!

San Marcos Estates

*A Quality, Planned Community
in the Old Presidio*

Seaside Living at Its Finest

J.D. wondered if Manoulian would bulldoze the palm trees and the old mansions.

As he turned a bend, the landscape opened up to a large, flat plain of raw upended earth and red clay deeply furrowed by mechanical tracks.

He rounded another curve and entered a small, beach town of dark, wood-shingle homes, white churches, and quaint stores. Maine by the Pacific. He slowed down, the city road narrowed, and soon he was actually crossing a fairway. J.D. braked for a cart full of elderly golfers.

In a moment, he was piloting his 'Stang up a hill, past rows of wooden houses and a city park, then past a two-story office complex covered in pink granite. A sign announced the complex as part of the San Marcos Group.

He turned onto a steep road that climbed through thick forest, rising until he could look back at a panoramic view of the beach town below and the flat expanse of the Pacific.

It was almost a shock when he turned the corner to face

a stone wall and a massive gate of thick metal bars. A guard sat in a glass booth watching closed circuit TV of the approaches to the property, the Manoulian mansion.

The guard checked J.D.'s driver's license and FBI consultant's special credentials before opening the gate.

The road to the house was steeper yet, at first crossing through a barren field of high scrub and stone. It flattened out at the top of the hill, and ran between twin rows of twenty-foot poplars. Between the trees, to the left, he caught a glimpse of white Ionic colonnades surrounding an Olympic-sized pool, overlooking the ocean.

The house appeared at the end of a gravel circular driveway. It was an Italianate mansion, three stories of balconied, Mediterranean splendor, with white cherubim recessed into niches below a tiled roof, a massive dark brown door that could have come from a castle or a monastery, twelve-foot Italian Cypress trees standing like sentries along the entry way. He pulled up in front and cut the ignition.

He rang the bell and waited a full minute for a smartly dressed young woman in a tan business suit to open the door.

"I'm Shannon Crocker, vice president and executive-director of the San Marcos Group." She shook hands firmly. "Let me take you to see Mr. Manoulian. He's very curious why the FBI needed an appointment so urgently. He's got to make a dinner tonight, so I'd appreciate it if we kept it to, say, twenty minutes."

"This is an FBI investigation. You'll offer me what I need."

"I can only guess you want to hear about Mike Hughes. Frank's fine with that, although I must tell you he hasn't really kept up with Mr. Hughes and is as mystified as anyone over what happened."

"Maybe he can demystify it for me."

He had a brief glimpse of an expansive, breathtaking sitting room, beautifully furnished with heavy, carved, dark-wood tables and chairs, polished to a sheen, a massive medieval tapestry dominating one wall, and a gleaming marble-tiled floor, before Shannon led him down a bright white hallway. The left side was lined with family photos, recent pictures of Manoulian's daughters and their respective families, early photos of his late wife. On the right side, by itself, was a large photo portrait of a handsome young man with bright blue eyes and dark, wavy hair. Manoulian's only son, dead at twenty-seven.

They reached a back wing, a small, wooden bar surrounded by cheap, tacky decorative items, mirrors embossed with slightly ribald sayings, then a conference room with a long, mahogany table and chairs, full ashtrays, stale cigar smoke. This was Frank Manoulian's part of the house, where he lives.

Shannon led into a large study where Manoulian sat on a black leather couch, looking at an issue of *Forbes* in his lap.

"Frank," Shannon said softly.

"Oh Shannon, thank you." He set the magazine to his side and stood up. At 6'1" in his tennis shoes, Frank Manoulian had an inch over J.D. He wore a white tennis shirt neatly tucked into a pair of pressed, khaki shorts. He had the muscular legs of a much younger man, and only a slight paunch about the belly.

The room had a lived-in warmth, with a faint odor of cigar smoke. The bookshelves were lined with potboiler novels, popular histories, the bindings creased by an avid reader.

The papers on his large desk were sorted and stacked into thick piles of work. The walls were dotted by photos of Frank Manoulian with his daughters or with movie stars. One photo, set off by itself, showed Manoulian on the rounded stern of his yacht, greeting Richard Nixon and Leonid Brezhnev.

J.D. noticed a slightly faded rectangular patch on the wall.

"Are you based in California?" Manoulian asked, smiling.

"I'm based out of Washington."

"You've made quite a trip. Okay, I'm ready. Hit me."

"The Bureau wants to close the Hughes file. You're an old friend and associate, I thought you might give us some insights into his recent life."

Manoulian's blue eyes were clear, yet impenetrable. "And you flew all the way from Washington just to ask me what little I know about the private demons of Michael Hughes? We could have talked for five minutes on the phone and spared you the trip."

"I have other interviews, up and down California." A convenient lie.

"Well, let's go outside. At least we can enjoy some of this fine weather." Manoulian led J.D. to a wooden veranda that gave a startling view of the ocean and adjacent cliffs.

Shannon Crocker joined them. J.D. glanced at her. Young and trying hard, almost a cool customer.

Manoulian pulled a long cigar from his pants pocket. "I would offer you a drink, but I'm sure you're on duty and as you know—"

"Mr. Manoulian must be on his way in no more than fifteen minutes," Shannon said.

J.D. let that pass. "What do you think history will make of Mike Hughes?"

Best to start with a softball.

Manoulian rubbed his jaw. "Mike was a unique guy. He was a thinker, a reader. He was that rare politician comfortable with ideas. Although he didn't go all the way, he opened the door for others like him, including our current president. I think he'll be remembered for that."

"What's your best memory of him?"

"Right here, in the mid-eighties, playing golf. We're talking politics with a couple of businessmen, several of them were big contributors of his," Manoulian said, sucking at the end of his cigar. "One of them pops off with a racist joke. I mean, something really ugly and mean. Some guys would have smiled and gone along. After all, no one would tell. But Mike, he shuts that guy down right then and there. He didn't care about the money."

"What were your impressions of how Mike Hughes handled defeat? Was he bitter? Was he angry at himself?"

A flash of irritation crossed Manoulian's face as if he wanted to say, *How the hell would I know?*

"Well, lemme see, we had dinner a few times after he lost. Mike seemed to have gotten over that rough patch after the election. He didn't blame the press so much. Or even his opponents. He seemed to blame himself. But I gotta tell you, I hardly had a window into the man's soul."

J.D. pressed on. "But you did deal with him often when he was a senator?"

"Of course. When you run one of the largest real estate ventures in California, you should get to know your representatives in Washington. Anything wrong with that?"

"And you were a major contributor to his presidential bid?"

"Yes, through proper, legal channels. I have a PAC. I have employees, who have minds of their own. If I'm doing something wrong, then we all are forced to work within a system that needs fixing. Politicians will tell you they're sick of dialing for dollars. Well let me tell you, I'm sick of being asked. Yeah, I gave Mike Hughes money. I thought he'd make a great president."

"I'd like to know a little more about him from your perspective. You, Hughes, and Barry Newhouse go back to the fifties, right?"

Manoulian stared at him again, the impassive look of an animal that might flee or might charge. "Yeah, I remember him as a kid in our frat. Charming young man, college debate champion. I remember thinking then that he would go far."

"But you only knew him... sporadically?"

"Yeah, that's a good word for it. Sporadically."

J.D. found himself staring at the sea, at the breaks and spurts of white foam against the jetties below.

"So when did Michael Hughes become your secret business partner in the Presidio?"

"What?" Manoulian looked startled. Shannon began to walk slowly forward, as if to interpose herself between her boss and J.D.

"He was a hidden investor in your real estate business."

"You're bringing up that old canard? Lousy press, oppo dirt guys, making stuff up, you buy that?"

Shannon broke in. "I'll give you a full list of investors if you like. You won't find his name anywhere."

"What about Barry Newhouse?"

"He's an investor, so what?" Manoulian didn't bother to disguise his irritation.

"You told us this would just be about background on Hughes," Shannon said, "I think this interview is over."

"This isn't an interview." J.D. was as calm as he was firm. "It's an interrogation. We could take it to the local FBI office if you like."

"Really? *Consultants* can do that?" The young lady had a talent for sarcasm.

"You'd be surprised what I can do."

"If you want more, we'll make another appointment and bring our lawyer." She led them back into the study. Manoulian stood squarely behind his desk.

J.D. pointed to the bare spot on the wall.

"Did you take down the picture of yourself and Mike Hughes before or after he was killed?"

Manoulian said nothing, his face revealed nothing.

"Goodbye," Shannon said.

CHAPTER
17

Shannon returned to the study to find Frank Manoulian sitting at the desk, his eyes unfocused, chin cradled in the palms of his hands.

"Frank?"

He looked up, cleared his throat, and settled back in his chair. "This is bad. Bad and getting worse."

"Frank, I've been doing some thinking, and it seems to me—"

Manoulian held up a hand. "You know what? We'd better take this to the pool."

He led her through the house, passing the housekeeper vacuuming the carpet, and then outside, where a yardman clipped bushes along the back wall.

The old man led the way to the dirt path lined with golden sage and blue-and-yellow perennials.

The remnants of the late-afternoon heat reflected off the white columns and white tiles of the swimming area. Shannon looked down into the vast coolness of the pool with longing. Manoulian chewed his cigar nervously, glancing at the low sun over the Pacific, the ocean already turning black at the edges.

"I knew better than to let Hughes in," he said. "Barry thought it would never be a problem, the way he and Mike had set it up, so many paper corporations, several times removed. Now the White House is in on this." He let out a sigh. "Politics. It'll be the death of me."

"Frank, I have to tell you something. You don't need to know how I know, but I can tell you with absolute confidence that Mike Hughes discussed this matter with only one other person—that reporter who was here earlier, Anne Carlson."

"Yeah, so what? No telling how many other reporters and editors Lois Lane has told. And now we got the feds on our ass."

"I wouldn't worry about that."

"You wouldn't worry about the FBI?"

"I did some checking through our own private investigator in Washington. This FBI man is not a real agent, he's some kind of half-assed PI."

"You called him a consultant."

"That's right, he's retired and living off the generosity of old friends in the government. He's just fishing around. And Anne Carlson? She has a hunch. She may even have shared it with her editors. But the fact that the two of them came here means they're empty-handed. They don't know where to look, or what to look for, and as executor of Mike's estate, Barry can clean things up for us."

"Yeah," Manoulian said and spit out black shreds of wet tobacco. "If he ever returns from Italy. We've got him scared shitless."

"Which is why we can relax about him. For the time being."

Manoulian shot a steely glance at her. "So what are you saying?"

"I am saying that everything is working out okay. It is still containable."

"How so?" Manoulian gave her a look of stern reproach. Shannon had to focus to keep her balance, to summon strength from the deepest sources of will and imagination, the way she did when she was half-a-lap behind in swim meets.

"Frank, this is one area in which delegation works best. I have the talent nearby and we're weighing options."

He continued to stare at her, Doctor Frankenstein looking at his terrible, new creation.

"C'mon Frank, he's not here. But he's nearby, on the Peninsula, and he's prepared if he's needed."

"Shannon, you don't know Dmitri like I do. He's good, but sometimes he lacks judgment, professionalism. He takes crazy risks. For God's sake, he kills people. And we've already taken such a big risk. Now a national reporter and an FBI agent? That's insane."

"What's insane is doing nothing. Our private investigator says the consultant and the reporter are working together. Who knows, they may even be lovers. When people spend time together, accidents can happen."

Manoulian shook his head. "You disappoint me."

"If it doesn't fall neatly into place, we'll let it go."

"I don't authorize anything."

"You don't forbid anything either."

"And if they get away?"

"If it doesn't line up just right, we're no worse off than we are now."

CHAPTER
18

Anne was yanked from sleep by a ringing telephone. The digital clock by her bed read 5:50 AM, the curtains of her hotel room illuminated by faint light.

"Good morning, Anne." It was Herb Smith, the national assignments editor.

"You may call this morning. I still call it night."

"I momentarily blanked on the fact that we're back in the same time zone. Sorry, you know how I gotta get my calls in early to reach the Washington bureau. Got to catch them before their three-hour lunches."

"What's up?"

"That's what I was going to ask you. Doing your first Washington assignment by interviewing Frank Manoulian back in California?"

"Well, I'm not sure," she sat upright, rubbed the sleep from the corners of her eyes and suppressed a yawn, "but I think in some way he's connected to Mike Hughes's suicide. And I think there's also a connection to Doctor Dirt."

"Manoulian's lawyer called Jim Miller, got him all upset. What you're working on sounds too good for a mere newspaper, better save this one for Oliver Stone."

"I'm sure there's a story here. "

"You've got a long way to go before you can do a story this big without training wheels." Click.

Twenty minutes later the phone rang again. It was Sid Sherman.

"How'd you find me?"

"Your office in D.C."

"What do you want?"

"Forgive me for calling so early, I just wanted to catch you before your day begins. I hope I didn't come on too strong the other night."

"You left welts on my arm."

"Sorry if I did. I was just excited to hear that you're on the trail so quick. The reason I called is to tell you I've been playing journalist again, done some poking around, and I think you're on to something with Manoulian."

"Anything specific you want to pass along?"

"Anne, if you break this story, I want to do the documentary. I mean it. My work here at the White House is almost done. I can get funding for a two-hour PBS investigative piece just like that. Book deal, too. You're on the right track. I got a sense for these things."

"Thanks. I'll let you know." This time, she clicked off.

She stared at the phone for a moment. No sleeping now. She stepped out of bed. Time for yoga. She raised her arms, drawing in prana, exhaling as she bent to touch her toes.

She stilled the relentless chatter of her mind, releasing her resentment of Herb Smith, her bafflement at Sid Sherman, let random thoughts cascade over her center of focus like river water over a stone. It usually took a minute to empty her mind, to slip into a meditative trance.

This time, she thought only of J.D., his smile, his banter, that confident, easy way that could make her laugh one second and irritate the hell out of her the next.

Last night she'd run into him in the lobby of her hotel on the highway on the outskirts of San Marcos. It seemed inevitable. So she let him take her to dinner to compare notes.

"I wonder if Ruth Thornburgh did it," Anne said in a low voice. After being so certain about Manoulian, momentarily suspecting Leonora Vasquez, she was back to the wife, at each turn starting to doubt her judgment.

"Why do you think that?" J.D. was poker-faced. No way was he going to share his thinking on suspects.

"For the money. To get rid of her husband, collect insurance, and sell Clarity to Ben for millions."

"What about Manoulian?"

She sighed. "Another good suspect. I don't know how he was with *you*, but he was very touchy. He seems afraid."

"So what do you do next?"

"There has to be some kind of underlying business connection between Mike Hughes and Manoulian, dating back to when Hughes was in the Senate."

"Beyond campaign contributions, beyond what Ben found out about Manoulian bankrolling Newhouse's agency?"

"Yeah, more than that. It's not enough. That's all public, if you dig like Ben did."

J.D. finished his second glass of wine and did not pour himself another. "Did Shannon Crocker offer you a list of investors? Hughes isn't one of them."

"So? I just need to dig deeper."

"You have experience in legal documents, deeds, and corporate papers?"

She stared at him a moment. "And you do?"

J.D. smiled. "No. But I've got the FBI, right?" Not necessarily.

"So what do we do next?"

He said nothing, but the answer, at least for her, was obvious. Get computer time from Grossman at Clarity.

"Let's order dessert and think about it," he said.

They shared a single slice of a key lime pie. Perhaps it was the atmosphere of the dark, candlelit restaurant, perhaps it was a matter of proximity, sitting at a table so small that their knees rubbed together. Whatever it was, she got J.D. to open up a little about himself.

She asked him about his family. He mentioned Sarah had graduated from St. John's—the great books college—and had stayed in Annapolis. She was smart, he said, and not just in liberal arts. She was smart with computers and science. He seemed proud.

"How long had you been married?"

"Twelve years. To a lawyer."

"What went wrong."

"I already told you, she was a lawyer."

Anne laughed at that. "No, really."

"Things just sort of felt apart. The marriage became a *menage à trois* between her schedule, my schedule, and her ambition. I also think being married to a mere gumshoe started to embarrass her after she made partner. Worst part of the divorce was what it did to Sarah. After that, she got in trouble in school, emotional problems, endless counseling sessions. You know the way kids can react. Her mother couldn't handle it. She gave the custody back to me."

"An FBI agent with a daughter. That couldn't have been easy."

"It wasn't. I had help of course. Mostly neighborhood moms. And Sarah's turning out fine."

"And your career?"

"I was getting a lot of pressure from the Bureau before I retired. I didn't do things their way. I was investigating political corruption, but I always felt there were limits to how far they'd let me go. So I took early retirement."

"And now you're a private investigator?" Anne took another forkful of key lime pie.

It was his turn. "What about you? Parents?"

"I talk to my mother a lot on the phone, although it's been ages since I've been down to Long Beach to see her. My dad died five years ago, right here, near San Marcos, where we had a cabin."

"Were you close?"

"At times. Looking back on it, I'm afraid I may have been a lot for him to handle."

A look passed across J.D.'s face, as if he were on the verge of making a smart-ass remark, but didn't.

They ate in silence for a moment, Anne savoring every bite, J.D. scooping the pie filling and leaving the crust. He was a strange one, she decided, smart, eccentric, not your standard issue.

He pushed the plate away. "What was the big love of your life?"

The question took her aback.

"You really want to know everything about me."

"I'm a trained investigator. Tell."

"Well, okay. There's a photo-dog—that's a news pho-tographer with the paper. He's real good, won a lot of awards during the riots. Almost moved in with him, until I found out that there was a reason why he liked to do so many *après*-game shots of players in the men's locker room."

J.D. sipped his coffee slowly. It was clearly time to change the subject.

"You're not leaving until late tomorrow morning, same 11 AM flight as me, right?" she asked.

He nodded.

"How would you feel if we were to get up super early and go on a little trip? Drive into the San Marcos headlands, take a look at my dad's old cabin? It's just off 121, about a half-hour both ways. It used to be beautiful out there. Bit of nostalgia for me."

"Fine, as long as we make the airport by eleven. Just one condition."

"Name it."

"I drive."

They were the first customers of the morning at the hotel coffee shop. Anne took a plate of fresh melons and straw-berries from the buffet, and added a blueberry muffin.

J.D. decided on a Denver omelet with dry toast and drank one black coffee after another, hardly saying a word, still sleepy and lost in thought.

Before Anne had come down, he had checked out, only

to have the receptionist hand him a faxed note marked "personal" from FBIHQ.

> Joseph P. DeVine, as of receipt of this message your
> contract can be considered fulfilled. Any assignments
> you are currently working on are terminated. Please
> return all invoices and your special credentials to the
> nearest FBI field office or resident agent.

The receptionist told J.D. he also had voice mail messages. He retrieved them on the house phone. The first was from the SAC, Carol Suarez.

"J.D., I guess you got an early start. Listen, I've got some bad news for you. The word's just come down from the top—and I mean the very top—that you're off the case. Contract done. Don't worry, you'll get the full payout. I'm also getting a lot of heat about files that Doctor Dirt may have been keeping. His people at Clarity insist that they don't know where he kept the really dirty stuff. The Bureau thinks they're lying. They also suspect you may have some of these files or copies. When you get home, you'll find a subpoena in your mailbox. I suggest you turn them over immediately. Sorry."

There was another message. He heard a cough, then a grinding sound like a Brillo pad against the receiver.

"Agent Hoover, I guess you heard that Ruth unloaded Clarity on Ben. Seems they inflated the equity value and both of them stand to make out like bandits in bed. Which they are."

While eating his breakfast, J.D. thought over what he'd heard, thoughts that made him anxious. It was time to transform anxiety into action. He excused himself while Anne ate and went to the pay phone by the men's room door. He called Clarity. Ben Grossman's secretary came on the line. J.D. demanded Grossman's cellphone number. He got it. Grossman answered on the first ring.

J.D. spoke first. "We have three minutes at most before this conversation goes public."

"Shoot."

"How long have you been fucking Ruth Thornburgh?"

"Are you out of your tree? Do I look like a gigolo?"

"You swear you never met her for a day rate at the Alexandria Hilton?"

"I can't believe this. Never."

"For the time being, you'll just have to forget I asked that. I'll explain later."

"You've got some explaining of your own to do, buddy. I finally checked up on who tried to hack into Cyclops. That paper you walked off with. Nice try."

"It was innocent."

"Uh huh. Right. I'll bet it was, just about as innocent as Chuck Beaumont."

"What do you mean?"

"Did some more work with Cyclops. Guess who was the House Republican counterpart to Mike Hughes on the Presidio deal, bought and paid for by Frank Manoulian?"

J.D. was silent.

"That's right, old Chucky."

"He's dead, and my daughter's out of politics."

"Yeah, I can see that."

"I give you my word she's not involved. The hacking thing was part stupid mistake, part freak accident."

"Bad mistake on her part, buddy."

"I know, but to hell with all that crap. We need to talk fast—about the nasty files. Don't give in to the Bureau. They can't subpoena you without a Congressional ruckus over the First Amendment, and that's the last thing Firelli wants. So, three things. First, don't give copies to anybody. Second, find out if Leonora Vasquez's days at Stanford gave her a taste for California real estate. Third, use your computer to search for a secret partnership between Mike Hughes and Frank Manoulian. Look for dummy companies, cut-outs, dead drops. Can you do that?"

"It'll take awhile. Computer time is tight."

"And on the Nixon-trip connection, look for a money trail back to Indonesia, maybe bankrolling the Presidio deal."

"I'll run the machine into the ground if it gets Todd's killer. But you gotta reestablish some trust, boy."

"You've got my word."

"Same thing on Anne Carlson?"

"Tell her nothing."

The driver's seat of the Mustang had been readjusted to the bottom setting, almost down to the carpet. There was an odor in the car, the scent of masculine sweat. There was also a stain on the floorboard—brown, grainy particles suspended in a spot of liquid on the floor mat.

"What is it?" Anne had just put her laptop in the trunk, not wanting to trust the bellman to keep it safe.

"Just looking for the heater." He smeared the spot with the heel of his penny loafers. "You tell me which way."

"Your voice is deeper in the morning." She seemed to like that.

They drove down the Pacific Coast Highway. Thick fog hid the surf that crashed just fifty feet away. They crossed a long bridge that Anne said she remembered driving over many times with her father.

A sign materialized out of the fog. J.D. braked hard, just making the left turn.

Now they were heading up a steep grade, gnarled eucalyptus trees and brush emerging out of the mist on both sides. J.D. flipped on the headlights.

The fog thickened with the steep grade. Now there was nothing to see, no mountains, no trees, just a gray curtain of fog.

He cut his speed to 25 mph, and kept his eyes trained on the rolling pavement, alert to any sudden shifts in direction.

"Some fun," he said.

"Beats watching you drink another cup of coffee."

J.D. kept his eyes concentrated on the patch of road in front of him. There was nothing else to look at.

The road seemed to come to a sudden stop—no, a sharp turn to the left. He cut left and slowed to 15 mph.

She blew out a breath. "One side of the road is a ditch, the other is a canyon. We don't need to find out which is which."

"You want to drive?" His voice was sharp.

They rode in silence for a few minutes until, in an instant, the gloom broke and they were in the cool shadow of a mountain, morning sunlight breaking around and above.

J.D. relaxed a little and increased his speed to 35 mph. There were, in fact, many mountains, vast, irregular purple cones clustered around a gorge thick with trees.

Behind them, the sun rose over a flat canopy of cloud that stretched out over the Pacific. The landscape of clouds stirred a vague memory of Anne's childhood imagination.

"I expect to see Jack's beanstalk." She untied her sweater from her shoulders and curled sideways, her face against the window. It suddenly seemed strange that they had snapped at each other just a moment ago.

"I just want to go about fifteen miles. That's where we used to go every summer. Then we should head back, make the flight."

J.D. looked into his rearview mirror and saw two evenly spaced lights gliding upward, the fog lamps of another vehicle.

"I love this mountain country," Anne said. "I wish I had known that all my life."

"That's a cryptic remark."

"It just has to do with my feelings about my folks, what it was like to grow up here in the summers. My parents didn't get along all that well. I rebelled, mostly against my dad."

They drove in silence.

"Was he hard on you? Mine sure as hell was."

"Just the opposite. He was the one who always wanted to take me hiking, fishing, to a movie. But because my mother was so emotionally distant, I guess I just took everything out on him. So your dad was tough?"

"My father, he's eighty-five and still running his little construction business on Long Island. We don't talk much. Mom's in a nursing home."

J.D. glanced at the rearview mirror and saw that it was a Cadillac El Dorado, and it was now two car lengths behind.

The headlights of the car were bright in the mountain shadows.

Anne pulled down the visor mirror and began to put on lipstick.

"Any brothers or sisters?"

"Just me."

"Me too. That guy sure is getting close."

"Yeah, to reach us so quickly, he has to be going at least sixty, and that's straight uphill."

"Can you imagine driving an orange Cadillac?"

The driver of the El Dorado hit his horn, which blasted the first few notes of *The Eyes of Texas* like a bugle. They laughed.

J.D. checked him out in the rear-view mirror again. "Get this, he also has longhorns mounted on his hood. Some kind of bowl-game idiot."

"His car has horns on it?" Anne turned and saw the curving horns mounted on the hood like massive tusks. She could see little more than the silhouette of the driver.

J.D. turned a corner, banking steeply uphill. A swath of sunlight swept across the driver's face and Anne saw a tough, raw-boned man, his hair combed straight back.

"J.D., I don't like this. Why don't you let the guy pass us?"

"Because he's an ass?"

The horn sounded again. *The Eyes of Texas Are Upon You.*

"This guy's a real psycho," J.D. said, speeding up, gripping the steering wheel as he made one tight turn right, another left.

The Cadillac pulled a tap away from his bumper, the

driver deftly making each turn by dominating the middle of the road.

"J.D., let him pass."

"I'll try." He looked at the speedometer and realized he had been bullied into driving 60 mph on a little mountain road.

The Eyes of Texas Are Upon You. The driver kept the horn down to the finishing notes of the refrain, *All the Live Long Day.*

The sharp points of the mounted bull horns raced closer to them. J.D.'s hands were white from gripping the steering wheel.

"Why don't you let him pass?" She was almost hysterical now.

"Too many hairpin turns. Can't pass here."

The driver blew his horn again. The Cadillac was closing on them, an enraged bull charging uphill.

"If I hear that sound again—" J.D. rounded the top of a hill and squinted through blinding morning sunlight to see a short straight-away ahead. He punched the tab for the emergency lights, slowed down to 40 mph, and edged the Mustang to the right. Gravel crunched under the outer edge of the right tires.

He reached down, snapped the Walther out of his ankle holster, and set the gun beside him.

The car began to pass. The Cadillac pulled even, and J.D. slowed to 35 mph, wanting to look the other man in the eyes, try to measure his capabilities and intention before reaching for the Walther.

The Cadillac stayed in the left lane, the front door handles of both cars perfectly parallel. J.D. turned to look at the driver, but the man was already giving him a glare, his eyes on J.D. as if he had no concern what was in front of him.

J.D. looked ahead and saw another hairpin turn, this one to the right and down, no more than 300 feet ahead. He slowed to 30 mph.

The other driver hit that horrible horn again, *The Eyes of Texas Are Upon You.*

"What is he doing now?"

All the Live Long Day.

The Cadillac began to speed up to pass them. J.D. exhaled as if he had been underwater for a minute. He resumed his speed. Was it over?

The other driver just stayed in the left lane. As they approached the turn, the immense orange bulk of the Cadillac swung into the middle of the road like a floating battleship. J.D. had the sensation that the harder he hit the brakes, the closer the other car came.

The Cadillac bumped him, but almost fishtailed out of control. Then it crashed against them hard, and the Mustang was spinning. A panorama of valley and cloud flew up before them, spinning faster, faster. The car slammed into a tree, its side crumpling as if hit by a giant wrecking ball. J.D.'s face smashed against the side window. He heard Anne scream, and a shot of nauseating white fear shot through him like an instant fever as he felt the car plunge.

CHAPTER
19

Three hundred feet below was dry-looking scrub and thick, gnarled trees—where they should have been. J.D. felt the matted blood on the side of his head. It was going to leave one helluva bruise. Above them, the Mustang lay on its roof, the only thing that stopped it slipping over the last ledge, a hundred feet from the road. J.D. shuddered at the memory of the terrifying free-fall—then the wheels coming into contact with a gravel slope at a forty-five degree slide. For a moment, the Mustang had rolled downward, almost as if it were actually meant to drive along the wall of a mountain before slamming into the earth with a jarring, bone-pulling lurch.

They had sat in the car a long time, listening to each other breathe. The gun had settled by the brake, J.D. reached down for it. Without saying a word, Anne heaved herself out the left door and J.D. followed.

Off in the distance successive, irregular mountains grew progressively more dun-colored and arid. There was no landscape of clouds on this side of the mountain, no Pacific. They had to be looking south and east.

"J.D., I know this place." Anne stood, shading her eyes.

"You've been here before?"

"Not right here. But way down there, by that river, up a mile or two. That's where my dad went fishing. Not half a mile from our lodge."

"Great. Now we can go fishing."

She turned to J.D. "Who was that asshole?"

"Someone with a hard-on for the Ford Motor Company, I suppose."

An eagle drifted by at eye level, caught an updraft, and sailed over the mountain.

"Really, why would someone do that?" Anne leaned back to keep from sliding.

"You're the conspiracy theorist. Because he was paid."

"So he's a hit man?"

"Maybe. The way he was looking at me, he meant for us to go over."

Anne sat next to J.D., very close.

"The Cadillac guy, could he come here? Shoot us?"

"At least I found my gun. Never forget the essentials."

They sat in silence for a full minute. They could not count on help. From where they were, the car could not be seen from the road. Maybe a Forest Ranger would pass by in an hour or so.

"What now? Back to the road?" she asked.

"And meet our friend? Or get run over?"

"Then we just have to go down there." Anne threw a large rock over the edge, checking the grade. It rolled awhile, then fell.

"It's too steep."

"Not if you stay on your butt."

"Good thing I'm an expert at that." He checked his Walther into his ankle holster. "I guess I should tell you I've never been a fan of heights."

"And they still let you in the FBI?" Anne laughed.

She took off, sliding on her buttocks down the hard surface of pebbles as easily as a child going down a snowy hillside. J.D. thought about the killer above them, swallowed some air, and followed her. Pain came immediately, his buttocks and groin bouncing against hard little rocks. At times, the surface went vertical and he fell, only to recover with a sharp slam into rock.

He kept right behind her. It was the only way.

Dmitri had begun by studying them at breakfast, noting the absent way in which the man slurped coffee, his face scrunched up with concern. The man was thinking about some problem. The pretty woman ate one piece of fruit at a time, also lost in thought.

The woman saw the world as clutter, as unwanted distractions from her tasks or thoughts. Such a person was easy prey.

The man was different. When he rose to make a phone call he showed a new alertness. Dmitri caught a glimpse of a slight bulge underneath the man's right trouser leg, a small gun. This one could be dangerous.

He decided to name the man Smarty. The woman could be Special.

From the moment Dmitri saw their tail lights almost disappear into fog, he knew he would earn his bonus. He stayed close behind. Then, going on the mountain road, into the heaviest fog, he pushed the lumbering beast upward, knowing they could not go far.

The instant the fog broke, he saw them a half-mile ahead and above. He jammed the accelerator flush to the floor, and felt the powerful surge of the car—stolen, as he had been taught to steal cars, to operate behind enemy lines, to strike like a lion or a cobra. True *spetznaz*.

First he intimidated them with his car, and then with his eyes. When he struck, he almost lost control of his own car. The enormous Cadillac swerved from the rear, but the forward momentum of the massive vehicle kept him on the road.

Dmitri drove on for half a mile or so, in no particular hurry, since he didn't want to face any other driver who might have seen him. And certainly, Smarty and Special could not go far away. He drove on leisurely until he came to a place to turn, eventually coming back to that wide patch of gravel by the side of the road.

He was relieved to see no other cars. It was easy to find the dark striations left by the Mustang's tires where it had spun and gone careening off the road.

He parked the Cadillac as far to the edge of the road as he could. He walked around. His back bumper had a V-shaped dent, and the trunk was slightly crumpled.

Many times since he left Los Angeles, he had almost regretted the Cadillac. It was certainly a violation of his training to use such a flamboyant car. He could be caught, despite changing the plates, despite keeping the horns in the trunk for the long drive up the California coast, remounting them only this morning, for the hunt.

It was still a dangerous way to travel.

But then great artists violated rules, took risks. He often thought of himself as a kind of jazz soloist who had the guts to make up the notes as he went along. Dmitri the Improviser.

This was also his last job. Manoulian's girl promised another hundred-grand, enough for him to get a good lawyer and work on becoming a citizen in America. They could help him with Hollywood connections, a place where he could get a start as a trainer to the stars, as an extra. From there, who knows how far Dmitri could go?

So—he could afford to end this old career with a flourish. And so far, his instincts had been right on target. The car had special magic. It had intimidated the driver and the woman. The car had been strong enough to heave itself uphill, strong enough to wipe anyone off the road.

After the kill the Cadillac would have one final mission, to get him back to the nearest airport. Dmitri was already mourning for the car, having to leave it, abandoned. Someday he would have to get another like it.

Dmitri ran his fingers around a huge, white gash in a giant tree by the road. The tender pulp was still wet with sap. Good, they had hit this tree.

And there, those ruts clearly show where the car went over.

Crouching, Dmitri looked down and almost cried out with disappointment. He could see them, alive, about ten meters down from their ruined car. He squatting, she standing on a tiny out-cropping from the cliff.

Killing them would not be difficult. But his instructions were firm, a believable accident or nothing. The hundred-thousand dollar bonus was for an *accident,* and an accident only.

Time for more improvisation.

When they came up the hill, he could surprise the man, break his neck, then the girl's, and throw them down beside the car. For all appearances, a perfect accident.

He looked over the rim again, and saw two elongated clouds of dust moving down the side of the mountain. At first, his heart raced with joy, thinking the pair had slipped to their death.

Then he saw Special taking the lead, sliding down on her ass at a fast pace. Smarty just behind. Although it was hard to judge, they had to be moving at almost 10 kilometers an hour.

Dmitri was impressed that they both managed to slide without losing their balance and tumbling.

Special slowed down and stopped at an easy gradient, waiting for Smarty. He came to the flat surface and stood. Each of them rubbed their buttocks and brushed the backs of their pants. Then they disappeared into a forest of twisted trees, under a parapet of vines.

He took it all in, tried to still his writhing thoughts.

His mind's eye saw another... *accident.*

He took a jimmy from the back seat, worked the crumpled Cadillac trunk, and removed the gas can. He had kept it filled. Another part of his training.

Dmitri tucked the jimmy into his jeans, sharp-side pressing out. He took the gas can under one arm and went over the rim.

He half-fell, half slid on his way down, caught a network of exposed roots, then raked by an outcropping of rock. This was easily the most dangerous part of his day. The climb back would be tough. If he sprained an ankle, he might as well jump off the nearest cliff himself.

Dmitri came to the ledge and landed as flat-footed as a cat. It would take some work, but he could ease the Mustang over the edge. Looking down, he was sure it would come to rest just above the forest.

He set the gas can down and wedged himself with his back against the hillside and his thick-soled tennis shoes against the car.

He strained like an Olympic weightlifter, red-faced and screaming. The car buckled and settled. He strained again, and moved the car a half-inch. He strained for the last time, closed his eyes, and imagined his future as a wealthy actor in Los Angeles.

The Mustang heaved backwards and slammed down, its wheels hanging over the rounded rim of the ledge. Dmitri slumped to the ground, weak and slick with sweat.

The car was dangling in such a way that pushing it over the edge was now easy, anyone could do it. He heaved against it, careful not to let his jeans get caught in the sharp edge of the bottom runner as the car turned over. Dmitri watched as the Mustang spun sideways, hitting boulders and jumping into the air, the trunk springing open and one door flinging wildly.

It came to rest on its side about twenty feet above where Smarty and Special had entered the forest. Beautiful.

Dmitri checked to make sure his new Glock was secure in his new shoulder holster. He slid down on his buttocks, holding the gas can flat on his stomach, and closed the three hundred foot drop in just over two minutes.

The underside of the car, with its greasy axles and exposed drive shaft, was facing the woods. He would have to be quick now, or they would get too far.

He set the gas can on the ground. With sudden violence, he ran forward and threw the sharp teeth of the jimmy into the fuel tank like a javelin.

It dented, but didn't tear. So he went after it again, aiming the sharp fingers of the crowbar into the metal.

He only succeeded in making a deeper dent. He stood next to the car and swung the jimmy like a baseball bat into the flat, metal canister. It burst open, raining a shower of golden fuel.

Dmitri walked behind the Mustang and pressed his shoulder against the top side of the roof. The car, already listing, heaved over and came to a resounding slam.

Dmitri allowed himself a small rest. He smelled the sharp odor of fuel. He heard the gallons of gasoline chug-chugging out of the ripped metal. He watched a shiny, silverish river splash over the rocks and roll downward, into kindling forest.

CHAPTER
20

Ben Grossman had decided not to occupy Todd Thornburgh's office.

In time, he might fill the office with a rabbit warren full of fast-trackers. But for the moment, he was content to leave his friend's office empty.

He ran a pencil down a line of figures, wondering how in hell he was going to produce enough research, at least in the short-term, to meet his costs. The problem wasn't lack of work, it was that he and Roman had bumped clients. They were using Cyclops to track Todd's killer, not draw up indictments of embarrassment against Democrats.

He pushed the tabulations aside and picked up a legal pad, on which he wrote himself a note. "L. Vasquez = J.D.'s decoy. Chk bkgrd Sarah DeVine. Place/murder/date."

There was a polite tap on the door.

"I've got it." Roman Grice stood at attention—his usual posture—just outside Ben Grossman's office, waving a stack of papers. "I've got it."

Grossman was continually amazed at how Grice could work an all-nighter, seven-day-a-week schedule, often sleeping on the couch, and always look as fresh, bright-eyed, and sharply pressed as the lead singer in a church choir.

"Well, come on in here. Let's see what you've got."

Grice handed him a stack of papers. "How about this? We got this from the probate court. It's Hughes's will. The key is here, in the listing of all his assets—a majority share of Golden Age, Inc., a real estate holding company. Guess where its properties are?"

"Tell me."

"The San Marcos Peninsula, managed by Manoulian's company. And guess who owns the minority shares?"

"Tell me."

"Sidney Bartholomew Sherman, purchased shortly before he joined the White House staff."

"Yes, yes, yes!" Grossman slapped the side of his chair and shouted like a preacher in a tent revival. "I should have known he was a part of this. I want everything on Sid Sherman, going back to his high school yearbook."

"I'm not done."

Roman Grice reached into his briefcase and handed him a copy of several original speeches drafted for the current president. Some went back as far as six years ago.

"How'd you get these?"

"Don't ask and I won't tell. Let's just say there're some people in this White House who'd leak anything for a price."

Grossman flipped through the papers—a draft of a toast to Suharto, several years before he was overthrown; a speech given by the president before the Los Angeles World Affairs Council, arguing for a relaxation of tariffs on East Asia, conspicuously mentioning Indonesia; an Executive Order supporting the IMF bailout for Indonesia; a draft of an Executive Order directing the Department of Interior to forever ban oil and gas mining in a national park in Utah.

"What am I looking at, Roman?"

"There's a direct link between all these Indonesian policies."

Grossman scanned the copies again. "I don't see it, not anagrams, diagrams, or pentagrams."

"With all due respect, sir, it really is right in front of you. Look at the top of each page."

There was a stamp across the top of each page, which on the original would have been in bright red ink. "The President Has Seen."

There were some other notations and writing at the top, all of it standard fare. Date of Receipt and Date to POTUS, the West Wing acronym for President of the United States. Then he saw it.

Draft: Final
Staff: Sherman

Grice hammered the point home. "With these speeches, sir, Sherman's created a distinct Indonesia policy. The Utah thing—the close-out of the mines—was strategically timed. It boosted world markets for oil, gas, and coal just as a major Indonesian conglomerate announced it was seeking capital for energy exploration." Grice paused to let this sink in. "Mr. Thornburgh had to know all this. The part we don't have is the Nixon connection. And one other thing. Golden Age does more than real estate. It handles large money transfers for the Indonesian government through an Anglo-Dutch bank. About $10 million worth."

"Enough to build homes for the president and all his friends."

"But that's not it. You see, the money's going the other way."

"Huh?"

"This president isn't *taking* payoffs from Jakarta. The White House is using Manoulian to *send* payoffs to Indonesia."

CHAPTER
21

"Are you following bread crumbs?" J.D. could barely keep pace with Anne. She led him down a winding deer trail that twisted under a dark canopy of interlacing limbs.

"Let's just hope we don't run into the big bad wolf," she replied. She was already unnerved by several loud crashing noises that had reverberated throughout the forest.

"Let's not mix fairy tales. If there were someone coming after us, could he find us in here?" It was quiet now in the thick brush, just the purring and trilling of insects and their own heartbeats.

Anne stopped before a particularly thick stand, almost a solid wall of trees and vines, contorted branches and spiny fingers of wood. "I can barely find myself."

"I've never seen such weird trees," J.D. said.

"Madrone. They shed their bark and turn red." Anne peeled a strip of skin from the tree as easily as shucking an ear of corn. The peeling revealed a shiny, ruby-colored core, sticky with sap and natural oils.

J.D. spotted a gangly eucalyptus to his right and drew in the tangy, almost sweet smell.

Anne walked around the stand and found another animal trail leading downward into the forest.

"Dad used to collect these." She snapped off a small, reddish-brown branch from a tree. "Folks around here call this mountain driftwood. If you look around, you'll also see some toyon—those shrubs over there, and manzanita."

She snapped off a gnarled branch from a manzanita tree. It looked more like a shrub, but its thick trunk was an even richer red-brown than the madrone.

"We're about five hundred feet from the top of the mountain. Descend another thousand, and we'll be in pine and fir. Another thousand feet after that, cedar and redwood. Then we'll know we're at the river."

"How far is that?"

"Probably another thirty-five hundred feet straight down. But this is a deer trail. It'll be a lot longer."

J.D. was thirsty, dreaming of a cold lager in a frozen stein. He thought about holding it to his throbbing head. His penny loafers sank into the soil, a smooth, blond sand like that at the beach.

They rounded a bend and came to a fork in the natural trail. Anne took the path to the right and soon they were descending steeply.

The forest grew darker, shafts of light only occasionally cutting through the inky shadow. While he looked around, Anne had disappeared down the trail. "Anne?"

"I'm right here." He found her sitting on a log, her head hanging almost between her legs, face cradled in her hands.

"Are you okay?"

She sniffed loudly and rubbed her nose with the side of her sleeve. "It's just been a hell of a day. Really nothing to do with you." She stood and started to lead the way again.

"Take a minute if you're upset."

She sat down again, the log was thick and hollow, bark covered with green mold and sprouting mushrooms. They were in a little clearing, not quite a glade, just a small opening between trees.

"It's just being back here. It's opened up some old wounds. I half expect to see Dad come bounding out of the forest with his compass and silly pith helmet." She laughed but her eyes shined with tears.

J.D. rested while she took a few minutes to collect herself. They were hungry and thirsty and needed to get to civilization soon.

"Anne, you better take a look at this," J.D. said. "We have a visitor."

He pointed at the base of a tree. A brown-and-black field rabbit looked back at them with big, black, liquid eyes.

Anne gave a teary laugh.

The rabbit jumped away. Then another black rabbit streaked by. Then a gray one.

"They move in packs?" J.D. asked.

"They don't." Anne was standing now, alert.

She stepped up on the log as dozens of field mice appeared and swirled about their feet, hundreds of tiny feet scratching across the leaves and sand.

"J.D., something's wrong."

A tiny but persistent squeal broke their conversation. It grew into a high-pitched screech that came from above them, an inhuman scream that grew louder, closer.

In an instant, a raccoon, its rump burnt black, rushed by them.

"Run, J.D.! Get down the mountain! Fast!"

J.D. stared at her, only beginning to understand.

"Fire!"

Heat and smoke rolled toward them like a wave. A ripping noise tore through the woods, the sound of shredding paper amplified by a thousand decibels, followed by an explosion.

The dry bush-like arms of manzanita bloomed into flame. The thick waists of the madrone and elegant limbs of eucalyptus burst one after another, spewing jets of burning oil.

Anne had run far ahead on the deer trail, while J.D. had tried to gauge the path of the blaze. But now he had to move. He threw himself over a ledge and into trees along the side of a steep wall. He cracked through a web of leaves and branches, falling until he hit sand and slid face first, stopped only by an outcropping of wild grass. J.D. lay there for a moment, surprised to still be alive.

He pushed himself up and realized his shirt was burned, and that his back and backside were stinging.

"Anne?" Had she made it over the ledge? Was she still up there, in the fire?

"Anne?" He heard a wail. He followed the sound to his right, through brambles and brush, until he almost tripped over what he took to be a curling, brown log.

He still hardly recognized her, rolled up in the fetal position, her shirt ripped and tattered; the white of her bra peeked through the front.

Her blonde hair was an uneven mop, burned in places halfway up to the root. Her face was smudged with soot and her eyes were sleepy and unfocused.

"Anne." She didn't respond.

J.D. grabbed her by the shoulder and pulled her to her feet. She was barely standing. He knew that if he withdrew his hands from under her armpits, she would collapse. He pulled her to him, raised her chin and looked into her unfocused eyes.

She was at best only semi-conscious.

The fire grew around them, the sound of crackling wood and gurgling sap building into a roar, a crescendo. She was just beginning to awaken, her eyes now sparkling with the reflected firelight rising around them.

Anne still couldn't stand on her own, although she could mutter in a barely audible voice, "Don't let me burn." J.D. pulled her to his chest, threw her over his back and ran downhill.

It was an obstacle course of roots, upended stone, and jags of wood bearing out of splintered trunks. He cursed himself for allowing her head and feet to be raked against branches, for the thorny vines that whipped her face.

He kept on running.

She curled around his shoulders and buried her face in the crook of his neck. His back felt like a wound of splitting skin.

He kept on, bouncing agilely on his feet like a boxer, downward to the left, downward to the right. He kept on and on, until the sound of the fire diminished and the trees began to change.

The sand was gone, replaced by a thick, black, loamy clay, damp and squishy under the soles of his feet. There were fewer manzanita and more pine, more ground foliage and large green fans sprouting from the mossy forest floor. Tiring, he started to pace himself, though still moving as quickly as he could downhill.

There were red huckleberry bushes and oak trees, many of them. Soon he found himself in a glade surrounded by an immense cathedral of thick redwoods that rose a hundred feet. The air was fresh, smelling of cedar. No sign of smoke.

Anne pulled her head up and slid off his shoulders. She tried to stand on her feet, but wobbled around until J.D. steadied her. She waved him away and went behind a tree to vomit.

She slowly regained her composure, walking around with her hands on her hips, breathing deeply, in and out. Anne finally stood in front of him, looking like a chimney sweep at the end of a busy day. Her tennis shoes were melted at the edges.

"Don't stare at me," she said. "You look like a campfire weenie that was cooked a minute too long."

J.D. smiled at that and was surprised when she took his hand. They walked under a cool canopy of high shade, until the ground leveled off and the grass gave way to stone.

Anne let go of him and took the lead again, her steps sure in the narrow slips between the jagged rocks, her balance as level as if nothing had happened. J.D. heard a roaring sound again, but Anne walked calmly on. Then he saw the river twenty feet below, a rushing green torrent laced with white foam and whirlpools by a rocky beach.

CHAPTER
22

They tried to wash in the cold river water, but it was too painful. Anne's face was red-raw from scratches. She inspected his back, but he wouldn't stand still while she rubbed cold water at the edges of two large, fist-sized blisters on either side of his spine. The flesh had turned slightly pink, like salmon.

"You've been scalded," she told him. "Not bad. Look, it's the same on my arms." Her forearms were mottled with little pink welts.

After a rest, they walked quietly for a long time along the stony beach, up river, stepping high to avoid the larger rocks.

"Are you sure that cabin's around here?"

"I think we've got only a half mile to go."

They came to a bend where the beach disappeared and had to trek up a hillock of wide, granite boulders. By the time they reached more beach on the other side, the heavy stroking blades of a helicopter could be heard.

J.D. turned and saw the mountain behind them, the fire obscured behind a thick white cumulus of smoke.

"At least they're onto the fire," she said. "And look. You see the river's moving up the rocks; they're releasing water from the reservoir. In case they need it for a break."

A C-130 lumbered across the sky until it was less than a hundred feet over them, the reverberation of its four churning propellers felt in the gut. Then it climbed high above them, releasing several tons of water and fire-retardant chemicals from the belly, a heavy white spray that plunged into the larger smoke cloud and disappeared. Around it, they could see a half-dozen helicopters like a swarm of mosquitoes. The largest of them had a one-ton bucket of water that it released as it made a dive over the fire.

The river cut to another sharp turn that led to the base of the next mountain. An ammonia smell wafted towards them.

"We're almost there," Anne said.

It took another half-hour. They clambered over a rockfield—the rocks made smooth by river water and slippery by slick green moss. They slogged through a knee-high marsh of reeds and tall water grass, while another helicopter buzzed overhead.

They finally arrived at a large cabin. The lawn was freshly mowed.

"This is it."

"Who lives here now?"

"Don't know."

She walked slowly up the wooden stairs.

"Feels weird, coming back like this."

There was a hummingbird feeder, cedar chairs on the deck. The front door had a panel with the family's name in yellow letters. "The Findlays. Dad knew them," she said.

Anne knocked repeatedly on the frame door. No answer.

With a grunt, J.D. began to unbutton his shirt until he realized that it was nothing but strips of heat-shriveled shreds in the back. He ripped it off, wrapped it around his hand like an enormous bandage, and punched through a window.

He extracted a large, jagged piece of glass, and punched again to widen the hole. He knocked away the shards, climbed in, and opened the door for Anne.

The interior of the house was warm and still. He saw wicker chairs and colonial-style furniture. A Navajo rug was thrown across the hardwood floor. A speckled rainbow trout, stuffed and varnished, was mounted on a wooden pallet above the mantle of the stone fireplace.

Anne looked around her. "So much smaller now."

J.D. shouted a hello.

Nobody home.

Anne walked around the room excitedly, telling him where things used to be. He went to the kitchen and made himself a peanut butter sandwich, washing it down with cold milk straight from the carton.

"Anne, got any aspirin?"

"I'll check the bathroom." She returned in an instant. "Catch." She tossed him a small bottle, and disappeared again into the master bedroom. He heard the door shut and the shower come on.

J.D. went into a room that he took to be a study—desk, chair, drawers. He sat down, opened a drawer, and started flipping through it looking for a cell phone or an extra pistol. All he found were a lot of empty file folders, a few uninteresting letters, random documents relating to the upkeep of the cabin. He read them anyway, with nothing better to do.

Ten minutes later, J.D. felt a presence behind him. He turned to see Anne standing in the doorway. Her tanned face was clean of soot, her full lips the color of red clay, the ugly burns in her hair smoothed out by combing her blonde hair straight back. No longer hidden by makeup, freckles appeared across the bridge of her nose. She wore a white terry cloth robe taken from a closet.

"Do you investigate in your sleep?"

J.D. liked the way she stood on one foot, her other leg slightly bent and protruding from the robe. She looked very tan against the white cloth.

"I look into everything," he said slowly, tired. "I'm finding out about our hosts. I can tell you they pay their bills."

"Fascinating. Remind me never to let you over to my place."

He stood up with a groan. "That shower sounds like a good idea."

As he walked by her, she placed a hand on his shoulder. He could smell her clean skin and hair. One thick scratch crossed her left check, another small one jutted out over her eyebrow. "It'll make you feel better," she said.

He went to the master bedroom, removed his Walther and ankle holster, and set them on the bedside table. He locked the door of the master bath, undid his khakis, black from burns and caked in mud, and started the shower.

He washed his hair and scrubbed down with soap, feeling clean again. He worked up the courage to gingerly turn around and let the water flow down his back.

The water felt good, soothing away the stinging sensation. J.D. just stood there for twenty minutes, until the water went too cold to endure.

He toweled off, combed his hair, finger-brushed his teeth. He wrapped himself in a large towel. The sting on his back was returning with a vengeance.

Anne was waiting for him on the bed. She half-sat, half-reclined, her legs stretched out. He had never seen her looking more relaxed.

"I need you to do something about my back," he said.

Anne went into the bathroom, rummaged through the medicine chest, coming back with cotton balls, rubbing alcohol, and a tube of salve. She went to the kitchen, filled a tin pie tray full of water and mixed the alcohol in it.

Anne ordered him to sit on the bed while she sat behind him and dabbed the edges of his burns with alcohol.

J.D. focused his attention on his hands, fists squeezing into balls of red knuckle and white flesh. Alcohol on his burns felt like a thousand, tiny, red-hot harpoons. "Sorry, but the wounds are starting to crack a bit around the edges," Anne said. "Got to keep it from getting infected."

She squirted a pungent, medicinal smelling glob into her palm and started to rub it in. The pain immediately began to fade. He felt his shoulders drop, the cessation of pain itself a euphoric pleasure.

Her hands gently caressed his back, balming the last of his pain under a coat of cold sticky goo. It was only a slight hurt now, a pulse to accompany the throb in his head.

"It seems like a year ago we were having breakfast in a hotel," she caressed his shoulders, feeling taut rope-like muscles built up from polishing cars and decks, lugging engine parts and hoisting sails.

"I wonder what our bosses are thinking," J.D. said.

"My national editor, Herb Smith—no telling what he's whispering into Jim Miller's ear."

J.D. wondered if the FBI would even bother looking for him after dropping his contract.

Anne got up, padded into the kitchen, and came back with two glasses of ice water.

J.D. looked at her. Her eyes filled with some kind of emotion that mystified him. He couldn't think of anything else to do, so he kissed her. It seemed to make everything all right.

"I just realized something," she said.

"What?"

"In all the excitement, I left my laptop in the car."

"My suitcase. We don't have anything to wear."

Something about what he'd just said made her smile.

CHAPTER
23

She woke suddenly, a hand over her mouth.

J.D. leaned above her, fingers tight and pressing down. "Someone's here."

It was dark, the inside of the cabin all shadows and vague shapes.

It took a few seconds for Anne to remember where she was.

There, she heard it too. A creaking sound, weight subtly shifting on the slats of the hardwood floors in the living room.

He reached slowly in the dark for his Walther, pulled the hammer back and made a mental note that the second shot would require a lot more trigger pull.

Anne quietly rolled over and knelt beside the bed.

For an instant, J.D. thought she was going to hide under the bed. Instead, she reached behind the bedside table and blindly felt for the plug to the Tiffany lamp. She pulled it out so hard that her hand banged against a wooden leg of the table.

She didn't mean to make so much noise. The creaking stopped.

The living room was dead quiet.

Anne stood and raised the lamp, wrapping the cord around the base. J.D., his eyes adjusting to the dark, could see her pull the lamp above and slightly behind her shoulder, wielding it high. She stayed behind him, by the bed.

He locked his arm, aiming at the door.

They heard hard footsteps, someone who no longer cared if he was heard or not.

J.D. shouted, "I'm a federal agent and I am armed."

"This is Anne, John's daughter. If you're the Findlays, let me explain."

The footsteps were loud and quick together, moving away from them. The front door opened and slammed.

J.D. turned on the bathroom light. Anne was ready to bring the lamp down on someone's skull.

"The more I think about this, it's got to be the Findlays," she said. "We scared them out of their own house."

"I'll check. Do not leave this room. For any reason."

She nodded.

The living room was black and silent, the door securely shut.

J.D. looked out the window. The lawn was dark in the moonless night, stars dimly reflected in the river. There was a smell of wood smoke in the air from the distant forest fire. He locked the front door and turned.

Anne had not stayed, she was curious, she just had to lean out the doorframe, just had to peek.

He could see where she stood, her white robe a pale radiance in the dim light at the bedroom door, a shadow growing behind her. J.D. aimed over her shoulder, but it was useless at this distance.

The blunt muzzle of a large pistol pressed hard against the bony nape at the back of her skull. Thick fingers wrapped across her mouth as she screamed.

Anne could feel the gunman against her back, his breath against the side of her face. He gave off a sour, burnt odor. The gun had shifted now to the side of her head. She was prey, helpless in the paws of a predator.

The gunman whispered. "Who is he?"

"FBI agent with a gun." She spoke loudly, wanting J.D. to hear it all.

The man's voice was almost inaudible, a strained whisper, as if he were speaking through deep pain.

"What kind of gun does he have?"

"Don't know guns," she said. "J.D., J.D., dear God, stop this."

"What is his full name?" The gun pressed hard. It would only take a flick of his finger to send a bullet grooving a channel through her skull.

"FBI Agent Joe DeVine, he's got his gun on you now."

The gunman grunted, unimpressed. He spoke again, this time in a normal tone of voice. "Drop it."

She bent her knees slightly and dropped the lamp hard on the floor.

He pulled her back from the bedroom door, toward the kitchen. J.D. advanced, Walther sighted at the indistinct shapes moving in front of him.

"Go back to bedroom," the gunman said to J.D.

J.D. was forced to retreat backward into the bedroom. The gunman advanced using Anne as his shield.

She could no longer feel the gun, but she could still feel the gunman's body. She walked toward the bedroom, ashamed of her helplessness, ashamed of her fear. J.D. waited for them, crouched behind the side of the bed, right arm stretched flat as a board, Walther sighted, firmly in hand.

J.D. caught a clean angle to the gunman's head as he walked Anne into the room. But the sight of the man's face in the half-light of the bathroom so startled him that J.D. lost his bead for an instant—enough time for the gunman to spin her body around for cover.

His upper lip had been ripped by a fall against stone, curling upward like a pulled curtain to reveal raw gum and rotten, discolored teeth. His nose was swollen, blackened, and blistered.

But the eyes were the same as the driver's, that same glint of hard determination, that same hairline sweep on a domed skull.

"Painkillers, do you have?" The man's voice did not match the intensity of his eyes. Red blisters covered his hands, and his arms trembled as he spoke.

"Yes," J.D. said. "Are you the man in the Cadillac?"

"I am Dmitri. Get me medicine."

Only in movies could an FBI man have the confidence to fire a pistol from across the room and expect to hit a target behind a hostage. For an instant, J.D. calculated the angles.

There were no options.

"Put gun under bed and get me medicine or you will see her brains. Now!"

Anne's eyes widened with terror. Jerks and twitches rippled across her arms and legs, gooseflesh spread across her body.

J.D. spoke in measured tones. "I am a federal agent. I'm trained never to put down my gun. Kill her and I'll put you down hard."

The wretched man's laugh was ragged and rough as a saw. "Go ahead, put Dmitri out of this pain."

The bluff had not worked. There were some situations that even the FBI's extensive training couldn't prepare you for. After a moment's hesitation, J.D. let his Walther pivot on his trigger finger, barrel pointing to the floor. He carefully set the gun on the bed, level to his shoulder.

"On floor. Kick to Dmitri."

J.D. had no choice. Dmitri's gun was on him. He did as he was told.

"Get me medicine for pain. Now!" Spittle flew out of his torn mouth.

J.D. saw Dmitri tighten his grasp on a bunch of her hair, pulling it hard by the roots. Anne wailed in pain.

Dmitri pointed the gun at J.D. as he walked to the bathroom medicine chest. At eye level, the gunman looked smaller, strange, a demonic puppet. The burns on his chest deepened from red into purple.

"What is it?" Dmitri croaked the words. "Why do you look at me like that?"

"Your face."

The gunman shoved Anne to the floor and turned to look in the mirror above the dresser.

He cried out and stared, gently touching the edges of

his burned nose, raising his hands to cover the horror of his reflection.

Dmitri spun back to put an end to this, to shoot the balls off the FBI fuck, kill the bitch, and then put a bullet into his own head. But J.D. had taken the second of distraction to lunge to the nightstand. He flung the contents of the tin pan—alcohol and water—into the raw, skinless wounds on Dmitri's face.

Liquid fire hit him, a fire that was both ice cold and furnace hot, alcohol fumes that forced his eyes shut and dug into his burned, cracked skin, inciting every nerve to agony. Dmitri clawed at his eyes and shrieked.

Anne tumbled over, out of his grasp, righted herself and ran in a crouch out of the room. J.D. rolled across to the foot of the bed and retrieved his Walther from the floor.

He screamed at the perp to drop his gun.

Dmitri raised a trembling arm, eyes still tightly closed. He made gurgling noises and half sobs. He said things in Russian, and then he spoke once in English.

"I wanted to live in America," his voice curled up and down an octave, like a child in a melodramatic rage. "I wanted to be in movies."

"Flinch and I'll blow you to hell." The man was effectively blind. J.D. had a clean shot at him, head and chest.

Dmitri thrust the blunt end of his Glock hard against the roof of his mouth. He stood there in silence for ten seconds, eyes closed, whimpering, half crying, muttering to himself. With a loud report, a bullet exploded through the top of his head and ejected a fist-size clump of red brain matter onto the dresser mirror.

The body collapsed to the floor on its haunches and sat upright against dresser drawers. Vacant eyes stared from a half-excavated skull.

His brains slid down the mirror.

J.D. stepped over the corpse and pointed his gun into the darkness as he walked low, feet carefully planted, out of the room. He crept past Anne and checked the door, the windows, all the rooms. There was no one else.

He went back to Anne who sat in the dark, shaking from fear and rage. It was only when he embraced her that he realized he had been shaking just as badly. Holding each other seemed to steady them both.

CHAPTER
24

Anne fished through a chest-of-drawers and came up with an adolescent boy's red T-shirt and a new pair of blue jeans.

They fit her perfectly.

The house was now ablaze with light. J.D. had switched on every light and lamp, and checked every window of every room. When he was satisfied Dmitri had been alone, he went to the kitchen and made coffee, the strong aroma permeating the cabin.

Anne found a bigger pair of jeans for J.D., but they were still too tight around his legs, and wouldn't zip. He wondered just how much weight he had put on since he was eighteen. He finally settled on a sweat shirt with a Raiders logo and a pair of gym shorts that fit fine, but looked perfectly ridiculous with his penny loafers.

He decided not to strap the ankle holster to his bare leg. No sooner had J.D. put his gun and holster in a plastic bag than he heard a noise from outside, the sound of a car crunching on gravel. Headlights shot through the back window.

J.D.'s training took over again. He pulled his Walther from the bag, went into a crouch, and turned off the kitchen light.

He watched a large SUV parked in the woods, lights on bright, power lamps mounted on top. A beam swept over the cabin.

The driver blinked his lights, very deliberately, three times. J.D. switched the kitchen light on and off twice. The lights in the truck blinked once more. J.D. went to open the door.

"FBI code?" Anne asked.

"Partner code. That's Agent McGuire out there."

"I wish you had something stronger than coffee." McGuire was repulsed by the bloody scene in the bedroom. Best to leave it for the guys from the crime-scene unit. He closed the bedroom door and walked into the kitchen, setting his shotgun against a wall.

Anne sat on the living room couch with her half-melted tennis shoes propped up on the coffee table. Her eyes were glazed, her mouth still tight with fear and anger.

"How do you like yours?" McGuire asked.

"Black," J.D. said, sitting down in a settee opposite Anne.

"Cream, sugar, and without a gun to my head."

McGuire walked slowly, holding two coffee cups in one hand, his own in the other. He set the coffee down on the table and pulled up a chair from the dining room.

"Who was he?" J.D. took a deep sip of coffee.

"Dmitri Popova, Russian national, whack specialist. Manoulian let his right-hand woman put out the contract on both of you yesterday."

"How could you know that?" Anne asked. The cup trembled slightly in her hands.

He ran his finger along the back of his collar, an "awe, shucks" gesture.

"Well, you see, Manoulian slipped out of his mansion—that danged fog again—and took off late this afternoon in his private jet. He's off to Armenia and I don't think he's coming back, unless we can catch him refueling somewhere along the way."

"But he'll lose everything," J.D. said. "The San Marcos Group, the Presidio, his house."

McGuire shook his head.

"He'll just lose what he keeps in this country. We'll be looking, but I'm sure Frank Manoulian has stashed enough money to be welcomed by the Armenian interior minister, not to mention some big cheeses in Moscow. Beats Folsom."

He took a sip, then McGuire broke out into a big smile, mustache curling.

"Shannon Crocker, well, she wasn't so lucky. Manoulian cut her loose and left her behind to take the fall. I look forward to that interrogation."

"Once again, how did you know they hired the hit man?" Anne curled up on the couch, watching the big man with undisguised skepticism.

"Well, I guess you do deserve to know. Whenever Manoulian wanted to talk about aspects of his business that were shady, he'd do it by the pool. You noticed those Greek columns? We had mikes in every one."

"So you knew he had a hit out on us?" J.D. stood up, shouting so abruptly that Anne, whose nerves were just beginning to steady, almost went to pieces again. "You used your old partner in a sting operation as *bait*?"

McGuire got that chagrined cowboy look again.

"You gotta understand, J.D., by then the Bureau had already decided to cut you back to civilian status. I had a tail on you all the time, waiting to see who'd pop out of the woodwork. I was in a van no more than a few clicks away. It's just that you threw us for a loop when you took off early and didn't go to the airport. We lost you in all that fog."

"Tell me more."

The agent made a scratching noise as he rubbed stubble along his jaw.

"When we lost the trail, Suarez went nuts. She was sure the Forest Service would find you all barbecued in the ashes. Then I remembered Anne's file, and figured out where you might be."

"I have an FBI file?"

"As for that fella in there," McGuire gestured at the bedroom, "when he got all burned up, he must have taken another path down to the river. That's when he saw you upstream, and followed you here. He had to have been one strong SOB, to move through all that hurt."

It was McGuire's turn to ask a question. "It was him, wasn't it, who ran you off the road?"

"The Cadillac killer," Anne said, nodding.

"Well, after that, the perpetrator, Dmitri, he sprayed gasoline all around you. Thought he'd made it look like your car spewed gas, caught fire and started a forest fire that burned you up. Not bad thinking, if you want to make it look like an accident."

"Do you know anything about my suitcases? My laptop?" Anne bit her bottom lip.

"Puddles of plastic. Anyway, he had a bright idea, but your friend in there—'the Cadillac Killer' you call him? I kinda like that—he didn't know much about forest fires. You see, when you start one, the gasoline may move down the hill, but the fire itself, it likes to move up.

"He thought he'd be safe, standing above the fire on solid rock. But what he didn't take into account was the way the forest curved up around both sides of his position."

"The fire went up the cliff?" J.D. asked.

"Not quite. A big forest fire draws in a lot of oxygen, creates a fierce suction. Sometimes the draft is like a hurricane in reverse. These forest rangers out here know how to deal with it. They pull out oxygen masks and run away in trucks. This old boy, well, by the time he knew what was happening, he got yanked halfway down the mountain. That fire wanted him, wanted him really bad."

"So where the hell did he get that car?" J.D. asked.

"Whacked a couple kids for it. He tried to make that look like an accident too. Victims were overdosed, like Hughes, then drowned. Coulda got away with it for a while. Kids were druggies following a rock band called Phish."

"Spelled with a ph," J.D. added, looking glum.

"Yeah. How the hell would you know that?"

J.D. shook his head.

25

McGuire had left the searchlights on, which made it easy to walk through the woods to his massive Chevy Tahoe. He turned off the beams and locked his shotgun into the gun rack.

Anne broke the silence halfway through the ride back to San Marcos with a blunt question. "Did Manoulian have Hughes killed?"

The mountain road back to Highway One was a nauseating array of unanticipated turns in the dark.

"I couldn't prove that, not yet," McGuire replied.

"But you suspect it?"

"I don't broadcast suspicions." He shot her an appraising eye. "You won't quote me?"

"No."

"The hit man resembles someone who left the bar with Hughes and the prostitute. We're working on it. We also hope to get some background on this from Barry Newhouse, who high-tailed it to Europe the minute he heard about Hughes. Now he wants to come home. Once we offer him protection and a deal, I bet we'll learn a lot more."

"You were also working on Todd Thornburgh's death, right?"

"I was doing the traditional homicide part while J.D. worked the political angle."

Anne looked back at J.D. in the dim cabin, as if to say, "Watch this."

"Okay," she said. "So tell me, why did Manoulian have Doctor Dirt killed?"

"He didn't."

The Tahoe bounced and rolled gently over a large pothole.

J.D. laughed at Anne's bafflement. She'd thought she had it all figured out.

The road had led them to the highway, only a few wisps of fog rose off the gullies. McGuire pulled into the light traffic, and J.D. looked out the window at the stars over the black Pacific. It made him want to be back home, on Spa Creek.

"How can you be sure of that?" Anne asked.

"He knows it because of the microphones around the pool," J.D. said. "Anne, you and I had a blind man's elephant by the tail, thinking it was a trunk. Manoulian knew we were on a false lead as far as the Nixon Library murder was concerned, but he didn't really care about our reasons. He just cared we were after him. For a long time, the FBI was squeezing on that elephant tail, too. Isn't that right, good buddy?"

"That's right," McGuire said. "By the way, that's a nasty burn you got. And your banged-up head looks ugly too."

"Thanks for making me feel better."

The darkness of the highway was suddenly violated by the bright lights of service stations and convenience stores. McGuire turned on the left-hand turn signal and stopped at the entrance to the hotel they had left that morning.

Anne was insistent. "If Manoulian didn't kill Thorn-burgh, who did?"

"Would you two do me a favor?" McGuire's smile crooked to one side. "When you find out, would you let me know?"

J.D. told Anne he wanted to talk privately with his old partner. She waited for him in the lobby. For more than a minute, the hum of the idling engine was the only sound in the cabin. That, and McGuire scraping the thick plastic of the steering wheel with a thumbnail. Finally, he spoke.

"What can I say, partner. I'm really, really sorry."

J.D. crumbled up the bag with his gun in it. "This one was close, closer than any tight moment you and I faced tracking down bank robbers. Even those guys in western Maryland."

McGuire nodded and grunted.

"Not that I fail to appreciate that you were under orders," J.D. said.

"You really got the Bureau spooked," McGuire replied. "The Airtels coming out from Washington in the last few days have been almost hysterical. They can't just pry open Clarity's files. They know you have copies and they want them."

"Which they could only know if Lou Firelli had me put under surveillance," J.D. said. "At least I appreciate the warning."

"Yeah," McGuire said, "I left you two."

"You left the light on in my office in Annapolis. Then you cranked the driver's side seat down in my car here in San Marcos. A wad of chewing tobacco on the floor. You know, you could've just taped your badge to the windshield. It would have been more subtle."

"I do get sloppy sometimes."

"That'd be a first."

Anne waited for him in the lobby.

"Did McGuire tell you anything I ought to know?" she smiled in a way that made him feel as if she were playing him for information. It was a feeling he never wanted, not even from a woman he liked.

"Anne, the old rules still apply. If you've got information to trade, I'll deal. If not, stay out of my investigation."

She looked as if he'd just slapped her. Her eyes teared, her face stiffened with anger. He hadn't meant to be so brusque, just set her straight, but there was no way to take it back.

If the desk clerk was surprised to see her again, he was astonished to see J.D. return beat up and bruised in gym clothes and penny loafers.

"Did you have an accident, sir?"

"Kinda."

"Do you have a new reservation?"

"No."

"But you need two rooms, nonsmoking?"

"We need two rooms," she said it first.

After they registered, the clerk told them they both had received a number of messages. He reached under the desk and pulled out a batch of pink message slips. "You're lucky. We usually don't do this for check-outs. But they were all so insistent. They had nowhere else to reach you."

Anne had three messages from Herb Smith and one from Jim Miller. J.D. had two messages from Carol Suarez, and another from Ben Grossman.

He tucked his messages in the pocket of his gym shorts and walked with her toward the elevator.

"Some day, huh?" he said.

Anne nodded, her voice almost inaudible. "Some day."

She got off on the third floor. J.D. rode up to the fourth.

CHAPTER
26

J.D. came down for a late breakfast and found the buffet to be wanting. The Sterno lighters had burned out, the eggs and sausages were cold. Even the best muffins had been picked, or picked apart.

He ordered the Hungry Hunter breakfast of two eggs over easy, hash browns, a side of ham, coffee, and toast. He told the waitress he'd be back in a moment.

He walked across the lobby, out by the pool, to a little covered walkway that connected the hotel to a strip mall. He went into a men's clothing shop, drawing the curiosity of the salesmen with his Raiders sweatshirt, gym shorts and penny loafers. Within five minutes, he had selected a white Oxford cloth shirt, a belt, new underwear, and socks to match his shoes. He even found a pair of khakis exactly like his old ones.

He dressed in the changing room of the men's store, paid the bill by credit card and returned to the front lobby. He drew $300 in cash off his card and went to the hotel shop to buy an *L.A. Times* and a bottle of aspirin.

J.D. reseated himself at the restaurant table, properly dressed and ready to read the paper as his breakfast arrived.

Before touching a bite, he spread out the front page and felt a tingle of satisfaction for Anne—and for himself, by forcing a situation the Bureau couldn't ignore.

Just above the fold, was a photo of Manoulian and the headline,

Billionaire Evades FBI Arrest, Leaves Businesses, Fabulous Wealth
FBI Sees Connection to Death of Hughes

It had Anne Carlson's byline, and she had put it together without any help from him.

J.D. had tried to call her through the hotel switchboard last night but her phone was busy. At eleven. At eleven-thirty. At ten minutes to midnight.

He called the desk clerk and asked for her room number. The man refused to give it out.

"But you saw us check in together?"

"We have a firm policy, and it's state law."

"Can you at least put me through?"

"Of course."

Anne's line was still busy. J.D. slammed down the phone in disgust. He could no longer use his FBI credential to pry the number out of the clerk, and he could not knock on every door on the third floor at midnight.

The phone rang, and he yanked the receiver.

It was Carol Suarez, still at her office.

"McGuire told me everything. I can't tell you how relieved I am. We pulled out all the stops, a dozen agents deployed in town, helicopters."

J.D. was sure she was telling the truth. Carol was like

that when one of her own was in jeopardy, even if it was just a PI some Bureau-Crat had taken off the company pad. He thanked her for her concern.

"I hate to bring up business now in this context," she said, "but Lou Firelli insists on getting those files now."

"Am I still under contract?"

She paused. "No."

"Carol, it's always a pleasure working with you. I sincerely hope to do it again someday." Click.

J.D. was finishing his last bite of toast when Anne sat next to him. She was still wearing a boy's jeans and red T-shirt.

"My, you look all dressed up." She dropped her copy of the *Times* on the table and ordered.

"So did you sleep in, too?" J.D. asked.

"No. I spent this morning explaining to Mrs. Findlay why the FBI woke her up last night, why we broke into her house, why we stole some of her son's clothes, and why we left a dead Russian hit man in the bedroom. I must say, she was very understanding about it, after the first half hour."

Anne ordered a breakfast of melon slices and a bagel.

"Did you see both of my pieces? I was up till midnight dictating it to our rewrite man. Not easy to do, with my laptop destroyed. Had to recite everything to him from memory. They stopped the presses, J.D., literally stopped them for me!"

He looked down at his copy of the *Times* again and noticed another bylined piece. It was a sidebar account that quoted an unnamed FBI source linking Manoulian to "a professional contract killer" who resembled a shadowy man seen with Mike Hughes and the woman the night of their deaths. It detailed the political connection between Hughes and Manoulian, and portrayed Barry Newhouse as their go-between.

The sidebar ran to an inside jump that included a more personal account of yesterday's harrowing events, with file photos of Anne. The inside headline read, *L.A. Times Reporter Barely Escapes Hit Man's Fury.*

The references to J.D. were few and somewhat elliptical. He asked the waitress for a refill of coffee.

"I tried to call you last night," she said. "Just to let you know that you'd be famous in the morning."

"I tried you too. Must've been when I was on the phone to Washington."

"Grossman, right?" Anne read no denial in his eyes. "I called him as soon as I got to my room, but he wouldn't tell me anything. Congratulations for turning him against me. I've made reservations for the noon commuter."

"So have I."

"See you." She gathered up her paper and went back to her room. A minute later, her bagel and melon slices arrived.

She barely spoke to him during the forty-minute commuter flight to San Jose.

The flight back to Washington was empty, and she took a seat far away from him, in the very back of the plane. J.D. walked down the aisle to get a cup of water for his aspirin, when he saw Anne stretched out across three seats, reading a magazine, her half-melted tennis shoes propped up against the window. She acknowledged him with a weak smile and went back to her reading.

They landed at Dulles, the sun low over the gentle, worn mountains of Virginia. J.D. stayed in his seat, letting passengers walk by. When Anne passed, he followed.

"I'm sorry if our jobs get in the way," J.D. said, and regretted it.

She looked at him, smiled in a perfunctory way, almost as if it pained her, and said, "It just feels different now, us working apart last night. You freezing me out on Grossman."

As they neared the exit, J.D. squinted at the brightness of the terminal, klieg lights that stabbed at his pupils. The crowd shuffled on, many people with arms raised to shield their eyes.

Anne was surrounded by burly men lugging hand-held cameras, lights, microphones. Reporters shouted questions at her.

Anne Carlson no longer just wrote the news. She had become the news.

CHAPTER

27

"So—tell me the whole story."

"I never know the whole story," Lindstrom said. "Just the Cliff Notes."

J.D. had pulled up a chair next to the large pieces of camouflage along the wall. He looked around the office and pitied the private investigator who attempted to sift through Lindstrom's garbage. It would be easier to paw through the entire city dump.

"Then tell me what you do know."

"Draw your own conclusions," Lindstrom said, "from this."

It was a month-old hotel receipt from the Alexandria Hilton showing that Ben Grossman had paid $225 for a suite. The print-out showed he had checked in at 11:35 AM and checked out at 2 PM.

"Ruth had thrown this out with the trash."

"What else?"

Lindstrom took a drag on a cigarette, and pulled out a raft of business appraisals filed with a local title and mortgage company.

"The cash value for Clarity is no more than two-million-five. And that's if you liquidate assets."

"Assets?"

"Yeah, including a million dollars for their robo-cop researcher."

"So?"

"Ben distributed equity shares to some big Republican donors for six million dollars. Half the money went to Ruth."

J.D. got up to leave.

Lindstrom looked surprised. "That's it? No more questions? Tell me what you think?"

J.D. turned at the door, "I don't need to know any more, Stinky. Thanks to you, I think we just caught ourselves a killer."

J.D. returned from a long morning sail only to find another subpoena under his door. He'd sent the last three to his lawyer. This one he folded into a paper airplane, the kind with a long nose and extended wings. It looked somewhat like a Concorde. He sent it sailing out over the docks. It glided almost twenty feet before diving nose first into Spa Creek.

He trotted down to his car, cell phone in one hand, a pad of foam in the other. He laid the foam on the backrest of the driver's seat to protect his wounds. Then he called Roman Grice.

"You talked to Anne?'

"Yes, she's coming."

"What did you tell her?"

"I told her Cyclops has given us all the pieces, but that we need help figuring them out, and that you wanted to count her in."

"She like that?"

"She was surprised, but she said yes."

"Good enough. I'm on my way."

Grossman's office had accumulated a few new curios, a six-foot-tall inflatable Godzilla in the corner, a vintage Howdy Doody, a table lamp in a Western motif.

"Now maybe you can explain just why in holy hell you thought I was making it with Ruth," Grossman said, brushing thick fingers through his Brylcremed hair.

J.D. handed him a single typed sheet summarizing what he had discovered. Grossman read it, pacing his office, absent-mindedly plucking a kachina doll from a bookshelf and waving it in his hand.

He had lost a little weight, but his shirt was tousled, the sleeves carelessly rolled up, a hairy navel peaking from where his shirt still failed to meet his pants, his yellow suspenders stained by newspaper ink.

"Classic poison pills. Good thing you didn't swallow 'em. Sure I went to that hotel—with Todd—to meet a corporate client who wouldn't come here. Ruth must have found the receipt when she cleaned out his pant pockets for Goodwill, that's all."

"And the money?"

"A seller's going to base a price on a business like this on the rate of growth, not on its cash value. So Ruth held out for six. I put in everything I had and raised the rest by selling shares. I didn't kill my best friend and boss so I could mortgage the rest of my life."

"Good to know that."

"This could only have come from Lindstrom." Grossman tossed the paper back to J.D.

"I can't tell you where it comes from."

"Why not?" Grossman asked, adjusting his pants. "I hear the FBI pulled your contract."

"I'm still going to finish this job."

"Well then, let's finish it. Roman and Anne are already back there."

They found Anne standing next to Grice, who, with white-gloved hands, meticulously inspected one disk after another.

Samurai Atwater was on Cyclops' screen awaiting instructions.

"All right, Roman, fill everybody in," Grossman said.

"Well, we know Todd was studying a trip Nixon made as a private citizen to Indonesia," Grice said, sliding a tray with a dozen disks into Cyclops. "While Nixon was touring the country, he made a stop east of Surabaya in Java, whereupon he immediately skeddadled, going straight to the airport. That's what Todd was looking into—why Nixon cut his trip short."

"You know the answer?" J.D. asked.

"Yes, sir. And here's the interesting part. We've found that when our current president was governor of his small southern state, he found time for no less than five Asian trade missions. Every one of them took him to Surabaya. And what's more, we've found that a lot of other American politicians, governors, representatives, senators, all somehow find their way there, and come home as pro-Indonesian as possible on every issue from human rights to trade."

"Honey trap?" J.D. asked.

"Brown sugar trap, young and sweet as molasses."

"Photos?"

"Don't have 'em, but you can bet they've got their white asses for sure, the way they never got Nixon's."

Grice quickly typed "samurai:relate\indonesiasurabaya\belledezuylen."

The Samurai Atwater bowed, drew his sword and attacked a row of icons.

"Todd had his first clue before he went to the Nixon Library, in the releases from the Watergate tapes from U.S. Archives. When things started heating up, Nixon raised the idea of sending the Plumbers Unit on a dirty tricks mission to Indonesia. That sparked Todd's interest. He wanted to know why."

Samurai Atwater bowed and slid his sword back in its sheath. "First datum."

They saw a black-and-white photo from the *New York Times* travel section of a gabled porch, a wooden plank verandah with ceiling fans, wicker chairs, and a hammock.

Grice raised a gloved finger to the screen. "The Belle de Zuylen, nineteenth century plantation home, converted to a luxury resort, and the Indonesian destination of every American pol for the last thirty-five years."

Samurai Atwater furiously worked his sword. Black-and-white documentary footage of Nixon appeared. He looked young, hair brushed back from his wide widow's peak. He managed to be both hunched over and yet bounding vigorously up the stairs to a waiting airplane. He turned briefly to wave to a small crowd of well-wishers, and turned back as if he couldn't get away fast enough.

"Incredible," Anne said. "They found the one vice Nixon didn't have."

"Unlike our current president," Grice replied. He keyed in "samurai: relate\potus\★★indonesia."

Grice explained, "In our disks we've digitized and cross-referenced all local Indonesian media, the four U.S. networks, plus PBS, CNN, MS-NBC."

"I still can't imagine how you find exactly what you're looking for in all those disks," Anne said.

"Cyclops's facial recognition software is the most advanced in the world," Grossman replied. "It can work out a face from most angles and perform a universal scan. Trouble is, we can get as many false matches as real hits."

Samurai Atwater slashed away at icons until another video news clip came on the screen, dated six years earlier. A newswoman's voice-over gushed about the success of the newly elected president's first major trip to Asia. There were rapid images of the young president clicking saki cups with the Japanese prime minister, touring a plant in Korea, meeting with Suharto. The computer's facial recognition software kept a blue frame around the president's face.

Grice twisted a dial, freezing the tape. He magnified the image.

Directly behind the president, barely visible over his left shoulder, was the white nimbus of Sid Sherman's hair, his face pink from sunburn, squinting under the equatorial sun.

"Recognize old Sid?" Grossman said, pointing a thick finger at the screen.

Grice fast-forwarded through clips of the president vacationing on a Javanese beach, talking to an old woman selling live crabs out of a crate, nodding thoughtfully as an Indonesian officer pointed to a tank turret.

Grice's fingers flew over the keyboard and another color video clip took over the screen. This one was three years old, from Indonesian television, showing the president exchanging toasts with Suharto, giving a speech, walking through a crowd of young people.

"This is from the Jakarta Normal School, which is a private high school for the best Indonesian families."

The president, walking through an auditorium, stopped suddenly, and, to the delight of the young men and women in the crowd, turned to shake their hands, slapping hi-fives, and then hugged a student standing in the front. As the president pulled away, the blue frame of the facial recogntion software cloned itself onto the face of the student.

"Hey, freeze it," J.D. said. "What's that?"

"Just the limitations of the software," Grice said. "When it sees similar features at similar angles we sometimes get the extra frame."

"Go back and roll it slowly."

The president glided in slow motion, made direct eye contact with the boy, smiled broadly, shook his hand, and pulled him into a hug.

"Do it again."

As the president slowly released the hug, he caressed the boy's scalp, a strong pinch between his thumb and fingers.

"Can you remove the blue frames?" J.D. asked.

Grice clicked a button and they disappeared.

"The president has his good points," J.D. sighed. "In fact, I feel sorry for him."

"You're not making sense," Anne said.

"We know if you rip away the dummy corporations, the real face of Golden Age is Sidney Sherman, and through him, the president. And what's the president want? A feathered nest, a nice retirement, and something else."

"Like what?"

"Magnify their faces," J.D. ordered. "At least double that size."

The boy was taller than the others, his sharp cheekbones offset by that distinctive, slightly bulbous nose. His coppery skin and short brown hair contrasted with eyes as blue as an Ozark mountain lake.

J.D. said. "No one can accuse this president of not loving his only son. He wants that boy safe and nearby."

CHAPTER
28

"Why did you bring me in on this?" Anne asked, as they stood on the curb outside Clarity.

"I don't trust the FBI and they no longer trust me," J.D. said. "You're the best hope we have." He flagged her a cab.

"J.D., it's just unexpected, after all that's happened."

He opened the door for her, and she gave him that indecipherable, searching look again, as if she was trying to find some secret in his eyes. He closed the door behind her.

"Were you guys an item or something?" Grice asked, as he came down the stairs from Clarity's offices.

J.D. shook his head and led Grice to his 356. He popped the trunk. "Roman, I want you to take this beer cooler and give it to Ben. Tell him to destroy it. And, Roman, tell him he ought to seriously think of destroying the originals. Got it?"

"Yes sir." Grice lifted the cooler and lugged it to Clarity, posture erect as if he were on parade.

J.D. jumped in the car, started the engine, and pulled onto the road. Then he called his old partner on his car phone.

"Listen, I need some info from your investigation."

"Sorry to have to point out the obvious, bro, but you can't ask me about Bureau business."

"Not even if I tell you who killed Doctor Dirt? Bro?"

The connection crackled.

"Now you've got me."

"I'll let you present this to Suarez as your collar," J.D. said. "I just need you to keep me current on what you've dug up. And I need you to do some more checking on the airline manifests around the time of the killing, from all Southern California airports."

"Tell anybody about this and Suarez will shitcan me."

"It'll be our secret."

"Deal," McGuire said. "Who is it?"

J.D. told him.

"What are you going to do?"

"I'm going to flush this one like quail."

"With a shotgun?"

"With e-mail."

"What's so important we couldn't discuss it on the phone?" J.D. said as he followed Anne into her cubicle.

She touched his sleeve. Her face was flush. "I think you should sit down."

"What is it?"

She had a downcast look, as if she faced a very unpleasant duty. She stepped behind her desk.

"Is it more trouble from your editor?" J.D. asked gruffly. "What does he need to get off your case?"

Anne opened her desk drawer and pulled out two sheets of paper.

"I'm terribly sorry," she said. "This came over the office fax, addressed to me. I think you need to know about it."

It was an old newspaper story, from the local Annapolis rag. He felt his face, neck, shoulders, go hot. It was like going out on the street and seeing the glaring eyes of an ex-con you'd put away long before. The headline read, "Eleven-year-old girl attacks classmate." Beneath that a subhead, "Assault with scissors wounds, does not maim."

Anger pooled in his chest like thickening blood. The paper shook in his hands, as he read about how a troubled young girl had snapped after being taunted about her parents' divorce. He turned to the next sheet. A news photo of Sarah, more than a decade later, in tears, at Chuck Beaumont's funeral. Beneath the photo a fax showed a handwritten, block-letter caption read, *"So who killed Doctor Dirt?"*

CHAPTER
29

"What is it?" Anne squinted at the image. It was a bright, blue day out on Spa Creek, excellent conditions for sight-seeing through the brass telescope J.D. kept on his deck.

The scope was trained on a long white pole set into a concrete base along the waterfront of the U.S. Naval Academy athletic field. Along one side of the pole ran metal plates twisted in grotesque shapes.

"Foremast from the Battleship Maine," J.D. said. "The mainmast is in Arlington Cemetery. Some 260 American sailors were killed when their own magazine exploded below decks. It took the yellow press little time to lead the country from that monumental screwup by our own U.S. Navy to kicking the crap out of Spain."

"The point being?"

"This whole business of twisting facts is nothing new. Disinformation is older than Hearst, older than Troy."

"But today it's faster, more effective, more personal."

"That it is."

Yesterday, J.D. had called McGuire to run some checks on the fax.

Then J.D. had some checking of his own to do.

Someone had dug up J.D.'s old divorce proceedings in which his ex-wife had made vague allegations about mental cruelty. At the time, he remembered, his attorney had advised him not to take her testimony personally. It was pro forma, he said, a way of securing the quickest possible divorce.

Now the "mental cruelty" portion of his ex-wife's testimony had been marked from the court transcript with a yellow highlighter and mailed to him. Read like this, out of context, his ex-wife's words made J.D. sound like a sadist.

There was a note attached, written by a blue felt tip pen in that same squarish script that had composed the "Speak No Evil" message in the Nixon Library. *DOES THE FBI KNOW ABOUT YOU?*

A light wind came in from the bay, enough to push the Morgan in a gentle glide leeward across Spa Creek.

Anne relaxed under the sun and wind, delighted by the sight of a racing spinnaker heading for the bay, mainsail full and proud as an out-thrust chest.

It took them less than twenty minutes to cross the creek and slice by the mouth of Ego Alley, the long, narrow rectangular inlet surrounded by the Annapolis city docks.

A warm late April morning like this brought out the Saturday sailors. They came in cigarette boats with bright metallic colors and racing stripes, in huge power boats with high cabins and wide berths. Women stretched out on the coaming around the cockpits in cut-offs and bikini tops, while the men went aft to ice down cases of beer, or oil their 260 horsepower Mercruiser engines.

Many of them, J.D. knew, had never even heard of the

International Regulations for the Prevention of Collision at Sea. They did not know the rules of the road, whether in overtaking or in crossing, nor did they have the faintest idea how to handle even a power boat in a squall.

Size, not skill, was all that really mattered here, the breadth of your beam and volume of your displacement.

Ego Alley.

Too many egos and too little skill in there for his Morgan. He took advantage of an offshore wind to steer at an acute angle toward a small quay near the Eastport Bridge, just below the intersection of Compromise Street and Duke of Gloucester.

He let the jib flap, spilling wind, and brought the boat full around, fast by a small quay. He lowered the sail and tied up the lines to rusty mooring cleats.

"J.D., this is fun but please tell me this has something to do with what we were talking about."

"Weren't we talking about a bite to eat? How about a waffle sandwich? Vanilla and chocolate ice cream packed in a waffle cone."

"No thanks."

"How about some fat free yogurt, then?"

"Chocolate," she said.

They finished their yogurts on park benches on the boardwalk at the very end of the rectangle of Ego Alley. The marina was thick with tourists, retirees in T-shirts and Bermuda shorts, college kids from St. John's, midshipmen in full dress uniform, dads and moms pushing strollers or pulling children along by the hand.

Behind them, a huge mastlike sign flapped in the wind over the town harbor declaring that the last leg of the Whitbread Round the World Race would commence in two weeks.

Annapolis in warm weather was an outdoor carnival.

Heavy metal blared from speakers mounted on a houseboat docked directly in front of them. Four college-age men, looking like pharaohs with their T-shirts flipped over their heads and flapping down their backs, emerged from the cabin, drinking clear rum from hurricane glasses. One of them started to undo the mooring, preparing to take the houseboat down the river and out into the bay.

"It's time you saw this," J.D. reached into the front pocket of his jeans and pulled out a folded sheet of paper. Anne unfolded it.

It was a printed e-mail message, "New on-line address necessary. Come to Annapolis city docks, Saturday, 11 AM to discuss Golden Age. Make no calls, tell no one. Too much curiosity from some quarters."

"What is this?"

"A little something I made up yesterday. I went on-line and created a new e-mail account called SSherman. Then I e-mailed it under that identity to my prime suspect."

"Who?"

"That fax about my daughter. I did some quick checking through McGuire after you called me. Turns out the stamp at the top shows it came from a Kinko's in Georgetown. I called the manager. As you'd expect, the person who sent you that little valentine had been smart enough to use cash. But the manager did remember that customer."

"And?"

"He said the man who sent the fax was dirty, unkempt, like a street person."

J.D. looked down at his watch. It was eleven o'clock.

Fifteen minutes after the hour, a 1964 Volkswagen Beetle convertible, top down, faded-blue paint job, pulled into a parking space behind the ice cream store near Ego Alley.

That would be just like Leo Lindstrom, J.D. thought. He'd be the sort to disdain the new Beetle as too bourgeois.

Leo'd have to have the original, pure, unsullied Bug.

Lindstrom wore a Baltimore Orioles baseball cap, his sandy-gray hair pulled back into a ponytail. He had let his scrawny beard grow back out, long enough to come to a point; several bits of food were caught in the wiry strands like flies in a spider's web. Lindstrom wore an untucked Hawaiian shirt that billowed in the wind over a pair of blue-jean cut-offs. His knobby feet, toenails long and yellow, were wrapped in sandals, the bottoms made from recycled tires.

"That's him?"

"That's the coward."

Lindstrom made eye contact with J.D. and smiled as if he had just spotted an old friend. He pulled a pack of Marlboros from his front shirt pocket, tamped out a cigarette, struck a match on a long, yellow thumbnail and cupped a hand around the flame while lighting up.

"I knew all along that was really you, getting me to come all the way to Annapolis," Lindstrom took a deep drag. "Don't know anyone else out here. So I came to ask, since you don't even work for the Bureau anymore, just what the fuck is all this harassment about?"

The college men cranked up the heavy metal on the houseboat speakers, forcing Lindstrom to almost shout to be heard. He had said the f-word loud enough to draw a glare from a couple with two kids eating ice cream on the next bench over.

"This is about the fact that my former partner in the FBI can place you in the Los Angeles area on the day of the murder," J.D. said. "Even though you paid cash, you still had to show your ID to the airlines. You were on an American Airlines manifest going out to LAX the day before the murder of Todd Thornburgh. You're on another one coming back from Ontario, the closest airport to Yorba Linda, the day after."

"Again, so what the fuck? L.A.'s got more people than forty-two states. You gonna arrest everybody who was in la-la land that day?" Lindstrom's cackling laugh cracked up into a smoker's cough.

"I have more pieces to this puzzle," J.D. said. "I also know it was you who sent the hate mail and hate faxes. Shannon Crocker broke down and told the feds that you also kept tabs on Anne and me for Manoulian. Now you've just added another piece yourself by coming here. You've just confirmed that you work for Sid Sherman through Golden Age."

"You ain't got shit," Lindstrom put a foot on a concrete parking block at the edge of the boardwalk and leaned forward. "You ain't even a real Hooverboy any more."

"And one other thing," J.D. said. "That tarp in your office got me to do some checking with your old soldier buddies. Seems you were a real devil with needle and thread, the one guy in the platoon who could patch up a pair of ripped pants or a backpack."

Lindstrom exhaled smoke and threw down his cigarette and ground it under the heel of a sandal. The fair skin of his cheeks went blood red, his eyes narrowed with hate.

"You're one stupid G-fuck gummyshoe," Lindstrom seemed oblivious how loud he was getting in public, didn't even notice the family next to them grabbing their children and fleeing. "Pig-eyed Hoover whore."

"And then, of course, you've been sharing dirt with Sid Sherman for years."

"You don't know that."

"A connection which, according to the papers of the late Michael Hughes now on full display in probate court, shows that you received a large payment from Golden Age just before you murdered Doctor Dirt."

Lindstrom's face was like a red tomato ready to burst. White mucus appeared at the corners of his mouth, spotted his beard as he leaned forward and shouted, "fuck you!" over and over.

"Not that Sherman expected you to go quite that far. Because deep down, Leo, few people realize that you've gotten stupid as you've gone crazy."

Lindstrom stood there, trembling, now too mad to even scream at him. J.D. smiled back, egging him on, just like Doctor Dirt must have done.

"What's it going to be, Leo, prison or the nut house?"

Lindstrom turned, stalked back to his Beetle and shut the door with a hard slam. He turned the key and a strong air-cooled, four-cylinder engine roared to life.

"McGuire can pick him later," J.D. said. "For now, it's best to leave him alone. Let him say and do things that will only incriminate him even more."

Lindstrom gunned the Beetle in neutral. The small, humped body rocked back and forth.

"What's he doing?" Anne was worried.

"He's just pissed off."

The car squealed in reverse, tires kicked up gravel, grinding blue smoke against the asphalt. The Beetle shot backward, and several pedestrians barely got out of the way before the rear end of the little car smashed a wide hole in the wooden wall of the ice cream shop.

"Lindstrom, you crazy shit!" J.D. pulled Anne to her feet.

The gears ground as he shifted into first.

J.D. locked onto Leo Lindstrom's eyes, an expression level under the brim of his baseball cap, the determined look of hatred and madness on the verge of fulfillment.

J.D. grabbed Anne by the waist and started to pull her along to the side boardwalk. No, that was a mistake, the boardwalk was a perfect straight-away.

The little car burst across the street like a cannon ball.

J.D. pulled Anne over the side, into the channel of water between the wharf and the departing houseboat. The shadow of the car passed over them as they plunged into the cold water. They could feel the percussion of an impact through the water, an impact both heard and felt as Lindstrom's car slammed into the houseboat.

They came to the surface. Anne choked, flailed at the water and sputtered, trying to catch her breath. He turned her around and placed a forearm under her chin. She coughed up water, her breathing steadied, and she quit thrashing.

Twenty-three years in the FBI, and he had never seen—never imagined—a sight like the one in front of them.

The car had smashed through the hull, into the forward cabin of the houseboat.

A padded bench and wooden galley table floated in the water, a lamp and television set toppling after them. The front of the Beetle hung on the shattered wood and fiberglass hull by its two front wheels, the back-wheel drive churned water, hot exhaust from the tailpipe bubbling up.

The Beetle roared in the water; the force of the impact was moving the houseboat further into the inlet. The four college men huddled on the aft deck, screaming in fury and terror.

Lindstrom frantically worked the clutch and the gas. It was useless, a rear-wheel drive with both back wheels in the water. The front two tires slipped on the broken fiberboard.

The weight of the Beetle was too much, the thin hull cracked into a car-sized shard.

The Beetle sank, heavy rear-end first. The hot metal of the engine sang and sputtered. Cool water rushed into the vents of the back hood, filled the hollows and chambers around the engine block.

J.D. remembered that Beetles had a unitized body, wouldn't sink easily. But this was a convertible. The car began to keel over, the solid plate under the car angling toward the sky, the convertible top rolling toward the water.

Lindstrom was caught in the roll of the car, tossed against the dash, his face against the rear-view mirror. He seemed to struggle, as if he were jammed in the seat as the car turned upside down.

Water poured into the back seat of the car, then rushed in to the front.

J.D. paddled against the current, holding Anne. He could still see Lindstrom through a translucent film of surface water.

Lindstrom looked angry, not at all afraid, as if he were trying to mouth one more "fuck you" before going to the muddy river bottom.

Water bubbled up around the tires. Lindstrom disappeared in a cloud of silt.

CHAPTER

30

Anne crossed Pennsylvania Avenue to the United States Botanic Garden. The humid air inside the giant, glass structure was thick with the earthy smells of growing, blooming, rotting things. Anne walked into the main building, on a walkway that was almost engulfed in jungle.

Several palm trees challenged the very top of the forty-foot glass ceiling. Every few years, the arboretum staff had to unscrew enormous bolts and slide out another foot or two of the louvered metal beams that extended the ceilings for more growth.

She turned to see Geoffrey, right on time. "I'm surprised you chose this spot. It doesn't exactly strike me as a Geoffrey kind of place."

"Anne, this whole town is a Geoffrey kind of place. I come here at least once a week to smell the roses, if you will. Good for the soul. Also the only place I can talk without fear that someone at the next table over is eavesdropping. By the way, if one more person tries to kill you, you'll win the Pulitzer."

"I'm finishing a story, my byline. The White House is doing everything possible to bury it through their spinmeisters, their lawyers."

"The White House?"

"I mean Sid Sherman."

"Tell me."

Anne told Geoffrey about Sherman's connection to Hughes, Golden Age, and the boy in Indonesia. She told him everything that had come out on Leo Lindstrom. The old man listened intently, asked about an occasional detail now and then, but otherwise seemed not to react. They walked along as Geoffrey used his folded umbrella like a cane, click-clacking with each slow step.

When she was through, they had walked from one end of the arboretum to the other, into the cactus room.

Finally, Geoffrey spoke.

"Well, that's just awful news about Sidney, terrible. Trying to kill a perfectly good story, I mean. Murder I can forgive. Frankly, I wouldn't have thought the old boy had any of that in him."

His attention was drawn to tall cacti planted in rocks and sand. A group of schoolchildren on a field trip were streaming around the edge of the plants, daring each other to touch a spine.

"Look at that one, will you? I saw plenty of those in the Marianas, let me tell you. And how about the flowers on this one over here, *Cereus giganteus*?"

The cactus had a good two feet on Geoffrey, its enormous arms covered with white, waxy flowers. The sign, which identified it as a Saguaro, read, "the flowers, which mature in summer, are generally solitary, stalkless, large, bisexual, and slightly fleshy."

Geoffrey chuckled to himself and patted the bottom of the plant with the tip of his umbrella, a gesture that drew a uniformed attendant to her feet. He stopped and walked toward the exit from the cactus room, on his way out bowing ever so slightly in a gesture of apology. The attendant held her peace and sat back down.

"That's it? Geoffrey, haven't you and Sid Sherman been friends for years?"

They reached the front entrance of the arboretum. No other visitor was in earshot.

"My dear girl, twenty years ago, the two of us were much more than friends. Does that surprise you? Anyway, it's long over now. Only the bantering and the insults remain. The important thing is if any of this is true, there's no forgiving him."

Geoffrey thought a moment, unfurled his umbrella, stepped out into the rain, and looked back at Anne.

"I believe it, I believe it all. I've always felt there was something missing in dear old Sidney. Oh, he's witty, he's clever. But I learned long ago that the man will do anything to scrunch another inch up the greasy pole."

Anne opened her umbrella and joined the old man in the slow procession down the sidewalk to Pennsylvania Avenue to catch their cabs.

"Anne, there's only one thing to do."

"What's that?"

"Come to dinner."

She laughed. Such a Geoffreyesque solution. But Geoffrey, who always wore a poker face, looked especially serious, like an undertaker on a busy day.

"Not just any dinner—a very special occasion, one that reporters rarely get to see. And those who do, have to take a vow of secrecy. Come tomorrow night. And I want you to bring that friend of yours, J.D. I want to meet him. More important, we need someone connected to the FBI to see what's about to happen."

"What's so special about this dinner?"

"It's the annual Ghosts and Toasts."

"Ghosts and Toasts, huh," said J.D. into the receiver. "Never heard of it."

"Not many have outside of Washington. It's a black-tie affair exclusively for present and former White House speechwriters. That's the Ghosts part, because they're all ghostwriters."

"I get it."

"And the Toast part—well, they seat everyone by administration. One by one, a speaker rises from each table to make a witty toast, defending his president and eviscerating the current occupant of the White House."

"Sounds like Washington kind of fun."

"It's more than fun. Geoffrey insists that we be there. We have to take an oath of silence. As a rule, they don't invite many outsiders. You'll come as my date."

"If Sid Sherman will be there, so will I."

They agreed to meet at the Hay Adams bar.

J.D. arrived at seven sharp, pleased that his tux, at least, still fit him so well. He looked up and down the bar for her, until he realized a second later that he had passed her right by. Anne Carlson sat alone, her short hair more elegantly styled than he'd ever seen it.

"You look good," she said. "Not at all like a penguin." Her cold, businesslike demeanor had evaporated.

"Anne?"

She stood up from the chair, resplendent in a red, satin gown that showed her smooth shoulders. A slit ran to within an inch of her hip, revealing the length of her slender, brown leg. She stood an inch taller in her elegant red pumps.

"Get over it. People dress like this all the time out here, right? Let's go to dinner." She said, snapping shut a small, red evening purse. "Besides, I had to find a good stylist to hide all the places where my hair is still burned to the root."

He escorted her to the stairs that led down to a private reception area, a large dark paneled room with elaborate plaster latticework across the ceiling. The room was full, mostly with old or middle-aged men, standing in clusters around ten tables.

There was loud talk and raucous laughter. A waiter came with a silver tray bearing champagne glasses.

Anne took one. "You, J.D., not drinking?"

"I'm not in the mood, at least not yet."

An elderly man shuffled forward and introduced himself. His famous face was crinkled, a mask of fleshy folds and creases. Wisps of white hair swirled around his bald crown like leftover strands of cotton candy. At ninety, the old man was the mandarin of Washington's gray eminences, a former Cabinet secretary and one of the most powerful lobbyists in America.

"Oh my, reporters. How did you get in here?" The old man said with feigned horror. "Actually, I kind of like the press. Back in the Truman years, we did whistlestops with you all. By day, I'd write these stem-winders for Harry in the presidential car at the back of the train. At night, we'd invite in the press boys," he looked to Anne and smiled apologetically, "and we'd smoke cigars, drink whisky, and play poker all night."

"Sounds like fun," she said. "Wish I could have been there."

"We could have used someone like you to lighten things up. Wonderful times. I'll never forget the poker game on the way out to Fulton. Played blackjack with the president, Winston Churchill, Byrnes. But the best times were with the boys in the press car."

He brandished his most charming smile and asked if by any chance they were seated at the Truman table.

Anne checked the invitation Geoffrey had messengered over.

"Of course you're sitting with me, the last of the last. They put all the guests at the Truman table. There's so much room. Ah, here comes my good friend."

He introduced them to a short, thin man in tortoise shell spectacles. He was one of the oldest and most distinguished sages of the Camelot brain-trust, his ringing words, for which he refused any credit, recited in high school civics classes across America.

"Welcome to Ghosts and Toasts," he said. "I trust you will not be the first guests to break our code of silence."

"Speechwriters do that, don't they?" Anne asked. "Live by a code of silence?"

"It's a code of honor," he said, stroking a hand across the fabric of his plaid, Edwardian vest. "Or at least it used to be."

"How do you stand it? I mean, doesn't your ego want to scream, 'I did that!'" Anne asked.

"Oh my inflamed ego can get along quite well thank you." He shook her hand, and then added, "Excuse us," as he led the Truman speechwriter shuffling away to whisper together.

"He's a bit full of himself, don't you think?"

"He should be," J.D. said. "There's a world of difference between that old man, and *him*."

J.D.'s nod directed Anne's eyes to Sid Sherman. He was working the crowd like a politician. In the dim light, his white hair had taken on a silverish glow.

"Sid certainly looks unconcerned. What did you tell him?" J.D. took a glass of red wine off a waiter's tray.

"I told him what I knew about Golden Age, Hughes, Lindstrom. Then I asked if he oversaw the payments for the president's son in Indonesia. He flipped, screaming at me before he hung up."

"That was it?"

"No. He called back and told me to look for a fax. He was breathing heavy, I think he was having one of his asthma attacks. A minute later, I received this." Anne unsnapped her purse and took out a folded sheet of paper.

J.D. unfolded the fax. It was from a prominent Washington law firm retained to defended the president on many previous allegations. The fax threatened suit against Ms. Anne Carlson and the *L.A. Times* for slander. The fax was cc'd to Jim Miller and Herb Smith.

J.D. looked up and made eye contact with Sid Sherman. Sherman smiled from across the room.

"Any static from your bosses?"

"You better believe it. Jim Miller is skeptical, always willing to give a reporter a chance to hang herself. He's worried that I'll fall flat on my tush. My national editor is hoping that I will."

"Why are we here?"

"Geoffrey wants us to see something, that's all I know."

A national columnist and former White House speech-writer asked everyone to take their seats. J.D., Anne, and the ancient Truman advisor were joined by Geoffrey, escorting a young man straight out of G. Q.-central casting—a preppy, Ivy league graduate in wire-rimmed glasses, eager to make his way in Washington.

Dinner was salmon poached in butter and sage, boiled potatoes, and green beans.

"Are you sure?" the old man from the Truman administration asked across the table, his rasping voice just above a whisper.

Geoffrey looked back at him, eyes level. "I am sure."

The waiters collected the dessert dishes. The first toast began as the last remaining speechwriter from the Truman administration pulled himself slowly to his feet.

"Colleagues, distinguished visitors, ghostly apparitions from administrations past." The old man steadied himself with one hand on a chair. "It is truly an honor for me to appear at this gathering. At my age, it is a matter of distinction to appear at any gathering."

He noted the mild laughter and continued.

"Soon, this speechwriter will be gone, and the Truman table will pass into history. The young whippersnappers sitting at Table One will no longer be the focus of our abuse. They themselves will be able to abuse a future administration, as they tell us all about what life was like in the good old days.

"The good old days are, of course, always a trick of memory." His voice was soft and rustling. Everyone in the room strained to hear. "We certainly were not always good. In my day, we were losing the Midwest to Dewey. And what did we do? Mr. Truman stood on the back of that train, somewhere in Kansas or Nebraska, and said that if elected, the Republicans would plunge a pitchfork into the backs of the American farmer.

"Now, I know you're not supposed to take credit here, but I am rather proud of that one." Laughter erupted around the room.

"I guess you could call that the original negative campaign. But there was a difference. Back then, when we spoke of an opponent's shortcomings, we weren't afraid to say it ourselves. It is one thing for a man to stand up against his opponent, and lash him to pieces. It is quite another to engage in the deceitful and effeminate art of skullduggery, of planting lies and harvesting hate, of delegating criticism to surrogates and slipping subliminal messages into television ads.

"Even worse, I fear for the Republic, there are those who are now so consumed by ambition that there is no deed they will not do, no law they will not break, no commandment they feel obligated to obey.

"As you know, in an old, celebrated court case, I was accused of breaking the ninth commandment on false witness. A jury of my peers exonerated me from that charge. But I fear there are those for whom even the sixth commandment is but a cobweb to be brushed aside."

He made no toast, merely sat down to light applause from a baffled audience. An old man from the Eisenhower table stood up and gave a simple, gracious toast, reminiscing about Ike.

The writer from the Kennedy table stood next. "The words of my colleague from the Truman table ring in my ears. The time has come for certain blunt truths to be spoken.

"My friends, when voices of eloquence are stilled, when the last cannons are silent, nothing of history remains but the word and the deed. We did not realize it at the time, but we were privileged to be coauthors of history, to write the words by which our times will be remembered.

"Not that we are here to honor ourselves. Those we honor are the true authors of these words. Our bosses, our editors-in-chief, our commanders-in-chief." There was applause.

"When they are gone, what remains? After a time, not even we remain. Again, all that remains is the word and the deed.

"The words of this administration are memorable." He turned and looked directly at Sid Sherman. "But the stench of its deeds will not be ignored by history."

A hush descended over the room as the old man kept his eyes on Sid Sherman, who smiled back idiotically, as if this were merely some kind of inside joke.

"Some in power today deserve to be cast out into the wilderness." He sat down, the room erupted into frenzied conversation.

After awhile, the columnist-emcee, smiling and pleasant as if nothing had happened, hushed everyone, turning attention to the Johnson table. A Johnson speechwriter stood and made a pro forma toast. The speechwriters representing Nixon, Ford, Carter, and the rest toasted without incident.

Sid Sherman rose to give the toast for Table One. He stood in a defiant posture, legs planted firmly apart, thumb hooked into a paisley cummerbund. He threw back a lock of white hair with a head jerk.

"This has been a very interesting evening. Until tonight, the worst that's been suggested is that our administration broke the law. Now we've had the tablets of Moses and the weight of history flung at us."

He waited half a beat for laughter that never came.

"It never fails to strike me as ironic that those who are the loudest denouncers of hate in our politics, are themselves the most hateful. Those who say they cherish history are themselves the great distorters. Those who speak as great moralists—"

Geoffrey stood up. "If you'll forgive a little impudence from a visitor and member of the fourth estate, I'd like to propose a toast."

Geoffrey raised his glass.

"To the late Michael Hughes."

"I'll be happy to toast Mike," Sherman said, voice choked with stress, his raised wine glass visibly shaking. Everyone followed suit, few seemed to know why. "Here, here," cried the old man at the Truman table.

With the last toast done, the program was over. The din of almost a hundred conversations rose, some people moving from table to table, others staying in their seats to finish off the last of the wine.

"I can't believe they actually did that," J.D. said.

"These men are the guardians of the liberal legacy," Anne said. "They've got the reputations of their own administrations on the line."

J.D. looked at Anne. He had first seen her as beautiful in the cabin, without makeup, in a white terry cloth robe.

Her beauty was something that came to you slowly, a dawning realization that something familiar isn't as common as you once thought. Tonight, in her radiant dress, she was drawing the notice of every man in the room.

Slowly, Anne and J.D. heard the conversations in the room start to hush. One table after another grew quiet as people realized something was happening. The silence opened around them until all that could be heard was a deep, grinding wheeze, the sound of someone struggling to draw air.

The entire room became still, as everyone looked at Table One, transfixed by the sight of Sherman seated in his chair, his fingers clawing at his shirt, fighting to breathe.

His eyes went white. He threw back his head and gasped and gulped for air. His brow glistened with sweat, spittle flaked about his lips.

"Oh my God, he's having a heart attack," a woman shouted. "Get some help." Several colleagues gathered around Sherman, fanning him with napkins, offering him words of encouragement and comfort. Anne and J.D. remained at their table, not wanting to gawk and yet not wanting to miss a thing.

Sherman was set on the floor, a small crowd of friends hovering over him. One man claimed to know CPR and began to beat about his chest. "Wait," someone said, "he's still breathing, his heart is pumping away, maybe it's a seizure. It's a seizure!"

Geoffrey poured himself a glass of cabernet and appraised his victim coolly. Anne poured herself a glass, looked to J.D., who nodded, and poured him one. They drank, embarrassed by the temptation to clink their wine glasses. Somehow they were not tempted to take charge of Sid's immediate health care crisis.

Within ten minutes, an ambulance crew came awkwardly down the stairs and worked a white stretcher through a narrow doorway. Sid Sherman was lifted to the stretcher as men in white suits checked his pupils, his pulse.

People stood in polite, quiet clusters, not willing to leave for fear of missing something or being rude, yet not willing to speak if someone might be dying in their presence.

Finally, after a few minutes, the columnist who had emceed for the evening spoke to a medical technician and then stood on a chair.

"Okay, let's call it a night," the emcee shouted. "They say Sid will be okay. Till next year, okay? Thank you, good night." The crew took Sherman out a back way, and everyone began to mill up the stairs, toward the lobby.

Geoffrey conferred with the writers from the Truman and Kennedy administrations. The three men hunched together so tightly, J.D. and Anne could barely hear them.

"Well, the son-of-a-bitch cut the match short by getting sick," the Kennedy writer said. "Although I wouldn't put it past him to play possum."

"What happened tonight will stick," Geoffrey said. "Anne here will see to it that the world knows it."

The three old men looked approvingly at her.

The old Truman aide said, "From here on out, it's a matter for the police to decide. One thing is for certain. He is no longer one of us."

J.D. and Anne rode in silence along Constitution Avenue.

The Capitol was bleached by floodlights. Bats could be seen swooping and swarming around the brightest lights near the crest of the dome.

As they passed the Senate office buildings, J.D. finally spoke. "You're going to go with the story soon, aren't you?"

"If I don't wrap it up by tomorrow afternoon, someone will beat me to it."

Now they were passing into the dark streets of Capitol Hill, surrounded by the hulking shadows of large brick Victorian townhouses.

He carefully parked the 356 in front of her townhouse.

"This street is not very well lit. Let me walk you to your door."

She got out without saying a word. J.D. followed as she opened the waist-high scrolled metal gate and walked down the sidewalk toward her townhouse. One set of stairs led up to the first-story apartments. The other led down, to Anne's little place in the basement.

She gave him a smile that was a little distant. "Good night, J.D., thanks for helping me wrap up this story."

She held out her hand. J.D. pulled her forward and kissed her lightly.

"Let's not—"

He kissed her again, his hands gripping her shoulders hard.

She stepped back. "That's not a good idea."

"It's more than an idea."

"Good night, J.D."

He flashed a smile, that playful look, and turned back to his car.

The single lightbulb that illuminated her front door had

burned out. She walked underneath the first-floor landing, descending into a pool of darkness.

Her dark and lonely apartment.

"J.D.?" He was half-way to his car, but it seemed to take him only a second to return to her side.

"It's dark down here, kind of spooks me out," she said. "It's not every day I can be let in by a law enforcement professional."

She took her keys out of her purse, fumbled for a moment in the dark, and finally found the right ones.

Anne opened the door and stepped inside the dark apartment. He didn't move.

"How many locks do you have on that door?" J.D. asked.

"Three."

"And once you're inside, if you didn't lock a single one, would I be right in assuming that you changed your mind and were leaving the door open for me?"

"Only if that's what I did."

"That you wanted me to kiss you again?"

"Dream on."

"That if I walked inside you'd greet me with open arms."

"Find out."

CHAPTER
31

The housekeeper entered the study and set a cup of Earl Grey on a coaster that was always on the right side of Mr. Sherman's desk.

He took the tea absentmindedly, without thanking Yolanda, a plump, polite, middle-aged woman who spoke little English. After she left, he stood and twisted the metal handle that opened the window to the garden. The recent May showers of the past few days had cleansed the city sky. He took a tiny sip of tea, savoring the tart flavor and the morning air.

It was going to be a good day. After all that, things were going to turn out okay after all.

The best news was that he did not have a heart attack. It certainly could have been one. Three days had passed since the Ghosts and Toasts dinner, three days since those awful moments when he ceased to hear the conversations around him, and felt his heart hammering insanely in his chest. He remembered struggling to breathe, vomiting, and then being afraid of vomiting again while trying to catch his breath.

Things were unclear after that, he must have blacked out. After coming to, he remembered too many helpful people getting close, touching him, opening his shirt, checking

his pulse. On the way to the hospital, he was sure he was going to die.

But Sid Sherman did not die. In fact, within a few hours the only condition he suffered from was acute embarrassment. After being kept overnight for observation, his doctor released him.

It was, he was told, a combination of alcohol, stress, and his underlying asthma that brought on the attack of nausea and breathing difficulty. Acute dyspnea. Sherman called it a breathing attack, and it was the first one that severe since he had scrubbed out of his high school gym class.

Now he was home, under strict orders from his doctor to keep a light schedule, drink no alcohol, eat healthy meals, and receive few visitors.

Like hell.

The only concessions he made to the doctor were to do his work at home and dress in his chinos, Topsiders, and an old golf shirt. Otherwise, he had to stay busy to keep on top of the world's latest attempt to tear down the president. And Sid Sherman.

So far, he had the world on the run.

That woman's story in the *L.A. Times* was tough. But Sherman's battery of lawyers and presidential flacks were tougher. In no time, they had gone into full spin cycle and convinced the press that this was a nonstory.

What about Golden Age? they asked. It was just a small-time investment company for people who'd worked together in campaigns and realized they didn't even have 401(k)s. Nothing more.

What about Leo Lindstrom? Sad story, the guy had been going downhill for a long time, till one day he really went off the deep end—oops, no pun intended.

What about these rumors that the president has a kid in Indonesia? Is there any lie so ridiculous that the president's critics won't try to sell it to the press? Really, you should be ashamed for allowing yourselves to be put up to ask such a silly question.

The story never migrated beyond the *L.A. Times*. A rumored second piece was said to have been spiked. And the word on the street was that Jim Miller was embarrassed and ready to fire the bitch who had dared to try and take down one of the most popular presidents in history on such flimsy evidence.

The story about him passing out at a Washington dinner got more play in the gossip pages than the *Times* piece did. It had all been embarrassing, but not fatal to his career. In fact, the president had called him from the Oval Office to ask him to personally spearhead the opposition research and counterspin on these latest allegations.

POTUS wasn't worried. He knew they'd turn this one around, just like they'd done so many times before.

And Geoffrey, insufferable, lovable old bastard, would owe him a public apology at next year's Ghosts and Toasts.

Ancient fart.

Sherman turned to his work. He leafed through some letters in the fax tray, testimonials to his integrity from friends in the media and on the Hill.

Then Sherman went to the door, called for more tea and turned on his computer.

He had e-mail.

Sherman deleted all the get-wells and read an encouraging e-mail from the vice president. The next message was from Doctor Dirt.

Yolanda brought another cup of Earl Grey. He took it as if the cup had simply materialized in his hand. He opened the message and waited while graphics downloaded onto his screen. He saw large Gothic font.

DID YOU KNOW LEO WOULD REALLY KILL ME?

He stared at the screen for the longest time. Attached to the message was a scanned-in copy of the Golden Age charter, page after page, with his name all over it. Could it have been some kind of delayed transmission, a timed message Thornburgh left in the system weeks ago?

There it was again, that breathing problem, a tightness about the chest, a dizziness, trouble standing up. Sherman held on to his chair to steady himself. He looked at his screen. There was another message from Doctor Dirt.

He leaned over and clicked it open.

SID SPEAK NO EVIL?

It had another scanned image attached to it, this one a copy of a canceled check for $20,000 signed by Sherman and made out to Leo Lindstrom. He instantly knew what this meant. Now that Leo was dead, his papers were also before a probate court, another set of papers in full public view. No telling how much incriminating stuff Leo had squirreled away. There was another message. He opened it.

There, too, were more attachments, dozens of pages from Leo's office, memos, checks, and notes from telephone conversations with Sid Sherman. In the middle of them, set conspicuously in a box, was a record of phone calls from Sherman's private home number to the San Marcos Group.

Put together, the papers connected him to Manoulian, proved a relationship between a wanted criminal and a White House Deputy Chief of Staff.

He couldn't decide what to do. Should he delete the messages or print them out? Who could he call? A lawyer or a flack? Can't bring anybody into this one. Best to leave it alone. He turned off the screen and started to walk around the study, extending his arms and rolling them in spirals like a pitcher warming up in the bull pen, trying to open his chest, trying to get some air in there.

It wasn't working. It was still getting hard to breathe. How could Thornburgh have left something like that? Was it an automatic program? Was it going to a hundred people?

Sherman tried to focus his mind on a wall full of awards and plaques. He went over to the telephone and hit the speed dial to his mother. A nice conversation with Lilly down in Myrtle Beach, that would calm him down.

The phone trilled, the old woman answered. But he couldn't say anything. He couldn't even say his name.

Sherman staggered out of the room, into the hall, looking for help. The last thing he remembered seeing before hitting the hard floor was the expression of horror on Yolanda's face.

"Breathing," he gasped, reaching for her.

"*Corazon?*" She backed away as if he might drag her down to hell.

"Breathing," he hissed, sinking to his knees.

"*Ambulancia?*"

Sarah waited for J.D., sunning on the deck of the Morgan, wearing the skimpiest of halter tops and cut-offs, her long legs slick with lotion and gleaming in the sun.

"Hiya, kiddo," J.D. said.

"Hi."

"You look like a french fry."

"Daddy."

J.D. set a tool kit on the deck. He had looked forward to an afternoon of maintenance, cleaning the deck, tightening some fittings. But there was more important maintenance to be done right in front of him.

"Can I have one of these?" J.D. reached into the cooler and pulled a Sam Adams.

It tasted good, as good as he had imagined a beer would be walking into the mountain forest under the hot California sun.

"How you been?"

"Worried," she said. "Worried sick about you. Catching crazy stories on the Net—news summaries about you almost killed."

"Greatly exaggerated."

"Still."

"Want one?"

She nodded. He passed her a beer. Now for the question.

"Why did you do it?" he asked. Now for the question. "And please don't disappoint me by saying 'do what?'"

Sarah sat up on her elbows, took a sip of beer.

Her nose crinkled and he knew that if he could see her eyes behind her Ray Bans, they'd be misting up.

"Well?"

She took another sip of beer. Her voice was flat and despondent.

"I guess I could tell you it was what they did to Beaumont or to get revenge over losing my job. But that would be a lie."

"So what's the truth?"

"I was curious. I knew you were looking into it, and I just wanted to know."

J.D. sat down.

That did have the ring of truth.

"Thanks for telling me. You just got me worried again. That's all."

She put down her beer and sat up. "Oh dad, I haven't had those strange thoughts or bad feelings in a long time. I know I can handle it now."

"Taking your medicine?"

"*Yes*, dad."

"Sorry, had to ask."

"It's all right." She went back to her elbows and faced the sun.

"Politics is a dirty business. A hard business. You don't need to test yourself that way. Okay?"

"'Kay."

They sat in silence for a while.

"I need to get a better job," she said finally. "I just blew all my savings."

"You did? On what!"

Sarah rose, poured the rest of her beer into the water and set the bottle in the trash can.

She gave him a hug and stepped out on the dock, walking toward her bike. J.D. paced his deck, looked out onto the water, watching the regatta forming across Spa Creek. What had she done now?

It was a good half-hour later before he found it on his way to the head, a package in bright wrapping set next to his bunk.

J.D. tore off the paper, but he knew what it was.

Fisher Ames, original, first edition.

J.D. parked the 356 well away from any other cars in the parking garage and walked through the main entrance to the George Washington University Hospital.

He went to the gift shop and bought a dozen long-stemmed roses in green wrapping paper. He took the elevator to the second floor and walked with confidence past nurses too busy to notice him. Thanks to some advance legwork from Roman Grice, he knew exactly where to find Sid Sherman.

J.D. knocked lightly on the wide door of the hospital room and heard a woman say, "Come in."

Sherman was on an elevated hospital bed, a thermometer clamped firmly in his mouth, and the TV remote in one hand. J.D. noticed a call button on the remote.

A nurse stood to his side taking his pulse.

"Hiya Sid," J.D. said.

Sherman nodded sullenly and tried to say something, but could only produce a humming sound.

J.D. looked up and saw that Sherman had been watching CNN. His bed and the visitor's chairs were covered in faxes.

"What do you want now?" Sherman growled after the nurse left. "You're not FBI anymore. They kicked you loose, like the asshole that you are."

J.D. walked over and extended his hand as if to shake, but reached past him and snatched the remote from the bed. J.D. pulled on it a few times, testing the strength of the cord. It snapped neatly out of the wall.

"You crazy shit, I can call Lou Firelli and have you arrested just like that!" Sherman thrashed in his bed like an angry boy. J.D. put a thumb on each side of Sherman's jaw and pressed in and up, immobilizing him.

"Forget the FBI. I'm here as a spiritual medium, the one who passed on a message to you from Doctor Dirt."

J.D. stayed on the man, making him think about it, making him worry about catching his next breath. "If you call for a nurse, you'll be punished."

J.D. let go. Sherman gasped and panted.

"*You* sent those messages?"

"Yes."

"Why?"

"Because I know you inspired Leo to commit a murder."

"You're out of your frigging, freaking mind."

"Do you want me to tell you how Leo did it, or why?"

Sherman glared at him, saying nothing.

"I'll take that as a why. We know why. Thornburgh was a day or two away from connecting all the dots. If he were alive, he would have found a clever way to draw out the story, to validate it more thoroughly than dumping one piece in the *L.A. Times*."

"That story was crap."

"*Your* story is crap. Anne Carlson is going after you again. Only this time, she has all the documentation to make it stick. Now, do you want me to tell you how Leo did it? I've even figured out the murder weapon."

Sherman started gasping again. J.D. smiled and threw the bouquet on the bed.

"Leo had done opposition research at the Nixon Library before. He could find his way around pretty easily.

"So he went there on your orders, to track down Doctor Dirt and confront the bastard with something from his past. Right? So Leo walks in the front door, but nobody notices him milling through the museum crowd with his hair rolled up and his baseball cap pulled down to his eyebrows.

"He had shaved that day. I bet he even bathed. For Stinky, a very effective disguise.

"He follows a hunch and takes the down elevator. He gets off at the basement, cuts into the microfiche room and shuts the door. Didn't he tell you all this?

"Your plan is for Leo to lay something on Doctor Dirt, some nasty that's supposed to make him think twice. The problem is, a guy like that really has few secrets himself. Given what he did for a living, I doubt he could be embarrassed.

"But Leo, you see, has a different take on reality. So when Doctor Dirt turns his back on Leo and patiently resumes his work to destroy all of you, Leo's addled brain kicks into gear.

"Without giving it a second thought, Leo reaches down, takes the wooden plate of a message spike into the palm of his hand and drives the spike into the back of Todd's skull."

Sherman's bottom lip quivered, the muscles around his mouth and eyes flickered.

"There he was, Leo Lindstrom, in a presidential library, standing with a block of wood in his hand, the metal spike broken off at the base, the rest stuck all the way into a man's skull.

"It had to have taken an incredible combination of hate and arrogance for Leo to do what he did next. Something he'd probably dreamed about doing for years.

"He locked the door from the inside. He had the presence of mind to slip the wooden base of the message spike into his jacket pocket. And then he took a needle and thread from a pocket darning case he used to patch up his old clothes, those old seats of his 1964 VW. We found that he'd kept it in his office as a killer's keepsake. And yes, a buddy of mine in the FBI says the fibers match. Then he did his amazing sick number, a move only Leo could have thought of."

J.D. let the last thought hang in the air for a moment.

"He shut up Doctor Dirt for all time."

Sherman looked pale and sick, like his yellow-white hair.

"It must have shocked you, to find out that a man you sent to do a simple muscle job was so crazy he actually killed the guy. You must have died to have him come back to you all proud, like a bird dog with a prize catch in his mouth.

"Now, I've got this old compadre in the FBI. Not your standard issue G-man at all. Real cowboy, Charlie Pride-type with a Marlboro mustache, wears boots to the office. He's been on the case from the get-go. I bet he'll be real interested in my story."

Sherman frantically slid from the bed, and staggered to the window. He snapped the latch, and pulled the window open from the bottom.

"You're not thinking about jumping, are you?" J.D. was three feet behind him. "If you are, go right ahead. Save everybody a lot of trouble."

"I just need some air."

"I bet you do. Anyway, I'm gonna take this to my old colleague in the FBI.

"Maybe he'll go with it, maybe he won't. There's a good chance you'll be prosecuted, especially if I push it. And I may decide to push it depending on what happens next."

"What do you want?"

J.D. was right behind him, speaking over his shoulder in a near whisper.

"Let me tell you what I don't want. I don't want one of those year-long celebrity trials on TV, the kind they run all day long. You'd be ruined. Your career would be over. But in the end, you'd hire one of those double-breasted orators who could convince an L.A. jury to let you off—maybe. Or maybe you'd be convicted as an accomplice to a murder. That's pretty high stakes. But I don't like to take chances. Do you?"

J.D. let his words sink in for a moment.

"Now, let me tell you what's going to happen. Tomorrow, another one of those articles will hit the stands. Anne Carlson is banking her career that the latest documentation will finally nail down the link between the president and the Presidio business, and to his bastard son in Jakarta. Are you all right? You look kind of peaked.

"Anyway, as much as I hate to play politics, I don't want to see this same bullshit continue under the president's hand-picked successor for another eight years. So I've come here to give you instructions. You're not going to fight back."

"What?" Sherman yelled, but it was a tired, hoarse yell.

"*You are not going to fight back*. You are not going to refute, rebut, spin, counterspin, or go after that story in any way. You are just going to quit the fight and let nature take its course. You'll find some phony excuse to give POTUS some new tactic, some rationale for holding off... until it's too late."

"The hell you say." The man bent over the window sill, his chest heaving. "Leave me alone."

"If you're lucky, the FBI won't find enough to prosecute, or they won't bother. If you're unlucky, you get the San Quentin aromatherapy."

Sherman hunched over the window, face on the sill, made a squeaking noise as he sobbed and gasped for air at the same time.

"You can keep the flowers."

CHAPTER
32

Anne watched the milling crowd of tourists and midshipmen on the Annapolis waterfront through the telescope lens. The still, cool air of early November seemed electrified by yesterday's election, a landslide at the beginning of a new millennium.

No one expected it, the way in which the administration had fallen apart at its very end and dragged down the campaign of its vice president.

Soon there would be a new president, a new Congress, a new story.

J.D. struck a match and lit the charcoal underneath the grill of the barbecue. For J.D. it was not yet too cold to barbeque. He put on a couple of sirloins and shrimp-kabobs, listening with satisfaction to the sound of sizzling meat.

Anne pushed up the sleeves of her Irish sweater, opened a bottle of good Chardonnay, and handed beers to Mike McGuire, Ben Grossman, and Sarah DeVine, the three of whom were talking about computer security and industrial espionage. J.D. drank the wine, listening in, admiring Sarah's intelligent comments, and thinking his girl would have made a good FBI agent after all. Geoffrey refused all offers of beer or white wine, preferring the red he'd brought for himself.

"Well, excuse me, everyone," said Geoffrey, raising his glass. "I'd like to propose a toast to justice, which has been ensured by this election."

"Hear, hear."

"What's the latest on Sid Sherman?" Anne asked Grossman. "I always knew there was something off about him."

Grossman took his time, taking a deep sip of beer. Another one of his dramatic pauses.

"Well," Geoffrey was so irritated with the wait that he answered the question himself. "Sid sold his house in Washington and wasted most of his money on lawyers. He wants to get back into journalism, but there's not a paper or magazine in the country that will touch him."

"It's only a matter of time before we catch up with him," McGuire said, his mustache trimmed to a neat rectangular patch since his promotion to counterintelligence at Bureau headquarters. "Sherman lives in terror that we're going to knock on his door any day now."

"Y'all want the icing on the cake?" Grossman said. "He's living in a Myrtle Beach condominium with his mom." Grossman laughed at the image of the once-great Sid Sherman eating his mother's baloney sandwiches. "And it was opposition research that finally found the relationships, the motive, and the killer."

"Oh for God's sake," said Sarah, setting down her beer bottle. "It wasn't your sleazy operation, it was my dad."

"Yes, indeed," Geoffrey added. "You can stuff your electric abacus. This case was solved by the application of good, old-fashioned shoe leather. Nothing more. Though I think the credit belongs to Anne as much as anyone."

balled them up, and tossed them back, as though he were sinking hoops. He took the lighter fluid, soaked the papers, threw in a match, and jumped back as it exploded into a thick, blue plume that shot up into the night. He set the cardboard box behind the can and took a seat on the concrete backsteps.

He took a sip of scotch and appraised the situation.

Each disk in the box had a label with a bar-code. Each one also had a handwritten number, which Ben knew by heart, as well as an "N" scribbled on the corner, identifying it as a "nasty."

"Do I really want to do this?" he said to himself, taking another pull of scotch.

He held up a disk. The firelight illuminated it, made it a round, crystalline kaleidoscope of flickering colors. He imagined he could see its secrets refracted by the firelight.

"I want to do this because I really don't care if you're keeping a mistress on Long Island."

Grossman threw the disk into the fire. He picked up another one.

"I don't care if you once celebrated Halloween in San Francisco by going out in drag."

He threw in another disk.

"I don't care if you had a DWI in Houston in 1974."

He threw in another disk.

"I don't care if you were a bag man for a New Orleans hood when you were fourteen.

"I don't care if your ex-husband was a real estate con artist. I release you. All."

He threw in another. Another. Many more.

Grossman sat on the backsteps, nursing his scotch, watching the embers from the newspapers rise out of the trash can, above the top of the townhouse, toward the stars. The old words came to him, *Yet man is born unto trouble, as the sparks fly upward*.

After a while, when the disks had melted into a plastic coating of goo over the crumbling, grey charcoal, Grossman hosed down the black, burned-out pit with a gardenhose.

Steam hissed and sputtered until the can was an inch full of water and the metal went cold and black. He rolled the trash can, sloshing water, over to its place by a brick wall. Then Grossman locked the townhouse and headed home.

The backyard was quiet except for the occasional snap of cooling metal from the trash can. It was completely dark now, city lights unable to wash out the brightness of the stars.

Five minutes went by before Roman Grice emerged from behind the carriage house, quiet and observant as a burglar.

He took his extra set of keys and opened the door, quickly disarming the alarm. He checked the disk shelves, and confirmed what he thought he'd seen. Grossman had completely cleaned out a whole shelf of the nasty files.

Then he closed up and headed for his car. Grice congratulated himself for seeing it coming, for seeing how Grossman was getting soft, the man's widening streak of sentimentalism and weakness.

No edge.

Grice congratulated himself again for secretly keeping the copies of the files J.D. had returned. Now, wealth was tapping him on the shoulder.

Grice would have to think of a reason to turn in his resignation.

He could be in business for himself in a month.

Big business.